"We're _____ *led*
Sexual _____

Melissa forced herself to sound professional. After all, she was simply teaching him the game. "We take turns touching each other. Whatever part of my body I place against yours has to stay where it is until the game is finished. That's where the paste part comes in. This is a kind of foreplay, so we can touch anywhere except the primary sexual zones."

Tony's eyes glinted with interest. "I'm all yours."

She stepped close and placed her hand on his right butt cheek. She felt the hard muscle flex under her touch. "See? Now I'm stuck to you." Her voice was fading on her. There didn't seem to be enough air when she got close to him.

"This could get very interesting," he said. The thickness in his voice betrayed him. He moved his hand upward and cupped the fullness of her left breast. Melissa nearly whimpered under his touch.

"There's a problem," he murmured. "A big one."

"A problem?" Then Melissa glanced down and saw what he meant.

"My primary sexual zone wants to play, too."

Blaze

Dear Reader,

What's your secret fantasy? Surely you have at least one delicious daydream that you would never discuss in polite company. I know I do. And so does Melissa Sanders, my heroine in *Unfinished Business*. I suppose I shouldn't say whether or not Melissa's fantasy is one of mine, but I can tell you that I had *way* too much fun researching this story. Writing it, too!

Melissa is a writer, herself. She spends her days dreaming up articles about erotic adventures for a popular women's magazine, and her nights dreaming of having one. After a cruel rejection in college and a mostly boyfriend-less life, she would dearly love to mesmerize a man with a bit of shoe dangling and hair tossing. She wants to be a vixen, not a victim—a woman whose hot body and cool indifference drives men wild with lust.

Melissa's dream comes true on her annual trip to Cancun with girlfriends. She takes their dare and tries out her vixen fantasy on Antonio Bond, a smolderingly gorgeous waiter—at least that's what she thinks he is. After one night with her dark-eyed demon lover—complete with a mock wedding—Melissa can barely summon the will to escape him. Little does she guess that Antonio has no intention of letting her go for long....

Well? Have I enticed you to read on and find out what happens? I hope so. If you don't already have a secret fantasy—or several—maybe Melissa and Tony's story will inspire you. Happy fantasizing!

All my best,

Suzanne Forster

Books by Suzanne Forster

HARLEQUIN BLAZE
101—BRIEF ENCOUNTERS

UNFINISHED BUSINESS

SUZANNE FORSTER

HARLEQUIN®

TORONTO • NEW YORK • LONDON
AMSTERDAM • PARIS • SYDNEY • HAMBURG
STOCKHOLM • ATHENS • TOKYO • MILAN • MADRID
PRAGUE • WARSAW • BUDAPEST • AUCKLAND

This one's for Ann, my dear friend, my sounding board,
and my shelter in the storm.

Your support means more to me than I could ever tell you.

ISBN 0-373-79129-1

UNFINISHED BUSINESS

Copyright © 2004 by Suzanne Forster.

This edition published by arrangement with Harlequin Books S.A.

® and TM are trademarks of the publisher. Trademarks indicated with
® are registered in the United States Patent and Trademark Office, the
Canadian Trade Marks Office and in other countries.

Visit us at www.eHarlequin.com

Printed in U.S.A.

1

Every woman is a pussycat doll, even if only in her own mind. Find that doll, wind her up and let her go.

101 Ways To Make Your Man Beg

"SO I'M OLD-FASHIONED," Melissa Sanders admitted as she lifted her Rum Mocambo cocktail to her lips. "So I'm waiting for marriage. So shoot me!"

A jet of cold water hit Melissa right between the eyes.

"Hey, I was only kidding!" she cried. Blinded, she felt around the table for a napkin while her three girlfriends dissolved in peals of laughter. She managed a good-natured smile through the water dripping off her nose.

But once her vision had cleared, Melissa fixed her old friend Kathy Crawford with a bemused look. She'd noticed Kath digging through her overstuffed tote, but hadn't expected her to whip out the squirt gun she kept there for self-defense. "What's with the water-gun assault?"

Kath's grin challenged her. "I say marry the guy, if you must," she said. "Whatever it takes, you have *got* to have sex with that beautiful man, Melissa. You lost the bet."

"If you can find him," Melissa said, "I'll do the honors right here on this table. Would that make you *bad* girls happy?"

"Yes," they all chirped at once.

"Well, shame on you." Melissa pretended to be busy

blotting rum from her much too demure cotton sundress. The girls had been giving her grief all evening about her sex life. She didn't have one, and they'd decided to make that their cause. They were trying to hook her up, and to that end, they'd approached almost every man in the restaurant, begging him to marry her for "just one night."

Melissa was used to their antics by now. The four of them had been friends since childhood and were currently in Cancún on their annual escape-from-civilization trip. But Melissa had not been prepared when one of the guys, a simply gorgeous waiter named Antonio, had dropped to one knee and proposed to her on the spot. She was mortified, but she was also a little tipsy—and okay, pleased. Mostly to show the girls, she'd accepted his proposal—and Antonio had seemed pleased, too. Obviously, he'd heard she wouldn't sleep with anyone she wasn't married to, and he loved a good challenge. It was even possible he'd been talked into the idea by her friends. But the way he'd lingered over kissing the back of her hand had made Melissa's stomach float like a cork on the Gulf of Mexico. Was that his tongue she'd felt? It could have been velvet.

Fortunately for Melissa, Antonio had returned her hand and disappeared with a bow of his sexy dark head. He'd probably thought it was a good joke, but Melissa was still trying to scoop herself off the floor. Now she knew how it felt to be an ice-cream sundae, melting under a puddle of hot fudge.

He'd surprised her almost as much the first time they'd met. The girls knew nothing about that, but Antonio had come to her aid three mornings ago while she'd been walking barefoot on the beach. She'd been gazing out to sea, perhaps a little wistfully, and had seen a stranger coming her way. He'd worn a billowing white shirt and a butcher's apron tightly knotted around his waist, and he'd looked like a man on a mission. She'd had no idea the mission was her until he'd reached her and told her there'd been a shark report. The sensual grate of his voice still resonated in her mind....

"The water's treacherous," he warned. "Don't go in, not even to wade."

He was treacherous, she realized, caught in the riptide of his inexplicable concern for her safety. That mouth, those incandescent black eyes. Just looking at him could pull you under. She would probably be safer with the sharks.

"Thank you," she said, realizing he had her by the hand and was guiding her farther from the water.

"What were you looking for out there?" he asked.

Something about him pulled the truth out of her. With a fleeting smile, she said, "My life."

A look came over him that made her catch her breath. Her mind couldn't process what she saw except to call it a glimpse of naked male power. The desire to protect, and something else too quick and electric to catch. She dug her toes into the sand for traction. He released her hand, and she didn't want him to go, but she had no reason to stop him. After all, he'd simply come there to warn her. She might have thought she'd dreamed him up, except that he was better than any of her fantasies.

"Don't look too long," he said. "You might miss it."

The next morning they'd met again, and she'd asked him what he'd meant. He'd just smiled and said she had pretty feet. She should always go barefoot.

"Melissa, are you daydreaming again?"

Melissa looked up to three sets of eyes fixed intently on her. "Still mopping up, thanks to Kath." She finished blotting her face, sipped what little was left of her drink, and held it up, signaling the waiter that she wanted another one.

The waiter who was not Antonio.

The charming waterfront restaurant had rapidly filled up. Saturday-night guests spilled out onto a tile patio, draped in crimson bougainvillea, where the girls were sequestered on a lovely, airy deck. The patio overlooked a placid blue-water inlet, and they'd planned to have dinner here after their cocktails, but, as far as the ladies were concerned, there only seemed to be one thing on the menu for Melissa: stud service.

"You heard me say yes," she told the girls with a hint of cockiness, then looked around to make sure Antonio was really gone. "You were all witnesses. If he hadn't chickened out, I might have married him. Hey, for one night? Why not?"

Her friends made scoffing sounds, and Melissa pretended to be hurt. "You doubt me? You think I wouldn't do something that impetuous? I'm not capable of sluttiness?"

Kath stood and raised her drink. "To the vestal virgin," she said, "who won't even kiss a guy unless he's wearing a condom."

The other two chimed in, and as much as Melissa wanted to protest, she couldn't. They all knew her, and Kath best of all. They'd grown up together and gone to the same schools, although Melissa had missed a year because of a childhood illness. That was probably why the girls mother henned her a bit and sometimes made her feel like the runt of the litter. They didn't want her to miss out on life.

She and Kath had always told each other everything and still did. Melissa had been through every one of Kath's romantic relationships. She knew her friend had slept with exactly five different men in her twenty-eight years, including a one-night stand. And Kath knew that Melissa hadn't.

Well, there had been one, but that was different. Melissa had thought she was going to marry Roger "Dodger" Boswell, and he'd agreed to wait. But once they were officially engaged, he'd argued that they might not be sexually compatible. He'd finally persuaded her, and it had been a disaster. Melissa had been nervous, and nothing had worked. He'd dumped her the next day, and of course, she'd blamed herself. But wouldn't the right guy have waited? Or at least been understanding?

She'd stubbornly clung to that notion, but there'd been no right guy since, and no sex either. Could a celibate woman burst like clogged plumbing?

The other girls had raised their glasses, too, but Melissa didn't want recognition for her lackluster love life, thank you.

"At least give me the benefit of the doubt." She pouted. "I *could* be a slut."

"Of course you could!" Pat Stafford raised her glass high. Pat was the beauty of the group, a slender blond cheerleader in their high-school days, and still much too lovely to live, in Melissa's opinion.

"You're already a diva of sluttiness by journalistic standards," Kath assured her. "How about all those steamy articles you write for *Women Only* magazine?"

Melissa winced at the reference to her secret life as the author of articles for women about how to be sexually fulfilled. Okay, a couple of them were pretty racy, but everything she wrote was straight out of her own unfulfilled fantasy life. Some women faked orgasms. She faked sex altogether. She probably would have run like a scared rabbit if Antonio had been serious. And she was tired of running, tired of feeling like a fraud.

Of course, he *wasn't* serious. This was all a crazy joke, but she rather liked the idea that he'd been willing to go to such extremes just for one night with her. In fact, it had always been one of her favorite fantasies. She'd always wondered what it would be like to have a powerful man willing to do anything for the chance to satisfy his lustful desires for her. And Antonio *was* powerful, in his way. She was pretty sure he had a few lustful desires, too. Otherwise, why did her mind go weak at the mere thought? And what was that other warm sensation? Were her panties damp?

Renee Tyler, the foursome's ponytailed tomboy, broke in with a bright idea. "Forget men. Let's go score ourselves some chocolate. It's better than sex anyway."

Four glasses shot into the air. "Hear, hear!"

Fortunately, Melissa's glass happened to be empty. Another drink and she would have been on her nose. As it was, she couldn't seem to find the silk shawl she'd worn, and the onshore breezes were getting chilly as the sun went down.

"I can taste the Peanut Butter Cup cheesecake now," Renee gushed. *"Vamanos, señoritas."*

"One sec." Melissa crouched to look under the table. Where could the shawl have gone?

"Melissa," Kath whispered, nudging her.

"What is it?" Melissa felt around the cool tile floor with her hand. It was dark under the table, and silk was so slippery.

"Look who's here! *Psssssst, Melisssssa.*"

Someone squealed and Melissa thumped her head against the underside of the table, nearly knocking herself cold. A moment later, as she peeked over the top, she saw that the waiter had come back. Not the waiter with her drink. Antonio. He'd changed into a white tuxedo shirt and black slacks, and he'd brought another man with him, one who looked suspiciously like…a priest?

Antonio smiled at her, and she considered going back under the table. But the girls were watching her every move.

"Hello, Melissa." Antonio pronounced her name perfectly.

She waggled her fingers at him. "Hi," she managed to say. Why did the floor feel as if it were tilting? Did they have earthquakes in Cancún?

"This is Father Domenici." Antonio's lush, husky voice held only a hint of foreign inflection. "He's offered to help us."

"Help us what?" she whispered.

"Get married, of course."

Melissa tried getting to her feet, fairly certain she wasn't going to make it. This had to be a joke, and her friends were probably behind it. The priest bore a suspicious resemblance to the older man who'd bussed their table when they'd arrived. The lengths those girls would go to!

Kath eased out of the way as Antonio held out his hand. "Father, this beautiful woman and I are going to be one tonight."

Joke or not, Melissa was aghast. She was also enchanted. Antonio helped her to her feet with a strong, reassuring grip. She wobbled only slightly as he presented her with a velvety red rose. He also had a delicate white lace veil for her head.

"For Melissa," he said, "the answer to a man's dreams."

Dream was right. The dulcet strains of a mariachi band filtered out from the restaurant, and Melissa could hear her friends buzzing in the background, but she had no idea what they were saying. Antonio's superior height forced her to tip her head back to see him, which made her dizzy—or was it the Mocambos?

This was her first opportunity for a good long look at him, and it *was*. Good, from his indecently sensual mouth to his dark, soulful eyes. The girls must have put him up to this. Otherwise, what could he want with her? Not that she was slim pickings, mind you. She had good teeth, shiny dark hair and long legs, which made her sound rather like a horse. She could still wear the same jeans she'd worn in high school. So what if she had to lie flat on her back and hold her breath to zip them up?

She doubted Antonio had ever had problems zipping up his pants. Or zipping them *down*. She smiled at the thought and glanced at him sideways. From what she could see, there wasn't an ounce of anything anywhere that wasn't absolutely necessary. His slacks fit as if they'd been tailored to his body. Narrow black satin bands ran the length of the outside seams, and the linen fabric caressed his thighs, straining ever so slightly when he moved. His snowy-white tuxedo shirt had a couple of buttons undone, which wasn't bad either, as long as you were partial to corded muscles and sun-bronzed skin.

Kath would have described him as yummy, and Melissa didn't doubt that any one of her friends would have leaped to switch places with her, in which case, the joke was on them. He'd chosen *her*. She didn't care to wonder why.

After a moment, Melissa realized that Antonio was leading her away from the table. Even more surprising, she was following, hand in hand. And she didn't seem to have any desire to stop him. Quite the opposite, it felt as if she could have gone anywhere with this man, done anything. How could that be?

She glanced back over her shoulder and smiled nervously at the girls.

"Where are you going?" Kath called.

"To the mission," Antonio replied.

"To the mission," Melissa echoed. "I lost the bet, remember."

"But you can't just marry him," Renee said. "You need a license and—"

"All I need is her." Antonio turned to face the three startled women and spoke in a voice of quiet resolve. "You begged every man in the restaurant to marry her and make a woman out of her," he said, "but that's not why I proposed. For some reason none of you can see it, but she *is* a woman—a beautiful, desirable woman who any red-blooded man would want—and I do."

You could hear the clunks all around the patio as jaws dropped.

Melissa was as bewildered as everyone else. Maybe this wasn't a joke. She looked at her friends, and fought back a tiny bubble of hysteria. They didn't seem to know what to do, and she certainly didn't either. They had bet they could get a cute guy to marry her for just one night. Well, he was more than cute. And he seemed to want to marry her. Really want to, for some reason.

Now would be the time to ask some questions and find out what was going on, she told herself. Even if her girlfriends weren't involved, this had to be a practical joke of some kind. If she stopped for a moment, cleared her head, maybe this crazy rush of feeling would disappear, and she could get her bearings. Then again, maybe she didn't want the crazy rush of feeling to disappear. *She'd waited her whole life to feel like this.*

Suddenly she understood how a woman could let herself be swept away by an impulse that didn't make sense and might even seem reckless. This was what she wrote about in her articles, but never dreamed she would experience. It was just a fantasy, right? Sexy, dark-eyed strangers didn't really ask for your hand and say that they were going to be one with you that night. Not if you were Melissa Sanders, the magazine writer. She was a recluse, a spectator, not a participant. She lived vicariously through others, courtesy of her imagination.

But her imagination, wild as it was, could never do this justice. And that must be why she was following him out of the restaurant, hand in hand. That must be why she didn't want to stop, not even for a second. For the first time in her life, she was going to do what she and her girlfriends had always said they would do when they took their annual trip. She was going native.

MELISSA'S EYES blinked open. She vaguely remembered being woozy and needing to lie down for a second, but that was it. Had she passed out? Those Rum Mocambos tasted like fruit punch, but hit like a hammer.

Whatever had happened, she wasn't dreaming though it was still dark, outside beyond the curtains. She was lying on a bed with a man, curled up in his arms, and they were both fully clothed. That last part struck her as odd. How could they be fully clothed if—

She lifted her head from his shoulder. "Antonio?"

He was awake—awake and gazing at her as if that's what he'd been doing for hours. Melissa struggled to dredge up details. There'd been a wedding ceremony in a small Mexican mission with not one word of English in the vows, which had not concerned her at all at the time. Antonio had slipped a delicate gold-filigree ring on her finger, and afterward she'd signed something written in Spanish that might have been a marriage license.

Antonio had found a way to make everything seem wonderfully authentic, but of course, it couldn't have been. No priest would marry two total strangers who barely spoke the same language. Nor could Melissa be legally bound to a document if she didn't know what she was signing. The ceremony wasn't real, just a crazy romantic adventure, which had led to this, whatever *this* was.

"We're in bed," she pointed out. They seemed to be in a hotel room, and one that no ordinary waiter could afford. The wrought-iron posts of the king-size bed swirled up to meet a red satin canopy. She'd never seen anything as vibrant or beautiful. Crimson clouds floated above them and a silk leopard-print comforter cushioned them from beneath. Scented candles flickered from every surface, giving off luscious notes that reminded her of warm vanilla flan with a dash of cognac. There was even a golden cornucopia, spilling exotic fruit on the dresser top.

Did Latin lovers seduce their women with food?

"*Sí, cama,*" he said, patting the comforter. "That's Spanish for bed."

"Did we—I mean, of course we did—we're in a *cama.* But did we—"

"Consummate the union?"

He might have nodded. She wasn't sure. His dark, soulful eyes had a tidal pull that made her feel as if she were made of nothing but liquid.

"Be nice if I could remember," she said.

"How could you remember? You were asleep," he teased in his deep voice.

"We did it while I was asleep?"

He laughed. "You must have very good dreams."

"So nothing happened? You were just watching me dream?"

"Watching you dream in my arms."

Apparently there was a huge difference, by the tone of his voice. He was just too romantic to be believed. She might write about this sort of thing in real life, but she never had any illusions that it could happen to her. It still didn't seem real.

She plucked at her linen sundress. "Antonio, we're both fully clothed."

"That's because we didn't take our clothes off."

"But you married me." She pointed to the ring on her finger. "Why would you do that and then not have sex with me?"

His eyes darkened, if that was possible. "I married you for many reasons, one being to discover what makes your heart run wild. But I also married you to solve the eternal mystery of Melissa, and to prove your friends wrong. They may think they know who you are, but they don't."

"And you do?"

"No, but…" He tilted his head in thought. "How can I explain? Let's just say I saw the wishing well in your smile, and I want to find out how deep it goes." He traced her *un*smiling lips with one finger. "I want this to be a night that neither one of us will easily forget."

"A night? Just one night?"

"It all starts with just one night, Melissa."

She began to laugh. She didn't know what else to do. "Are you sure I actually woke up? That I'm not still dreaming?"

Pinch him, she thought. *If he yells, it's real.* But somehow she never got the chance. He took her hand as if she'd offered it to him on a platter. Was that how he would take the rest of her? As if she were something succulent that he wanted to sample and savor? That wouldn't be so bad. It wasn't like she'd ever been savored before.

"What makes Melissa's heart run wild?"

She tried not to react as he turned her hand over, exposing the inside of her wrist. She could see the delicate blue veins, the rapid pulse. She was watching her own heart flutter in crazy anticipation of what he might do.

He touched his lips to the tiny pulse and made it jump.

"Kissing wrists seems to work," she murmured, aware of the rasp in her voice.

Steady as she goes, Melissa. If you're going to write about this stuff, maybe you should give some of it a try. All the wicked things you've thrilled to in your mind. Bare lips on naked skin. A man's hands, hot and slow. That first forbidden cry of excitement.

"Want to bet it works with elbows, too?" he said with a slow smile.

She shook her head. "Not the same—" And quickly realized her mistake.

He trailed baby kisses up the inside of her arm. His breath was hot and moist—and his teeth deliciously sharp. When he got to the tingling flesh on the inside of her elbow, he helped himself. The nip sent a bolt of fire through her veins that made her dizzy and weak.

When she tumbled into his arms, he whispered, "Welcome home."

They rolled across the big bed, and Melissa's dress crept up to her panties. Antonio tried to preserve her modesty by pulling it down, but she barely noticed his efforts. They were flush up against each other, and her nerve endings had turned into friction sparks. The fire bolt zinged through her, its velocity thrilling. So this was what unbridled lust felt like. She hadn't realized it could come upon you that suddenly. Like a sneeze. You were fine one minute and reaching for a tissue the next.

Somebody should give her a box of tissues. She was on

the verge of a fit. She wanted to kiss and bite. Be kissed and bitten.

"Why did you marry me?" he asked, watching her face.

Apparently he wanted to talk.

She swallowed a tiny sigh of frustration and shrugged. "Because I would very much like to get into as much trouble as possible."

"You married me to get into trouble?"

"Yes, definitely."

"What kind of trouble?"

"The kind where you do things you've only imagined doing."

His jet eyes sparkled with intrigue. "What's stopping you?"

"I've never been in trouble. I'm not sure I'd know how to get out."

"Let's get you *in* first."

He feathered the silky tops of her breasts with the backs of his fingers. His boldness left Melissa momentarily speechless, and the sensations left her shaking inside. He was playing in the neckline of her sundress. He hadn't even kissed her yet. They hadn't kissed and he was headed for first base!

The fire bolt flared in her belly. No part of her body was safe.

She watched with fascination the bronze hands that teased her blushing skin. Her nipples drew tight in anticipation of what he might do next. She made no effort to stop him, which only increased the tension. She'd always wondered what it would be like to let a man have his way with her, to be a wanton love toy, existing only for his pleasure, at least for a couple hours.

What an article this would make. *Let the man have his*

way, let him kiss and touch and play, and he'll be randy, night and day.

It took too much energy to compose bad poetry, especially with the sensations spiraling through her. The fire bolt had split into ribbons of light, and she could barely concentrate on anything but their brightness.

Antonio seemed pretty intent, too. Apparently he enjoyed watching her breath catch in response to his touch. She trembled with delight as he bent to drop a kiss in the delicate cleft between her breasts. His mouth was warm and steamy, and she wondered if it could take her to the places where only her imagination had gone. She could still feel the way he'd caressed the back of her hand with his lips and his tongue. It had tickled so sweetly.

She made a purring sound as the lights ribboned through her again.

He met her gaze. "You remind me of a kitten," he said. "Big, innocent eyes, sharp little claws and very curious. What kind of trouble do you want to get into, kitten?"

She would rather have been a wild cat, but it was a start. "French-kissing, maybe?" She'd done it, of course, but a very long time ago, and she was anxious to get on with this makeup course in sexual fulfillment. Maybe she could write this off as research, and even if she couldn't, at least she wouldn't feel like a fraud anymore. She would finally have had some thrilling experiences of her own.

She decided to get more adventures. "Or fantasy role playing?"

"Rolling and playing?" He didn't seem to know what she was talking about.

"Maybe it would be easier if I showed you," she said. "Can I borrow one of these sheets?"

Together they worked the top sheet loose, a black silk

beauty that would easily make a half dozen of the skimpy costume she had in mind.

"Don't go anywhere," she told him as she disappeared into the bathroom with the sheet. The marbled dressing room had a full-length mirror that Melissa couldn't avoid as she slipped out of her clothes. She wasn't totally uncomfortable with her rather average figure, but she didn't often look at herself naked. Her tummy could have used a few emergency crunches, and there would be no cheating with a push-up bra to enhance her B-cup breasts. Her butt wasn't bad, though, and her calves were nicely shaped, thanks to the yoga, no doubt.

Gaaaah. Was she really getting naked in the bathroom of a hotel suite with a man lying in wait on a jungle-print bed just outside the door? Did sexual fulfillment have to be this thrilling, *this* wild? She wanted the experience, but this was nuts. Blame it on the Mocambos. And she'd almost forgotten about that knock to her head under the table at the restaurant. Call her crazy, call her drunk, call this the school for sluts. *Or call it her chance to find out who she really was, as opposed to who she'd been pretending to be.*

She undressed down to her panties, knotted the ends of the sheet together over one shoulder like a black silk toga, and let the length of it trail after her like a train. She thought about leaving one breast wantonly exposed, but that kind of brazenness would have taken another thump to the head. She'd never behaved like this before and she wasn't going to hold back now, after almost thirty years of holding back. Moments later, she opened the bathroom door, raised her arms above her head and touched the frame on each side, as if she were lashed there by ropes.

Antonio had rolled to his side, facing her, and propped his chin with his fist. He could have been a *Playgirl* centerfold, except that he wasn't showing enough skin. He could have been one anyway.

He smiled inquisitively.

"Have mercy, Lord," she whispered. She almost giggled but swallowed the urge and continued. "Don't ravish me and fling me into the volcano."

Antonio cocked his head. "Excuse me?"

"I *said* don't ravish me and fling me into the volcano. You're the tribal king, and I'm the only maiden left in the village. You have to sacrifice me to appease the volcano gods."

He cocked an eyebrow. "Couldn't I just ravish you?"

"No! There has to be a blood sacrifice."

"Sounds a little harsh, don't you think?"

"No, actually, it's *wonderful,* see, because you can't do it. You can't fling me to my death, so you fling yourself instead. Oh my God," she whispered. "I love that. It's so noble. It's so you, Antonio."

He sat up and swung his bare feet off the bed. "I appreciate the vote of confidence, fair maiden, but I'm not *that* noble, and I have a much better idea. Let's keep it simple. Why don't we tease you until you beg me to ravish you?"

"What fantasy is that?"

He began unbuttoning his shirt. "It's the prim-and-proper-lady fantasy, where you pretend you're immune to my fondling and wicked suggestions, and I, being a gentleman pirate, do my best to prove that you're not."

"Not bad." Except that Melissa had a wicked idea of her own. She struck a wanton pose then blew him a kiss. Next, she gave her shoulders a little shake, startling herself with her own boldness. The move made her breasts bounce, and while she had his attention fixed on her décolletage, she reached under the sheet and gave her panties a tug.

Could she really do this?

His dark eyes lit with anticipation.

"Like what you see?" Encouraged by his interest, she began to rotate her hips and draw the sheet up her leg, exposing a bit of creamy thigh.

Antonio watched her every move. "What's this fantasy called?"

"Shameless hussy."

"I like it."

His smoky voice could have set off a fire alarm. It brushed her senses with enough sparks to make her crazy with lust.

Antonio's shirt fell open as he rose from the bed, and the stark white material brought the tawny tones of his skin into sharp contrast. Unfair, she thought. His abs could have been classified as concealed weapons. They weren't just rippled. They were corrugated steel.

Show him what you've got, hussy. Level the playing field, so to speak.

Breathless, Melissa flashed more thigh and wriggled her hips, gyrating until the panties she'd tugged down were free of her hips. The silk material began to slide down her legs, and a thrill shot through her as it pooled around her ankles.

His gaze flared with passion. His beautiful mouth twitched.

With two strides, he closed the distance between them. Melissa's heart caught. She expected to be swept into his arms, kissed and plundered. Instead he smiled, watching her jump as he caressed her shoulder with his long fingers.

"You're toying with me," she murmured.

He gazed down at her, and she defied him with her eyes.

If his soul was as black as his pupils, they were in terrible trouble, both of them.

"Like what you see?" she asked coyly. Two could play at that game.

"Oh, yeah."

"Then take it...if you can."

She tried to step out of the panties, but the touch of his lips sent her swaying toward him. He locked his legs, bracing her, and reached up to place a hand over hers on the door frame. His other hand stole inside the sheet that protected her.

Melissa gasped. Not pretending anymore.

He growled softly as he found her naked skin.

The shameless hussy was shaking like a leaf. A moan welled in her throat. She kissed him back, and lights zoomed in her depths. Fountains splashed. This was better than her fantasies. A connection this thrilling couldn't be imagined. You had to feel it and let it feel you. You had to succumb.

Warm fingers found the small of her back, urging her closer. They crept down, those marauding fingers, getting more and more intimate with her defenseless derriere. But Melissa couldn't think about anything except the way he was laying sweet claim to her mouth.

His tongue swept her parted lips, and she moaned in appreciation, more eager than a shameless hussy should ever be to accommodate him. He drew back before she was anywhere near ready for the kiss to be over. She searched his eyes and saw the molten sparks of desire. *Good.* He was aroused, and that stoked her courage. Not breathing fire yet, but he would be.

She wanted this to happen. She needed it to. It would prove that she could push past her fears to her desires.

Back to the game. Now would begin the slow assault

on his defenses, and she intended to be merciless. She would dangle the prize and then snatch it away. Give him sips but never let him drink his fill. This would be no easy conquest. He would have to take the prize from her...and make her glad that he did.

She willed the sheet to fall away and leave her totally naked. How lovely to brush her breasts and thighs against him, and watch the fireworks. She swallowed heavily, imagining the way he would kiss her and fondle her when she was nude in the doorway. Who would be at whose mercy then? she wondered.

"Has a woman ever driven you crazy with lust?" she asked.

"Never."

"Good." Her knee crept up the inside of his thigh. "Let me be the first."

She tried not to look surprised as she nestled his burgeoning erection. This night promised to fulfill her fantasies in many ways. In her book, she had once described the pleasures of a well-endowed man, but she'd never experienced them. Never experienced much of anything, really. Her pirate would have to be slow and patient with her, although she wasn't going to tell him that just yet. Let him strain at the leash a little more.

She pressed her lips together in a pouty smile and rubbed her leg against his shaft. It was hot enough to burn a hole in his jeans. "Shameless enough for you?"

"I could devour you right here in the doorway."

Passion made his voice throaty and harsh. Melissa had to struggle to find hers. "Where would you like to start?"

"All of the really tasty places, like here—" Hot breath burned her ear as he whispered along her jaw to her mouth.

How could she hide her trembling breath from him? How could she hide anything? Her pulse was a mess, and if she'd been wearing panties, they would have been soaked by now.

"You can do better than that," she said. But she didn't sound terribly convincing, and he must have sensed weakness. He pressed his advantage, his fingers rimming the cleft of her buttocks and dipping between her legs to find the wetness there.

Pleasure zinged through her in a dizzying current.

"How's this?" His lips moved over hers, and the reverberations in his throat sounded like a sensual snarl. Long fingers pleasured her so sharply that her legs wanted to melt underneath her. Only she was trapped. The silk panties held her ankles, making it impossible to move without stumbling.

"Not bad," she got out.

But the whimper must have given her away.

In the space of the next several moments, she experienced one first after another, all of them at Antonio's sweetly plundering mouth and hands. He released her arms, and she waited for him to undo the sheet and let it fall from her body. Instead he knelt and raised it as slowly as a theater curtain, exposing her bare feet and unsteady ankles, the secrets of her calves and the pink baby skin behind her knees.

With a sound of satisfaction, he tucked the sheet behind her and secured it there.

His fingertips caressed the sensitive cords at the back of her ankles, purling upward to the bend of her knees. Melissa could feel her knees lock as he feathered the entire length of her shins. Heavenly. She didn't want him to stop, and yet it was maddening the way he drew out each touch to the breaking point.

Her thighs tightened almost painfully as he unveiled them. She wasn't sure she could handle much more, but he'd barely started. He opened the sheet to her waist and glanced up, as if preparing her for what came next. He pressed his lips to her mound and kissed her through the soft cap of curls. The sudden heat made her shiver with ecstasy. Her hands were still clutching the door frame, now the thing holding her up, or she would have buried them in his rich black hair. When had she lost control of this fantasy? She was supposed to be driving *him* mad with desire.

He cupped her buttocks, anchoring her as he brushed her still-hidden labia with his lips. His tongue stroked her secrets, searching for the nectar hidden in the rose. It swirled into crevices and flicked over nerve endings, nearly driving her over the edge. His warm breath dampened the dark curls, turning them into shiny ringlets. Or was it her own excitement making them so wet?

"Open your legs for me," he said.

She stepped out of the panties, anxious to give him access. She could have cried it was so delicious. But suddenly he rose—and left her aching for one more kiss.

"Not bad," she said faintly.

He laughed and picked her up in his arms, flinging away the dangling panties as if he never wanted to see them again. The sheet trailed behind them as he carried her to the bed. There wasn't time to protest as he laid her out, sheet and all, and took a moment to admire her that way. He dropped down to her feet and came up from there, spiriting the black silk away as he exposed her belly and breasts. He sprinkled kisses all the way up, lingering to let his tongue dip into her belly button and leisurely encircle her areolas. Velvet, that tongue.

He didn't stop until he had the sheet above her head, and she realized that her arms were entangled. Her breath snagged in her throat. He was going to leave her this way. "You're a devil," she cried softly.

She watched him rise from the bed to undo his belt and the clasp of his slacks. And he watched her watching. Talk about shameless. She couldn't believe the way he stripped down to the skin for her, clearly aware of her staring at him with wide, wondering eyes. He stepped out of his briefs, and she lost the breath she was holding. He was more than impressively built. He was intimidating. He moved toward her, but nothing bounced with his steps. His muscles were far too rigid for that. All of them.

"Think you're in enough trouble yet?" he asked her.

He ravished her senses slowly, arousing her until she could do nothing but whimper and plead with him to spare her. Even with the leisurely pace, she swiftly reached a point where one sensation burst like a star and melted into another, and soon it was all one glorious, mindless blur. Still, she was exquisitely conscious of the moment he mounted her, the moment he entered. The sudden pressure made her throw back her head in ecstasy. The aching sweetness brought tears to her eyes.

The experience of losing her virginity had been rushed, furtive and painful. This was as thrilling as her dreams. *More.* She begged him to pump faster and release her. But like a good pirate, he showed no mercy. He took his trembling prize all the way to the stars and back with slow and deliberate thoroughness—and made her desperately glad that he did.

Afterward, Melissa lay limp and breathing softly in his arms. But the vixen wasn't vanquished. She was only catching her breath. Some time later, as Antonio lay spent on the bed, she moved over him with the grace and cunning of a she-demon and aroused him to the same screaming pitch of desire that he had her.

Her sneak attack left *both* of them trembling, and when it was over, they slept for hours, but Melissa's body never truly quieted. It quivered in ecstasy the entire time she dozed, and at some point, deep in the night, he kissed the nape of her neck and whispered one last wedding vow, "I promise to keep you in trouble for as long as we both shall live."

MELISSA AWOKE with a soft gasp of surprise. She saw the man lying next to her in bed and realized she hadn't been dreaming. He was there. She'd married him. Or maybe she hadn't, but he *was* there. Dear God, what had she done? He could have been a serial killer, and she wouldn't have known. Everything was confused and fuzzy, but if she remembered correctly, she'd been more intimate with him than with any dream lover and she barely knew him. People sometimes poured out their hearts to total strangers. Was that what she'd done?

No, she hadn't poured out her heart. She'd poured out her most erotic fantasies.

How had this happened? Had she been drugged? Kidnapped? Sold into slave labor? Taken hostage and brainwashed?

Nothing so convenient as any of that, Melissa. Try consenting adult.

Careful not to wake him, she crept out of bed and looked around for her clothing. Panic rose inside her as she clutched a corner of the comforter to her naked body. Finally it came to her that she'd undressed in the bathroom. Maybe she *had* been dreaming. It was all so fuzzy in her mind.

No more Mocambos for her. Ever.

In the bathroom's full-length mirror, she checked herself for telltale marks. She did look slightly flushed and swollen in certain intimate places. Were those teeth bites on the inside of her thighs? She was lucky she hadn't pulled a muscle. All kinds of crazy questions buzzed through her head as she rushed to get into her clothing. Panic stirred again. All the more reason to leave before he woke up and confirmed her worst fears. If they'd really done the things she remembered, she didn't want to know.

She thought about leaving him a note, but there wasn't time. Something told her she had to get out of there before he woke and discovered her. Otherwise, she might not go. *Might not go?* What kind of crazy notion was that? He had incredible powers of persuasion, but she was sober now, with all her wits about her. Of course she was going. Just watch her go.

She straightened the straps of her dress and felt something snag on the linen. The ring. She'd almost left wearing the ring! A couple quick tugs on the band told her it wasn't going to come off easily. Desperate, she tried soaping her hand, but that didn't loosen it, either. She twisted and pulled, wincing in pain as the ring caught on her knuckle. Nothing short of metal shears was going to work, she realized in despair. She would have to find a way to return it to him later.

He was lying on his stomach as she came out of the bathroom. He'd thrown the pillow on the floor and twisted around so that the sheet just covered his sinfully sexy backside. She told herself not to look at anything, especially him, but a piece of paper on the bureau caught her eye. It was the marriage license. She picked it up on impulse and slipped it into her bag. The writer in her had taken over. Someday this would make a good story, if she ever had the courage to tell it.

She slipped out the door into the pink light of dawn, still unsure whether the odd warm glow that pervaded her body was really from sex or just from dreaming about it so vividly. By the time she got back to her hotel, she realized she'd left her shawl behind, the one she'd been searching for under the table when he'd arrived with the priest. Maybe she was destined to lose that shawl. Better than a few other things she could have lost. Like her mind. Or her heart. So much of what had happened confused and frightened her, but one thing she knew for sure. She wasn't going back for the shawl.

2

What's sexier to a man? A hot imagination or a hot body? If you said imagination, you're right! And he's one lucky guy.

101 Ways To Make Your Man Beg

Kansas City
Two years later...

MELISSA SANDERS WAS in the stork position when her bedroom phone rang. She'd raised her left leg, bent it at the knee and grabbed hold of her foot, which sounded easy but wasn't. With her other arm she reached for the sky. She'd been working on the posture for six months, and this was the first time she'd managed to hold it without timbering like a felled tree. She was not the most coordinated of women, which was why she'd taken up yoga. Well, that and to help with her runaway imagination. She'd heard yoga centered the mind as well as the body.

Let the phone ring. This was a milestone. She wanted to hold the position for at least two—maybe even three—minutes. That was a mere fraction of the time that Tara, her yoga teacher, could hold it, but still impressive. Tara was a goddess.

"Melissa, you there? It's Jeanie from Searchlight Publishing, and I have to talk to you! Call me the second you get in. I have great news!"

Exhale slowly from the center of your being. Breath is the divine life force.

Melissa's life force hissed out of her like a punctured tire. She tried to abandon the position and felt a sudden, agonizing tightness in her lower back. She'd pulled something.

"I'm coming," she said, knowing Jeanie couldn't hear her. She worked the heel of her hand into the tenderness, wondering if she had any liniment in the medicine cabinet—and felt like thirty going on one hundred and five.

She hobbled to the night table next to her four-poster bed with the heirloom patchwork quilt her mother had given her. But all she got for her trouble was a dial tone. Jeanie was long gone. The woman did everything at warp speed, including talk, but then she probably had to. She worked for Melissa's publishing company, and she was in charge of the publicity campaign for *101 Ways To Make Your Man Beg,* Melissa's first book.

My first book. Melissa marveled, smiling through the pain. She was still a little bewildered by her good fortune. She'd been making her living for years writing freelance articles for women's magazines. The articles had gotten her noticed, and she'd been invited to submit a book proposal to Searchlight because of several pieces on imaginative sex she'd done for *Women Only* magazine. But she hadn't dreamed the publisher would actually want to buy it. That was a year ago, and just last week, *101 Ways* had been released.

Melissa punched in the number and got Jeanie on the first try.

"Are you sitting down, Melissa? Maybe you should," the publicist said.

Melissa groaned in anticipation. Sitting was going to hurt. Her back didn't seem to want to do anything *but* the stork position. She worked the area vigorously, with her fist.

"Okay, I'm on the bed. If I fall over, it'll be a soft landing. What is it?"

"Your first week's sales in the chain bookstores are phenomenal, and marketing wants to run with it. They're sending you on a two-week, ten-city media tour, and I'm coming with you. Isn't that the best?"

"Two weeks?"

"At least. We'll fly you into New York on Thursday, but here's the really exciting part. You're going to be on *Wake Up, America* Friday morning. Are you getting this?"

"*Thursday?* Two days from now?" Melissa had never been to New York, and she'd certainly never been on a media tour. Other than her yearly escapes with the girls, she didn't travel at all. Her writing assignments allowed her to work from home, and she did most of her research on the Internet. Besides, the trips she took inside her own mind were exotic enough.

"It's okay," Jeanie said. "I'll meet you at the airport and get you settled in your hotel, and I'll be there first thing Friday morning to pick you up for the show."

Melissa was too agitated to stay on the bed. A twinge made her groan as she rose.

"Melissa? Is there a problem?"

"I hurt myself, Jeanie. Where's your spleen anyway? Lower back near the kidneys? I think I may have bruised mine."

"Oh pooh, Melissa. You're always ailing with something. I think spleens are like appendixes, aren't they? Not really necessary? Besides, being hurt is out of the question. We've already booked you on almost every daytime show in existence. The airline is e-mailing you the tickets, so get yourself packed. It'll be fine.''

''Jeanie, I really did hurt—''

But she was gone again, before Melissa could defend herself. And it was probably true that she had a tendency to exaggerate medical symptoms. Her friends had stopped discussing their various conditions in front of her because she would invariably come down with them within days— TMJ, ADD, the heartbreak of psoriasis, which had turned out to be a couple of bug bites. Her damn imagination was always getting her into trouble. But it was also her bread and butter. She spent her time thinking up ways to make women's love lives more exciting. She, who'd had no sex in two years, and then it had been just a crazy fluke.

The phone rang again, and she jumped about a foot off the floor. *Ouch.* She really did need to get a grip. She'd be doing the tour in a back brace.

''Sorry,'' Jeanie said. ''I forgot the most important part. Marketing wants you to bring Antonio with you.''

''Antonio?''

''Your gorgeous husband, silly. The man you dedicated the book to.''

Melissa sank down on the bed. This couldn't be happening. There *was* no husband, not the way Jeanie was thinking. Two years ago she'd married a man on a dare, and her one night with him had inspired the idea for the book. But it wasn't a real marriage, just a night of unbelievable passion. The man had driven her mad in the best possible way. He'd had her as naked as the day she was born and perspiring through every pore, and she hadn't even given a thought to catching a cold. There'd been moments when she couldn't remember her own name.

At any rate, she'd dedicated the book about revitalizing

marital sex to her "husband" to give it credibility. Who would listen to a woman who'd never been married?

"Your readers will be crazy to meet him," Jeanie was saying. "Everyone at Searchlight is crazy to meet him. I mean, this is the guy who gives you orgasms by whispering in your ear, right? Wasn't that chapter eight—'How to Turn Him into the Lover of Your Dreams in One Night'?"

"Yes," said Melissa weakly. "Chapter eight."

Melissa forgot her bruised spleen. In the next thirty seconds, she debated every possible excuse she could think of. She was pregnant, she was dying, she was gay. She put her vivid imagination to the test, but nothing made sense. Nothing but the truth.

"Jeanie, don't hang up, okay? I need to tell you something."

"Oh my God, more marriage-bed secrets? You two will be a smash on the talk-show circuit."

Melissa wet her lips. "Jeanie, I've got something to tell you." She paused a moment, then biting the bullet, she blurted out, "There is no husband. Antonio does not exist."

Over the din of her pounding heart, Melissa heard a thud. Fortunately, it turned out to be Jeanie's phone, not Jeanie, herself.

"I'm okay," the publicist said, breathing hard. "I got up too fast. How can there be no Antonio? You dedicated the book to him! He lovingly waxes the hair from your inner thighs, Melissa! He nibbles on your elbows and removes your underwear with his teeth. I've been fantasizing about the man for a year, and now you're telling me he *doesn't exist?*"

"I can explain." And she tried. She told Jeanie everything. About the dare, about the one crazy night, about the most incredible sex of her life—well, almost everything—

she did not mention that it was the only sex of her life worth mentioning.

"It wasn't a total fabrication," Melissa pointed out. "We did get married, sort of."

"You married him and never saw him again?"

Now Melissa heard repetitive thuds and imagined Jeanie pacing back and forth over her floor. Her poor publicist was clearly desperate to salvage the tour—and the book sales. Strong sellers weren't easy to come by, and it wasn't just Melissa's credibility on the line. It was Jeanie's, too, and the publishing company's. They had obviously never bothered to check on their author's credentials.

"Maybe we can still make this work," Jeanie said. "It was a bona fide union, right? Was there a marriage license?"

"Well, I signed something, a document in Spanish that looked sort of legal, but it was in Mexico. I'm not a citizen. It wouldn't be valid here, would it?" *Please say it wouldn't.*

"Do you still have it? And don't say 'sort of'!"

Melissa sighed. "Yes, somewhere."

"Fax it to me. Fax it to me *now,* along with all the information you have about the man—his full name, his nationality, the name of the restaurant where he worked, and when you last saw him. Send me everything."

"All right...but why?"

"Because I'm going to find your mystery husband, and I'm going to find him fast."

"Do you think that's a good idea?" She spoke to a buzzing dial tone. Jeanie was already hot on Antonio's trail, and there was probably nothing she could do about it.

Melissa fell on the bed, moaning at the twinge in her back. She tugged futilely at the delicate gold band that was still stuck on her finger after two years. She'd never been able to get it off, and she hadn't had the heart to have the band cut off. She'd explained it to her parents as a ring she'd had to buy because it got stuck on her finger, the wrong finger. They knew nothing about Antonio or the book she'd dedicated to him, and given that they lived a very isolated existence on their farm, with one television that hadn't worked in years, she didn't expect them to find out. On those infrequent occasions when she dated, she resorted to the "wrong finger" story, or wore a Band-Aid.

Maybe the ring had jinxed her. And what had she been thinking about anyway, pretending that she had a real husband? If Jeannie didn't find Antonio, her book was down the drain. The publisher might even sue her for misrepresentation. But if the publicist did find him, what was Melissa expected to do? Pretend she and Antonio were still married—and that they were the blissfully satisfied couple she'd written about, whose relationship was so hot they used their cell phones to leave each other erotic text messages?

She'd hoped writing the book would resolve her feelings about that night—kind of like exorcising demons—but it hadn't. She dreaded the possibility that Jeanie might find him. How crazy and complicated and *dangerous* would that be? Melissa had no idea how he felt about her after all this time. What if he was angry at her, or worse, delusional in some way? He could destroy her career with a word. It was a terrifying thought, but at the same time, she felt an undeniable fascination with the idea of seeing him again. How could she not? He was the catalyst for her wildest fantasies and a source of pleasure beyond description. His smoldering intensity was as sharply imprinted on her nervous system as it was vivid in her mind.

Antonio. Dear God.

Melissa sprang up and rushed out of the bedroom, heading down the hall to her office. She was supposed to be looking for a marriage license, but she had to find a copy of her own book first. What else had she written in that thing?

"I'LL BE FINE. I can do this," Melissa said. She sat next to Jeanie on the greenroom couch of *Wake Up, America,* patting the publicist's tightly clasped hands. "I really like the idea of picking couples from the audience and giving them the Naughty-Sex Quiz. That should be fun," she enthused, despite in truth feeling a bit leery about the idea.

"Are you ready for some tough questions?" Jeanie asked. "In the last segment, Bobbi will take questions from the audience, but even she doesn't know what they're going to be. The show's producers don't want to lose the element of surprise."

"I don't think I could be surprised," Melissa said dryly. "I've memorized the damn book."

"Where's your hubby, Ms. Sanders? How are you going to answer that one?"

"He's in London on business travel. I'm hoping he can join me soon." Melissa smiled and flashed the band on her finger at Jeanie. "See, I'm ready for anything. I'm even wearing a wedding ring."

"Hey, *good* thinking," Jeanie said. "That didn't occur to me."

Melissa felt an uneasy twinge as the gold ring glinted in the lights, but decided not to share its history with Jeanie. Maybe that's why it was still on her finger—to help her pull off this crazy tour.

"You thought of everything else," she told Jeanie. "It's going to be fine."

Of course, Melissa was certain she would be stricken

with hysterical blindness during the broadcast and run screaming off the set. But other than that, it was a classic case of role reversal. Jeanie seemed more nervous than Melissa. There was more at stake than Melissa wanted to think about, so she was concentrating on being grateful that the booking hadn't been canceled. Antonio still hadn't been located, but the marketing department had made an executive decision to go ahead without him. *Wake Up, America* was too good a gig to pass up, and Melissa had finally convinced them she would be able make excuses for her missing husband.

Please, God, let him stay missing. It was much safer that way.

The greenroom door popped open, and the show's guest-wrangler—the harried young woman who'd been squiring them around all morning—beckoned for Melissa. "C'mon! You're up next!"

Melissa squeezed Jeanie's hand. "I can do this," she whispered. "I won't let you down."

Jeanie squeezed back, and some color returned to her ashen face. She began to straighten Melissa's clothing, dusting the shoulders of her navy pin-stripe pantsuit and straightening the starched collar of her man-tailored blouse. She even gave Melissa's shiny brunette pageboy a smoothing. It was probably a reflex action, but Melissa was encouraged that Jeanie was acting more like herself. Jeanie was about thirty-five and the perfect publicist, part brilliant sales strategist and part mother hen. There hadn't been much strategizing going on this morning, but at least she was starting to make familiar clucking noises.

The guest-wrangler grabbed Melissa's hand, dragged her out of Jeanie's clutches and quickly led her through the wings. Melissa heard a countdown, and then she was gently pushed onto a television set to tumultuous applause.

The lights were surreal, like the spaceship landing in *Close Encounters,* but she could see a woman who looked like Bobbi Start rising from a couch and waving at her. She'd never seen the host through anything but her television screen. Now she looked as if she were a mile away.

Was that a symptom of hysterical blindness?

Melissa wouldn't have placed a bet on her chances of getting over there, but somehow she made the trip in seconds, and miraculously, there were no disasters. She didn't trip or fall. Her fly didn't unzip itself and her jacket didn't catch on anything and rip off her body like stunt clothing.

Did they have obedience schools for imaginations? She should have sent hers years ago. *Down, imagination, down.*

''Here's our sex expert!'' Bobbi rushed over and hugged Melissa as she stepped up on the pedestal set. Bobbi's exuberance nearly knocked them both over, which the audience loved. They clapped and cheered, making Melissa feel as if she was in friendly company. She wasn't surprised the show was a hit. Bobbi projected that same sort of welcome to everyone. Tiny and boundlessly perky, the former Olympic gymnast was morning television's bright new face. She'd brought *Wake Up* to the number-two spot in the ratings, and the show was swiftly gaining on number one.

Who needs coffee, with Bobbi Start in the morning? That was the show's teaser.

''Melissa, Melissa, *Melissa,*'' Bobbi gushed as they sat down. ''You naughty girl! This book of yours is quite an eye-opener. Or should I say mind-opener?''

Bobbi held up *101 Ways,* and Melissa blushed, mostly with pleasure. She'd been coached by Jeanie to think of herself as excited rather than nervous, which must mean she was *really* excited. Her insides were vibrating like one of those coin-operated motel beds.

"Please, yes, call it a mind-opener," Melissa said. "My goal with the book is to help women think out of the box, so to speak, when it comes to their love lives. I believe we should be as creative in our quest for sexual enjoyment as we are in our quest for bargains at the mall. Think how happy everyone would be—and how skinny. You know sex burns nearly seven hundred calories an hour. That's better than the treadmill."

Bobbi chortled. "But who could have sex for an hour?"

She doesn't know Antonio, Melissa thought.

One of the cameras had a blinking red light, which Melissa had been told meant it was on. She glanced at it and smiled, hoping to send Jeanie a signal. *See, I'm doing fine out here. Piece of cake.*

"Why don't we have some fun with the folks in our audience," Bobbi suggested. "Let's give a lucky couple the Naughty-Sex Quiz and see how they do. Do we have any volunteers?"

Hands shot up all over the studio, but one of the show's pages was already out in the audience with a couple who'd volunteered before the taping. The page introduced the couple as in their thirties, married ten years and stuck in the sexual doldrums.

Melissa scanned the crowd nervously. Okay, so she'd invented the quiz for her book, but it hadn't occurred to her that she'd be conducting man-on-the-street-type interviews. She greeted the couple with a smile, pretending it wasn't at all unusual to be casually probing into the intimate details of their lives.

"Do you indulge in sexual afterplay as well as sexual foreplay?" she asked them. "In other words, do you talk about your lovemaking afterward and tell each other what you liked?"

The man blushed, but the woman spoke right up. "What I'd like is to *have* sex," she said.

The audience tittered, and Melissa found herself grinning, too. "Not to worry," she said. "It sounds like a case of sexual batteries going dead. What you need is a jump start." She rubbed her hands as if warming them. "To get the current flowing again, try something I call erotic flash-forwards. They're fun, highly stimulating, and they'll help you discover your own secret turn-ons."

"What are erotic flash-forwards?" Bobbi asked.

The husband seemed perplexed, too. "I flashed someone once," he said uncertainly. "There was a census taker at the door and it was hotter 'n hell that day, so I flapped my bathrobe to create a breeze—"

Bobbi jumped in again, apparently to save the audience's delicate sensibilities. "I'm guessing Melissa is talking about visualizing the kind of sex you'd like to have with your partner. Right, Melissa? Fantasizing?"

"Yes, exactly." She turned to the crowd. "And here's a homework assignment for *all* of you. Next time you're stuck in traffic or waiting in a line, use that time to daydream about what would thrill your soul if you were alone somewhere with your partner. It could be something you saw at the movies or read in a book, but don't limit it to the obvious. Sure, you could have your partner brush your hair, but maybe you'd rather have him warm your bottom with that hairbrush."

"Just when it was getting interesting!" Bobbi clucked with disappointment as the show's theme music began to play. "We have to take a short break, but stay tuned. Coming up next? How to make him sit up and *beg* for booty."

As soon as the cameras were off, the set buzzed with activity. A rather morose young man refreshed Melissa's water glass and Bobbi's iced tea. Flowers were fluffed and pillows plumped. A soundwoman checked the boom mikes, and a group of staffers huddled in discussions off to one side.

Melissa looked to Bobbi for approval and got a thumbs-up as the host leafed through her notes. "The next segment should be even better," she said. "I see we have some great surprises in store. These producers of mine are geniuses."

The guest-wrangler dashed out to powder Melissa's nose, so there was no chance to find out what Bobbi meant, but she wasn't too concerned. Things seemed to be going pretty well. Even the married couple had been cute without trying to be. When you talked about sex, you had a real advantage, she'd discovered. The subject was a minefield of double entendres. You couldn't go far without stepping on something. It was dangerous—and exciting.

"...three, two, one—"

Melissa barely got a sip of water before they were back on the air. Bobbi held up the book again, and one of the cameras zoomed in for a close-up. The cover appeared on the monitor, and the name Melissa Sanders appeared on the screen. It gave her quite a jolt. That was *her* book! There'd been a flurry of activity getting ready, and it hadn't dawned on her until now that she'd be seeing her own book on TV. It almost felt as if they were talking about someone else, and she was here by mistake.

"Let's talk about chapter five, Melissa. Some of these games sound like carnival rides—Joyride, Spin Cycle, Express Train to Blissville, Wing-Ding Swing and Sexual Paste. Oh, and how about this one—the Velvet Tongue. Care to tell us about any of those?" Bobbi said with a coy wink.

"Well, the Wing-Ding Swing involves having your partner push you in the swing, but not with his hands."

"My, my." Bobbi laughed. "Sounds like good coordination is required. How about Sexual Paste, hmm? You must tell us about that one."

Melissa laughed, too. "Sorry, you'll have to read the book. Sexual Paste is triple-X-rated and much too hot for daytime TV."

"Okay, but tell us this at least—which one of these games made your husband beg for more? Was it the Velvet Tongue, maybe?"

Melissa blushed. The interlude that had sparked the name Velvet Tongue was still achingly vivid in her mind, even after two years.

"Actually, Antonio inspired that game," she said softly, "but I'm not sure I should tell you how."

Bobbi rose, glancing toward the wings from which Melissa had emerged. "Well, then," she said in a tone lilting with intrigue, "maybe Antonio will tell us himself."

"What?" Melissa stared at Bobbi, who was now talking directly to the camera.

"Yes, folks, we have a surprise for Melissa. She doesn't know anything about this, but we've brought her husband over from London, where he was traveling on business. We thought everyone would want to meet the man who inspired the Velvet Tongue."

Bobbi flung out an arm. "Welcome, Antonio Bond!"

NO ONE GASPED louder than Melissa as a tall, dark and exotically handsome man walked onto the set of the talk show. His glossy black hair was a little longer than current trends dictated, but he'd never seemed the type who cared about trends. It caressed the nape of his neck and fell onto his forehead, making him look ever so slightly disreputable, but in the sexiest possible way.

On the other hand, he could have been a spokesperson

for the line of clothes he wore. The casually tailored slacks, black silk shirt and woven leather sandals gave him the look of a man who'd just flown in from the south of France. The shadowed jaw beautifully carved his angular face. This was not the waiter who'd dropped to his knees in front of her and proposed. And yet, it was. This was Antonio. He had that same intense, prepare-to-be-swept-off-your-feet quality.

He walked to Bobbi first and shook her hand, then turned to Melissa, who had not yet managed to stand up. His dark gaze locked in on her, glinting with dangerous lights. Apparently he was in no rush. The set's blinking red bulbs and ticking time clocks didn't seem to faze him as, with undisguised interest, he watched her efforts to rise.

With a tug of his hand, he pulled her to her feet and said for everyone to hear, "*Cara,* it feels like years since I've held you."

The audience sighed as he drew her into his arms. Melissa couldn't even breathe. Her pulse throbbed so hard it hurt, but this wasn't pleasure. She didn't know what it was. Fear, excitement, wild anticipation?

The audience couldn't hear what he whispered, and Melissa didn't catch all of it either, but it sounded like, "Don't expect to walk away from me again. Ever."

She glanced up at him, startled, but all she caught was his fleeting smile. Lord, he was impossibly gorgeous. Still. That mouth of his was every bit as smolderingly gorgeous as the night he'd laid a trail of fiery kisses all over her nude, trembling body. Why was this happening to her? On national television?

"It's just as beautiful as the night I put it on your finger," he said.

Melissa wasn't sure what he meant until he brought her fingers to his lips and kissed the woven gold band she

wore. Her heart froze like a stone. It was the ring. She was
jinxed, cursed. She would never escape him as long as that
ring was on her finger. She could feel her imagination
spinning away with her, and she made a desperate effort
to stop it. Jinxes and curses were pure superstition. It was
him, not the ring. *He* was her problem.

She needed some distance from him, but it felt as if
she'd stepped onto a merry-go-round. If not for his arms
around her, she would have tumbled off. The set swirled,
and so did her thoughts. What had he actually said, and
more to the point, what did he want from her? Maybe she
was spinning out again, but could this be some kind of
blackmail attempt? Was he after money? He'd never struck
Melissa as that kind of man, but how well did she know
his true character?

Jeanie should have thought of all this before she tracked
him down.

Why didn't she tell me she'd found him?

Antonio sat down next to her, and never in her life had
Melissa been forced to gather her wits so quickly. She
knew Jeanie had been looking for him, but she hadn't been
prepared for him to show up this way. In all honesty, she
hadn't been prepared for him to show up at all. She hoped
he'd been coached and knew what he was supposed to say
and not say, but there'd been no sign of that so far.

She had no idea what to say either, especially to him.
*Have mercy, Lord, don't ravish me and fling me into the
volcano.* That should bring down the house.

"I can see this really is a surprise for Melissa," Bobbi
chirped. "Just look at her. She looks— Are you all right,
Melissa?"

"I'm speechless," Melissa managed to say. "How did
you find him?"

No, never mind! Don't answer that.

Bobbi was already addressing the audience. "Somehow, I have trouble imagining Antonio begging for anything, don't you?" she asked them. Heads nodded.

"Call me Tony, please," he said. He graced Bobbi with a fleeting smile, then shot a penetrating glance at Melissa. "I think my bride should answer that. Have you ever heard *me* beg, Melissa?"

Melissa tossed him a bawdy wink. "Well, of course." She turned back to Bobbi. "My whole book is based on personal experience." She was not going to let this man intimidate her on national television. He was supposed to be her well-satisfied husband, according to the book, and if he didn't know it, she would have to make that point somehow.

He leaned over and whispered in her ear, "Tell the truth, if you dare. And by the way, according to your book, I can arouse you to the point of orgasm this way. Is it working? Maybe you'd better let the audience think it is if you want to sell books."

Melissa whimpered, but not in ecstasy. Every single eye was glued on her. She considered doing her best imitation of Meg Ryan in *When Harry Met Sally,* but the humiliation factor was too great. She couldn't make those noises when she was having sex. Well, except with him, the rat, and she didn't intend to give him that satisfaction now. She was already having flashbacks of their wedding night. In Technicolor and Surround Sound.

She could hear the sensual growl in his throat when he'd stolen inside her toga with his hand and found her naked skin for the first time. She could smell the body heat rising off his skin, and feel the rush of her own blood as she realized how addictive his touch could be.

Somehow she had to hit Rewind and turn this video off! Stalling for time, she reached for her cup of ice water.

Her hand was shaking so hard, she could barely hold it steady, which gave her an idea. But could she do something that crazy? No, it was outrageous, much too risky.

Yes, she could do it. She had to. It was the only way to put him off balance and regain any kind of control.

She sucked in some air, flashed Antonio a nervous smile—and emptied the entire mug into his lap. It had to be freezing cold, but he didn't move a muscle that she could see. He just sat there, breathing through his nostrils, and did nothing while the audience gasped.

Bobbi sprang into action, looking for something to blot up the mess, and the guest-wrangler dashed over with a towel. She held it out to Tony, but Melissa grabbed it.

"It's okay!" She held up the towel, addressing Bobbi and the audience. "We're playing a game called Oops! You spill something on the gentleman's lap, and then you get to clean him up. It's very sexy. Right, Tony?"

Tony's glance had gone darker than a creature of the night's. Dracula didn't have eyes that black and endless. In an ominous voice, he said, "I don't know about Oops! but we have played a few games. The one I like best is the Runaway Bride and the Furious Groom—who takes his revenge when he catches up with her."

Melissa gulped audibly. She had little doubt that he was furious, and that she would pay for this in some unspeakable way. But that wasn't the only thing that concerned her at the moment. The audience had all been given free copies of *101 Ways*. She hoped no one would notice there was no such game in the book.

3

Fighting is an underrated activity among lovers. It cleans the pipes and clears the air, and then there's make-up sex!

101 Ways To Make Your Man Beg

IT ALL BROKE LOOSE right after the show. Tony stood behind a screen, pulling on a dry pair of pants, which the guest-wrangler had found for him. On the other side of the screen, he could hear Melissa pacing, muttering about how she'd been betrayed and how Jeanie would hear about this. As far as Tony was concerned, Melissa had a few things to learn about betrayal, but that could wait until they were alone.

Alone. He could hardly wait.

The door opened and someone entered the greenroom. "Hey, terrific show!"

Tony recognized the voice as Jeanie's, the publicist from Searchlight. But Melissa didn't seem to share her enthusiasm for the show. She nearly squeaked with indignation.

"Why didn't you tell me about him?" she asked Jeanie.

Her anger gave Tony a small measure of satisfaction. If he had his way, she would squeak often and with feeling. And he *would* have his way.

"The producers wanted him to be a surprise," Jeanie said. "What could I do?"

Tony zipped up his pants. As he emerged from behind the screen, the two women were circling each other like combatants. He didn't realize they'd noticed him until Melissa stabbed a finger in his direction.

"A surprise?" she said. "He's not a surprise. He's a fatal mistake from my past. How could you spring something like this on me?"

Jeanie clasped her hands in an act of contrition. "I'm *sorry*. The show wouldn't take you without him, Melissa. They were going to cancel our booking. I found him at the last minute, and they made me promise not to tell you."

"And you agreed to that? Knowing my history with him, you still agreed?"

"I thought you'd want me to. It's for the book. Everything we're doing is for the good of the book, right?"

Tony wasn't exactly happy with either one of these women, but he was rooting for the one who hadn't just dumped ice water on him. The vestal virgin had changed, he acknowledged, watching her stamp her black spectator pumps. She'd gotten better at standing up for herself.

So much for trying to protect damsels being badgered by their girlfriends. At first his proposal two years ago had been nothing more than a gallant move to quiet her friends. But when he'd knelt down to ask for her hand and seen the look of utter disbelief in her eyes, he'd known he was going through with it. She didn't believe any man could want her.

And he couldn't believe that.

She was beautiful. Her translucent skin was tinged with the hot pink of blooming roses, her expression one of wonderment. When he'd run into her on the beach, she'd seemed as wistful as the Madonnas in the mission, but once they were alone in his room, she'd confounded him with the way she'd thrown caution to the winds. She'd sent his heart and various other parts of his body soaring, and he hadn't caught up with them since.

The guest-wrangler popped her head in the greenroom at that moment and made various hand signals that Jeanie seemed to understand.

"The limo's here," Jeanie said, beckoning to Melissa and Tony. "It will take us to the hotel, and we can talk this over there."

"What hotel?" Melissa asked.

"The hotel where you and Tony are staying."

"He and I are *not* staying at the same hotel."

Tony caught Melissa's glance, the one that said this was all his fault.

"It's just for appearances," Jeannie explained. "We need people to think you're married—and by the way, you are."

"Are what?"

"Married."

Melissa went as pale as death. "It's legal? Is that what you're saying?"

She tugged on the ring as if trying to pull it off, which Tony found highly ironic. The band had been in his family for years, and there was an interesting legend attached to it, if you believed in such things. He'd always wondered why she'd taken the ring with her. He could never really fathom that she'd stolen it, but now it was also hard to imagine that she'd kept the ring all this time.

Jeanie nodded with the authority of a magistrate. "Legal and binding. You signed your name to the marriage license."

Melissa gave out a little choking sound. "How is that possible? I thought it was all a joke, and the license was in Spanish. I didn't know what I was signing."

"No judge is going to buy that, Melissa. You stood with

Tony before the priest, recited the vows and signed your name to the certificate. You knew it wasn't a funeral.''

Tony had some sympathy for Melissa at that moment. News of her had certainly come as a shock to him, too. He had obligations that didn't allow for treks to New York—binding obligations, both business and personal. He should have been furious at the news, but he hadn't been, not totally. Melissa had signed the form, but her last name was illegible. That apparently didn't make the union any less legal, but it was why he hadn't been able to trace her. She didn't know that, however, and he wasn't going to be the one to tell her. He was here because he had to be. Her publicist had made him a deal he couldn't refuse. But there was one other reason: He wanted to know how a woman could give herself to a man with such complete abandon and then walk away without a word.

"Melissa, are you all right?" Jeanie asked.

She held her chest and made little panting sounds. "I can't seem to breathe," she said. "There's something wrong."

Jeanie gave an exasperated shake of her head. Apparently she'd dealt with this before. "Melissa, you're fine. Now, let's get out of here. The limo's waiting for us."

Melissa's pants became gasps, and it sounded to Tony like the breathing problems he'd had as a child. Moving quickly, he came up behind her, clamped one hand over her mouth and held her nose with the other. His forearm pressed into the softness of her breast, and he could feel every crazy beat of her heart. He wasn't copping a feel, much as he might like to. He was trying to keep her from passing out, but apparently she didn't appreciate the good deed. Within seconds she'd broken out of his hold and was whirling on him.

"What do you think you're doing?"

"Just trying to help," he said. "It's an old remedy my mother used to use. You seem to be breathing better now."

Jeanie made a tiny gurgling noise that sounded like laughter, but Melissa didn't seem to be amused. She had her arms crossed over her breasts, and he knew exactly what that felt like. His skin still resonated with the steam heat of her flesh and the quick, hard beats of her heart. Two years ago she'd wanted his touch. She'd begged him for it, but he'd made her wait. He knew all about pleasure withheld. Its potential. Its power.

She'd been making him wait ever since.

"Let's go." He reached for her arm. "I'll help you."

She drew back, her eyes spitting fire. "I don't need help, thank you. Why don't you just throw me over your shoulder like a caveman and stomp off with me?" Obviously realizing what she'd said, she thrust out a hand. "Don't you dare!"

Tony's smile held little in the way of mirth. She had no idea how much he wanted to throw her over his shoulder and carry her off. His runaway bride had left him wondering what hit him. She'd given him a gift—one night of heaven—and then she'd snatched it away. He'd spent two years unable to get her out of his mind, two years obsessed with her wanton body and her heart-shaped face.

He and Melissa Sanders had some catching up to do. Call it unfinished business.

Her book was all about how to make men beg, but that wasn't how it was going to work. Someone might be begging, but it wouldn't be him. And he couldn't wait to be there when she found out.

THE BLACK LINCOLN sluiced its way through the rain-snarled streets of midday Manhattan, traversing the honking cabs, jaywalking pedestrians and death-defying bike messengers. It was exactly noon, and the storm clouds had picked the busiest hour of the day to burst. Runoff drains were overflowing and the block-long city buses drenched everything in their wake with their spray.

Spring had sprung a leak, and tempers were coming to a quick boil. Sirens wailed, and cabbies rolled down windows to shout curses in every language imaginable. But inside the limo the atmosphere was more restrained—quiet and tense. No one said much of anything, except Jeanie, who was on the phone with booking agents, trying to juggle appointments.

Melissa was just grateful to have the show over and nothing else scheduled today. She had a book signing tomorrow morning and two interviews in the afternoon, back-to-back, and there would probably be more when Jeanie was done. But at least they had time to get this mess straightened out, the mess being Antonio—or rather, Tony—Bond.

Jeanie had done her best to put a good face on things. "The show was a huge success," she'd told them when they'd first got into the limo. "The audience was on the edge of their seats."

"At least their seats were dry," Tony had observed in a low, dangerous tone.

"Accidents happen," Melissa was quick to insist. "I had to make the best of it, didn't I?"

Fortunately, Jeannie had positioned herself in the middle of the squabbling couple. Otherwise, Melissa might have been singed by the look she got from Tony. It was as hot as the steam coming off the streets.

Now he was busy jotting notes on a legal pad, and Melissa was trying to peek over Jeanie's lap to see what he was up to. Naturally his handwriting was illegible. Someone else might have called it bold and dramatic, but Melissa wasn't feeling very charitable right now. It didn't surprise her, though, that he wrote boldly. He did lots of things that way.

"Excellent," Jeanie said to whomever was on the line. "You want Mel and Tony there two hours early for makeup and wardrobe? You got it. Thank you!"

She clicked off the phone, all smiles. "You guys are hot! Melissa, they've already shortened your name to Mel. Isn't that adorable? And apparently every booking agent in the country was watching *Wake Up*, because they're crazy for you two. I just firmed up four more shows, with six pending."

"Not so fast," Melissa said. "We have to talk about this."

"And we will talk." Jeanie dropped her cell phone in her huge Louis Vuitton backpack. "But first a word of warning, kids. I haven't had a reaction to an author appearance like this in years. Something is happening here that is bigger than all three of us, and if anybody in this limo is thinking about chickening out, let me just say this. *Don't.*"

"Thanks for taking the pressure off," Melissa mumbled.

Tony, however, seemed more than ready to negotiate. "I want game approval prior to the shows," he told Jeanie. "No more surprises like that Oops! game. Without that stipulation, I can't agree to the terms you've laid out."

"What terms?" Melissa asked Jeanie. "What agreement have you made with him? And why wasn't I told about any of this?"

"As I said in the greenroom, I wasn't free to tell you." Jeanie's tone was one of calm forbearance. *Hey, relax, everything's under control,* she seemed to be saying. "And as for Tony," she added, "we dragged him away from his very busy life. We had to find some way to compensate him.''

Melissa peered at the two of them suspiciously. "And what way was that?"

Jeanie shrugged. "I can't really discuss the details of our arrangement with Tony, now, can I?''

Tony hadn't cracked a smile, but Melissa sensed that he wanted to. His expression, his whole demeanor, was a bit too innocent for her taste. He and Jeanie were in league in some way, and that struck her as just downright wicked. How could a publisher turn on their author like this? Of course, she was the one who'd started this whole thing by dedicating the book to him, but that didn't justify a conspiracy.

"Well, maybe I have some terms, too," Melissa said, thinking fast to come up with a whopper of a list. "If we really are expected to stay in the same hotel room, then it has to be a suite. I want my own bedroom and bath. I'd also like a daily rundown of the schedule with background information on whom we'll be dealing with at each interview. Plus, Tony and I are obviously going to need some rehearsal time if we're to pull off this blissfully happy couple thing. And last, when all this is over, I want a divorce.''

"No problem with any of that, including the divorce,'' Jeanie said amiably.

Melissa looked at her sharply. She hadn't expected it to be this easy. She'd thought someone would protest, possibly even Tony, but he seemed to be taking it all in stride, too. Maybe she should have added a little something like: *And meanwhile, there's to be absolutely no sex!* See if that got his attention.

"This is a two-week tour?'' Tony asked, apparently confirming what he already knew.

Jeanie nodded. "However, Searchlight would like you both to be available for joint interviews for the next three months."

Melissa dropped back in the seat with a gasp.

Both Jeanie and Tony glanced over at her, and at least Jeanie had the decency to show some concern. "You don't have to live together," she told Melissa, "but you do have to be willing to make media appearances."

"How about two months?" Antonio suggested.

"One month," Melissa croaked when she found her voice.

"I'll leave it open for now," Jeanie said, "but whatever period we agree upon is final. If you want a quick and quiet annulment of the marriage after that, go ahead. I assume that's what you both want, isn't it? An annulment?"

"Of course," Melissa said, aware that Tony had echoed her. Apparently, with the right kind of connections, they could get an annulment even though the marriage had been consummated. She'd heard these things could be arranged with the consent of both parties.

Jeanie's relief was audible. "At least we agree about that. And by the way," she said, "I've been trying to recall if that Oops! game is in the book. If it isn't, we'll have to add it to the next edition."

The driver's voice came through the intercom as the limo pulled over. "Hotel Da Vinci."

Melissa was seated on the street side, and as she grabbed her bag and got ready to make a dash for it, the driver got out and came back for her with an umbrella. It was still pouring, and she would have to hurry if she wanted to save her brand-new suit and boots. Unfortunately, just as he opened the door, a cab roared by, and she was instantly drenched.

By the time Melissa got around the car and under the hotel's protective canopy, she was dripping like a drowned cat, and of course, there was Antonio, standing by the door, bone dry and looking impossibly dapper. Some people had all the damn luck.

"Things have a way of balancing out, don't they?" he said as she shook off the water and walked over to him.

"Beast," she whispered. "I am not having sex with you, so don't even think about that."

He gave her a puzzled look. "I haven't thought about it in two years. Why should I start now?"

"Yeah, like I believe that. You've been thinking about it every damn day, just as I have."

"Really?" The smile that had been lying in wait suddenly appeared.

Melissa's heart quickened. She clearly had his attention now. He was eyeing her as if she were a cream puff on a dessert tray.

"Every damn day?" he said. "I can't wait to hear about it."

A HOT, STEAMING BATH with essential oil of jasmine and mounds of lovely bubbles. That was the way to beat stress. Melissa's sense of well-being seeped back into her by degrees as she soaked in the deep well of the claw-footed tub, behind locked bathroom doors. She'd found a basket of bath accessories in the hotel suite's sumptuous marble bathroom, and she'd immediately chosen that room and the adjoining bedroom for herself. When she was done with her bath, she was going to have a glass of white wine from the ice bucket on the coffee table. When they'd entered the suite, the wine and a tray of appetizers had been waiting for her and Tony, compliments of Searchlight.

Jeanie was the one who'd chickened out. Once she'd

arranged for the suite, she'd left them at the elevator, suggesting that they needed some time alone to talk. In theory, yes. But, in reality, Melissa wasn't ready to talk to the man she'd exposed so much of herself to. It was a dare, a crazy dream of a night, and she'd had too much to drink. Maybe it had seemed like a chance to experience all her fantasies with no one the wiser, but that was supposed to be the beginning and the end of it. She'd never imagined he would show up in the flesh, and she would have to deal with him, not to mention everything she'd done with him.

Well, that wasn't exactly true. She'd imagined it all right. She'd even thought about waking up one morning to find him standing in the doorway of her bedroom, one arm braced above his head, watching her with the deliberate calm of a wolf on the hunt.

Think you're in enough trouble yet?

Melissa let out a soft moan of despair. She closed her eyes to the disturbing image, but she couldn't shut him out of her senses. He'd kept his promise. She was in plenty of trouble now. But was she going to pay the rest of her life for one reckless night of pleasure? While she was writing the book, she'd tried to tell herself that it had been about research. But that was ridiculous—an excuse, not a reason. She'd wanted to be with him. Wanted it with every cell of her being. But that still didn't explain why she'd done it. Why with him and no one else? Why that night? And why had she gone so far? Abandoned didn't begin to describe her behavior.

Something about him had allowed her to take the risk of claiming what she wanted, and that's what alarmed her now. She'd walked through the doorway of her own volition, but it felt as if someone else had opened the door, as if *he'd* opened it.

How could she be sure he wouldn't do it again?

Suddenly everything was spinning. She was back on the merry-go-round, her heart racing, her thoughts awhirl. The force of it should have made her dizzy. She *was* dizzy, but there was something strangely exhilarating about it, too. She felt alive, empowered.

She didn't want him to open that door again…did she? *No! No, of course not.* And even if she did, there was too much at stake.

Melissa sank lower in the tub, trying to relax and recapture the serenity. Remembering had brought back all the confusing feelings, and she needed to let them dissipate. But the steaming bath had done everything it could. In fact, it might be making things worse. She needed a glass of wine and a good night's sleep. If only she could talk to Kath. She and her friend had always confided in each other, and men were Kath's area of expertise. But the suite seemed eerily quiet, and hotel walls were notoriously thin. She didn't want to chance being overheard.

She left the tub, having already decided the phone call would have to wait for a better time. Tonight it would be the wine and the good night's sleep.

Moments later, still damp and jasmine-scented, she slipped into a fluffy terry robe, tied it around her and let herself out of the locked bathroom. She was almost surprised to discover that there was no one waiting outside the door, poised to ambush her. She was being silly. He'd probably put that night behind him, too. But then why was he here? She didn't know why he'd bother, unless money or some kind of revenge was involved. He couldn't make much on a waiter's salary—unless he wasn't a waiter anymore. There was a lot she didn't know about Tony Bond. But did she want to know?

The wine seemed like a better and better idea.

She slipped into the main room of the suite and found

it glimmering with afternoon sunlight. The focal point was a sunken living room with a drop-out window seat that seemed to rest on top of the city. Melissa's gaze was drawn to the man standing in front of the panoramic view, looking out at Central Park. He'd already opened the wine, poured himself a glass and put the bottle back in the bucket. He'd obviously decided to get comfortable, too.

He was wearing a T-shirt and jeans that rode the crest of his hips. Maybe it was his stance, but she didn't remember him being quite so tall and imposing. The room had a Kentia palm that had to be close to six feet, but he had it beat. Of course, she'd been horizontal most of the time she was with him.

She brushed the distracting thought aside and concentrated on him, her mortal foe. Either he was one of the fortunate few who had natural tone, or he'd spent time in a gym. Waiters did some heavy lifting, but not enough to create those biceps. His muscled arms were golden in the light, and even his bare feet had taken on a bronze cast against the plush white carpet.

Bare feet. Plush pile. Was there something incredibly sexy about that? Or was she still suffering from posttraumatic stress disorder where he was concerned?

He had his back to her, but the picture that zinged into her mind was quite different. She saw him turning and walking toward her, a man crossing the room to join a woman lying on a bed. A naked man, muscled and golden from head to toe. Aroused like a stallion from head to toe. Even his nostrils were flared.

Melissa's thoughts came screeching to a halt. She couldn't go there. Could not. She shouldn't even be in the living room with him. It wasn't safe. The flashbacks flew like bullets when he was around. Maybe she could pour herself some wine and disappear. If she was quiet he would never notice.

"You're sneaking off again?"

Melissa froze. That was his voice, but she wasn't sure how he'd caught her until she saw her own reflection in the mirrored windows. He'd known she was in the room from her first tiptoe.

"Sneaking off?" she said.

He turned around, framed by the sunlight. His gaze was unflinching. "You know what I mean."

Of course she did, but— "I didn't sneak off. I just left."

"Without a note? Without a word?"

She hesitated in an effort to steady her voice. "I should have left a note. I meant to, but I was embarrassed, and I thought you might be, too. I wanted to spare both of us that awkwardness."

Did he believe her? She hoped so because she had just realized it was true. She had been trying to spare them. "I wasn't sure you were any more ready to face me than I was to face you." It didn't explain why she'd left, but it did explain how.

He gazed at her, perplexed. "Not ready to face you because I'd made love to you?"

"Well, it was a little more than the missionary position."

She shuddered, hoping to dodge the bullets of memory and knowing she wasn't fast enough. Had he forgotten how he'd laid her out on the leopard-print spread with her hands entangled in the sheet above her head? He didn't remember how helpless she'd been, and how she'd nearly cried because his touch was so sweet, so wicked, so right, so wrong...*so everything?*

"We let our imaginations run," he said. "We didn't

throw up barriers. Maybe that was a little adventurous for a woman like you, a little dangerous.''

''A *little* dangerous?''

''Melissa, I got down on one knee and proposed to you. That was dangerous.''

She glanced up at him, startled and flushed. ''That was a gesture. You were just being kind.''

''I don't marry all the women I feel kindly toward. In fact, I haven't married any of them but you.''

''Why did you marry me?'' She met his gaze and saw her reflection swirling behind him, as if the room had moved. Uncanny, but that happened all the time with him. The whole world felt as if it were moving, like the horses on a carousel, galloping around the cornice at the center. Somehow, he made her feel as if he was the only stable element on the plane where they existed, wherever that plane might be. He was the cornice. Everything else fell away.

She glanced at the gold band on her finger and wondered if wearing it had anything to do with the effect he had on her. Wishful thinking, that. If the ring was responsible, then all she had to do was get it off, and she was free. It couldn't be that simple, could it?

''I'm not sure,'' he said in measured tones. ''Why did you leave?''

She had a plane ticket? He hadn't asked her to stay? She didn't think the marriage was real? He was such an accomplished lover she thought he might be a gigolo? She was scared to death?

''It all happened so fast.'' She took a sip of the wine, more to see if her hands were shaking than for any other reason. ''It was chivalry, right? You were trying to rescue me.''

He frowned at her. ''Is that wrong?''

''Probably not wrong, but hardly the basis for a lasting marriage.''

''I've heard worse reasons.''

What did that mean? Melissa didn't understand him. He didn't operate according to any rational rules. Her gut was telling her that he was some kind of Don Quixote, rescuing the needy. He had a savior complex, and she had made the mistake of needing to be saved that night, at least from her girlfriends.

''Why are you here?'' she asked him.

He walked toward her, the sunlight at his back, masking his expression. ''Maybe I'm curious. Would that be reason enough for you? I saw a woman on the beach, and I thought I knew who she was. No one else had a clue, but I had several—and a strong desire to solve the mystery.''

Melissa tried to speak, but her voice had lost its strength again. Amazing how he could do that to her. Amazing how he could make the earth move. But she had to make it stop moving. She had to, or someone was going to fall off the edge. And she knew it would be her.

She cleared her throat. ''How could you possibly know who I was?''

''The better question is how could I not know? It was right there, crying out for recognition. I'm surprised everyone didn't see it.''

''What was crying out? You just said I was a mystery.''

''Maybe I said too much.''

''You're not going to answer my question?'' That brought a flash of anger. ''If this is some kind of game, I don't want to play.''

''I saw needs, your needs. I saw a hunger in you for more, but something was holding you back. That was the mystery. I didn't understand why you didn't go after what you wanted, claim it.''

"I did go after it," she insisted. "I'm the expert on that, if you'll remember. I've written an entire book about women going after what they want."

He smiled. "You did, and you didn't, which is all part of the puzzle."

"So that's what turns you on, a good mystery?"

"No, it's the hungers of the human spirit that turn me on. It's unrequited love and lost dreams. But mostly, it's women who are terrified of being needy."

Melissa gaped at him. So this *was* about her being needy. That's how he'd seen her, as desperate for his attention? In need of sexual healing, maybe? She turned away from him, wondering if she should be as deeply offended as she felt. In fact, she *had* been needy and desperate that night. But she could have lived her whole life without having him know it.

Her hands were shaking, and she kept thinking she should set her wineglass down. Instead, she took a good long drink.

"I'd really like to put that night behind us, if we could."

"Why? It happened."

The wine ripped at her throat. "Just because something happened is no reason to drag it out and analyze it to death. Sometimes it's just as good a reason not to. I'm going to bed."

She didn't bother to look back as she walked out of the room, still clutching her glass. She was more than likely wrong about him anyway. Unrequited love? Needy women? Don Quixote was beginning to bear a passing resemblance to Don Juan, and that wouldn't have surprised her, either. Nobody got that good in bed without some experience.

Personally she liked a guy who tilted at windmills.

But the real question was why she cared which one he was.

4

Retire your vibrator, girls. His tongue is trainable!
101 Ways To Make Your Man Beg

SHE WAS ENCHANTING. Marching out of the room with her dark hair pinned up and bouncing on her head. Her slender body drowning in the white robe. Trailing a mist of jasmine. Haughty. Hot. And everything the word implied.

She had enchanted him. Tonight. Two years ago.

Maybe it was those Bambi eyes. When she'd turned them on him in the restaurant, he would have fought mythical dragons to save her from harm. But tonight those big brown eyes had suddenly looked wounded and accusatory, and he had no idea what he'd done to hurt her. Or that he *could* hurt her.

Tony glanced down at the swirling wine, lifted the glass and took a swallow. Now, *there* was a twisted yet strangely exhilarating thought. He had the power to hurt her. Would he want to hurt her? She had hurt him and, human nature being what it was, he wouldn't mind a little payback. But this was more than that. If he was right, she had just inadvertently revealed a vulnerability—and that's what had him intrigued. Maybe she still had some feelings for him. The way she'd disappeared that day two years ago had made him question whether she'd ever had any.

A platter of appetizers—everything from pâté and oysters to Norwegian smoked salmon stuffed with cream cheese and chives—waited on the wet bar. He was duly impressed, even for a man who knew his way around a restaurant kitchen. He helped himself to some salmon, savoring the pungent flavors and tender texture—and fleetingly thought about ordering up some dinner. Melissa's publisher had flown him in late last night, and he'd been up early this morning for the talk-show taping. There hadn't been time to think about food, and he should have been hungry, but he wasn't.

He poured himself more wine, although chardonnay wasn't a real favorite. Most Americans had yet to discover the pleasures of a really fine rosé. In Europe some prized it more than red or white, but here it was largely thought of as unsophisticated. Just one of the many things about this country that mystified him, that and one particular woman.

The slant of the sun's rays through the living-room windows said it must be around seven. Sundown. Too early to retire to the bedroom with her book, but that was exactly the plan. Jeanie had given him a copy with instructions to get it read and quickly, but he'd only had time to skim the chapters. It amused him that Melissa had made him sound like a porn star. The woman had quite an imagination. Their night together had been erotic, to say the least, but she'd given him credit for things he'd never heard of. He was going to have to do his homework to find out exactly what the Velvet Tongue was, although he could imagine.

Maybe he should go directly to the author.

He'd become fairly familiar with her tongue that night, as she had with his. And he could still remember exactly how she tasted—delicate and sweet, yet as deeply intoxicating as the finest French rosé. He could have drunk her all night long. She had made his head swim and his muscles go mindlessly hard. What more pleasure could a man want than that? Vital signs on full alert. Vital juices flooding his loins.

That's probably why he wasn't hungry tonight. His blood was rushing elsewhere. And why he couldn't sustain a thought that wasn't about her.

He set down the wine. He didn't need anything else blunting his instincts. She was doing a fine job. Two years and she was still in his blood? That was too long for any man to be preoccupied. Okay, obsessed.

He walked to the bedroom at the opposite end of the suite from hers and thought about the distance between them. Not just the span of a hotel room. They were from different worlds although he'd done enough traveling to feel comfortable in most situations. He wasn't just the backwater waiter that she might think. And more important, his life had changed in the past two years. He had moved on, and obviously so had she. He knew what the crystal ball had in store for him, and it didn't include a runaway wife who wrote about sex games but was afraid to play them.

Accomplish what you came to do and go, he told himself. *Make it a clean break and go back to your life. Your real life.*

But there was just one thing stopping him. One question he had to ask.

One question that only she could answer.

A LONG EVENING stretched ahead of Melissa. That should have been a relaxing thought, but she dreaded the unscheduled time. With her imagination, who wouldn't? It wasn't even 7:00 p.m., which gave her the entire night to think about how many different ways things could go wrong, and they all started with Antonio. If he was after revenge and trying to ruin her career by exposing her as a fraud, he might well bring down Jeanie and Searchlight as well. He could also be a double-dealing blackmailer, intending to strip her of every penny she made. Or he could decide to take up where they left off—and strip her of other things, like her clothes. Forget about her virtue. That was long gone.

Of course, there was always the possibility that he might be here simply to get the marriage annulled so he could move on with his life. She had a news reporter's tendency to gloss over mundane realities in favor of catastrophic possibilities. But regardless of his motives, one thing was clear. She was going to be forced to submit to all the possible risks and indignities of Antonio Bond, because without him the book could bomb.

She'd been lying on the bed leafing through magazines, and she grabbed one to fan herself. Either the room was stuffy or she was coming down with a fever. With any luck it was some virulent new strain of flu, and they would have to cancel the tour. Of course, fevers also signaled dread diseases like meningitis and malaria. She hadn't been bitten by any mosquitoes lately, so it was probably meningitis.

An inflammation of the lining of the brain. Oh, joy.

She whisked her cell phone off the night table to check her voice mail. That should distract her. If any of her friends had caught the show, she expected some startled messages. Kath and the girls knew about the book tour, but nothing about Antonio, the well-kept secret.

The first message was from Kath, followed by one from the whole gang, who were at a restaurant where the four of them met for dinner whenever they could. Listening to her friends' excitement worked like a tonic, and Melissa found herself laughing with them. Kath did the talking, but the other two could be heard cheering her on, and occasionally stealing the phone to make some cheeky comment.

"Melissa, you bad girl, you vixen, you *slut!*" Kath said. "You didn't tell us your 'husband' was going to show up. You didn't even tell us you *had* a husband. Isn't that the waiter from Mexico? Did you actually marry him for real, or is this just a great publicity stunt?"

Both, Melissa thought. Apparently, fate reveled in mixing the bad with the good, just to keep things interesting.

"Melissa, it's Renee. Congratulations on the book *and* the man. An*tonnnnio*. Just saying his name makes me lubricate. I can imagine what shape you must be in. And speaking of that, I spilled some water in my date's lap last night. He loved it!"

Melissa rolled her eyes. Crazy women.

Pat Stafford added her two cents'. "So, are you two on your second honeymoon? I hope it's every bit as wicked as the first. You *have* to call and tell us everything!"

Melissa had never gone into detail with her friends about the night with Antonio, not even Kath. She'd been too thrown by the whole experience. It had taken her months to come to terms with what she'd done, but eventually, just so the girls would stop bugging her, she'd begun referring to it as the night of her life. That had started them guessing, and some of those guesses had inspired ideas for her book. But in reality the girls never got close to guessing at the sheer wild heat of that night, which was saying something.

No wonder I'm nervous, Melissa thought, clicking off her messages. Her friends knew very little about the dark side of Melissa Sanders. Only a near stranger knew how truly slutty she could be.

She called Kath back, knowing this was her friend's

investment-club night, and left her a message that Antonio was a surprise arranged by her publisher—more of a shock, actually—but everything was fine. She couldn't say much more than that. There was no explaining this mess in a voice mail, and she really didn't want to encourage any more group messages. Besides, there were those thin walls to think about.

She couldn't call her parents, either. They also knew nothing about Antonio. She'd intentionally left them with the impression that her book was a self-help tome about the perils of dating. That had seemed a safe enough story. Their farm was light-years from the nearest bookstore, and they didn't have a TV that worked.

Melissa fell back against the pillows. The bedroom had French doors that opened onto the balcony, which really wasn't a balcony at all. The heavy wrought-iron railings allowed just enough space to open the doors and step out. But the bedroom *was* stuffy, and she didn't want to go in search of a thermostat and run the risk of encountering him again. Better to let some fresh air in, no matter how noisy it was out there.

She rose from the bed and opened the doors to the din of traffic. It was well after rush hour, but the taxis were still honking and squealing their tires, jockeying for position. Fifteen floors up, she tilted over the railing to look down and had a horrifying vision of a woman leaping to her death and the morning papers announcing that it was the newly infamous author of a kinky sex manual trying to escape her whispering husband.

Overcome by dizziness, she stepped back from the balcony. A breeze washed over her, warm and steamy from the rain, but nothing could have cleared her buzzing head. Her composure had evaporated. She turned back to the room, wondering what in the world she could do to distract herself. She had a book signing in the morning and radio interviews in the afternoon. She'd already laid out what she was going to wear and come up with some cute phrases to inscribe in the books.

She really ought to try her hand at conspiracy thrillers instead of self-help books. That might be a way to put her antsy imagination to practical use.

The chilly sound of her own laughter made her shiver. She had on nothing but her silk nightgown, and her bare arms were clammy with goose bumps. Her skin prickled and stung, making her wonder if she really had come down with something. Was that a rash on her hands? Wasn't that one of the symptoms of Lyme disease? She pictured Tony calling 911 and riding with her in an ambulance to the emergency room. Searchlight would send flowers, of course.

Time for a physical, she thought, heading for the bathroom.

The rash didn't show up well in the soft lights of the bathroom. In fact, she couldn't see it at all, which was a relief. That didn't mean she wasn't sick, though. The green coating on her tongue was very suspect, although it might have been from the green-apple candy she'd been nursing earlier, but she didn't think so. Her eyes looked a little yellowish, too, as she pulled down the lower lids. Yellow eyes meant hepatitis, didn't it?

Her pulse was too fast and her skin damp. This wasn't good.

She grabbed a cloth and soaked it in cold water to mop her forehead, but when she looked up, she thought she saw another reflection in the mirror. It didn't go away, even when she blinked. Now she was seeing double? What was that a symptom of? No, wait, it looked like a man's reflection. Someone had come up behind her!

She screamed, twisting the rug beneath her as she turned. Her feet flew out from under her, and she tumbled into his arms.

"Tony," she gasped. "What are you doing here?"

He scooped her into an embrace, cradling her with the tenderness that a wide receiver would a football. "I thought I heard you screaming," he said.

"I'm screaming because you're in my bathroom."

She was too off balance to push him away, but she wanted to. He helped her get to her feet, and she hurried to extricate herself. Her nightgown was all over the place—everywhere except where it should be. Nearly exposed breasts blushed at him, one nipple peaking from behind a silk strap.

"I'm fine," she said, pressing her hands to his chest for leverage. That might have worked, but she made the mistake of glancing up at him as she stepped back. It was as far as either one of them got. Their gazes caught and drew them back together like rebounding springs.

All the crazy energy of that electric moment surrounded them like an aura and held them exactly where they were. She didn't want to push him away anymore. She didn't even try to save herself as he cupped her face and whispered something low and sexy in a language she didn't understand. It sounded like French. How many languages did this man speak?

There was a section on kissing in her book, but it didn't begin to do this justice. His lips touched down tentatively, brushing sparks across the surface of hers. He made a noise that sounded like relief, and she yearned to hear it again. He didn't actually lift her off the floor. It just felt that way. His hand stroked her face, urging her to give him more. His mouth coaxed and beguiled, seducing her to open up and surrender everything he wanted. Everything she had. And suddenly it was everything she wanted, too.

"You taste like apples," he whispered, "and I'm hungry."

I am, too. Her throat tightened and ached with longing. She wasn't even sure she'd heard him right, but the feelings suffused her. They reminded her of her one and only night with him, and suddenly she couldn't imagine why she'd felt compelled to run away. His mouth was perfection. How could anything ever surpass this need to be lost in drowning passion?

She was just about to wrap her arms around his neck when he broke the kiss and released her. She panted for breath. "Why did you do that?"

"Kiss you," he asked, "or stop kissing you?"

"The first thing." She wasn't sure herself.

When he finally spoke, his voice was almost as breathless as hers. "There were times when I thought I'd dreamed that night. I had to know."

She could see by his expression that he was serious. His dark eyes shimmered with intensity. He'd come in here and kissed her because he thought it might have been a dream. That was exactly how she felt. How she'd always felt. But they couldn't both have dreamed what happened. It *had* happened and she'd been staggered by the passion that had ignited between two virtual strangers. It could have burned her to ashes. And even though she'd run away, being with him had forced her to question nearly everything about herself and her life.

After days and weeks of wondering if she might hear something from him, or even—romantic fool that she was—if he might come in search of her, she'd finally decided it had been spontaneous combustion, like what could happen to leaves piled up too long. She'd gone too long without sex and, in the heat of the moment, she'd burst into flames. The insight had helped her set her fantasies aside, but the experience had stayed with her, nonetheless. It had motivated her to write an entire book, and perhaps she owed him something for that.

"Listen, I'm sorry," he said.

"No, it's all right." She drew a breath and cast her eyes down. "The truth is, I need to tell you something. There wouldn't be a book if I hadn't met you. It feels a little awkward saying that, considering the way things began, and the way they ended, but it's true, and—Tony?"

She'd felt him step away, but it startled her when she looked up and saw him disappearing through the door. She had the feeling he hadn't heard anything she'd said, but she didn't have the strength to stop him and start again.

Let it go, Melissa. You tried. Center yourself and give it a couple of good breaths. A yoga position was out of the question, but she did manage some slow deep breaths, which calmed her a bit. Even if she'd been able to kid him about this having anything to do with the book, she couldn't kid herself. One kiss, and they'd been very close to another meltdown—or at least she had. That kind of erotic chaos wasn't going to work for this book tour, no matter how sexy her book was. There was too much at stake, not the least of which was her famously shaky grip on reality.

She drew a nightgown strap off her shoulder and peered at her reflection, turning in front of the mirror to check her back. She didn't find any visible marks, although it seemed as if there should have been some after something so shattering. She really did have to get things under control—herself at the very least. Under the circumstances, she couldn't trust Jeanie to help. She and her publicist seemed to be at cross-purposes lately, which meant she, Melissa, would have to do it herself.

Rules of engagement. That's what she needed. Ironclad rules so that no one was in any way confused about acceptable tour conduct. And she knew exactly what the first rule would be: No kissing except in public places!

TONY HAD THE SHOWER going full bore before he had his clothes off. Conveniently, he wasn't wearing much. He pulled the T-shirt over his head and shucked his jeans, practically in one motion, leaving everything in a pile on the floor of the bathroom. He was already barefoot.

The shower stall was a work of art, its floor-to-ceiling glass textured like ocean waves, with a heavy door held by two gleaming brass hinges. It appeared to be free-floating, swinging shut behind him with soundless force. The steaming hot spray needled him in three different places along the length of his body—his shoulders, his lower back and his bum.

He imagined the showerhead was meant to massage aching muscles, but all he needed right now was water, and the more the better. Showers had been known to save his sanity. They cleared his head when life crashed through the center divider of the road and sideswiped him. In this case, he may have been the one who'd gone through the divider, but he had definitely been sideswiped. And by a kiss.

The trembling leaf was still a temptress in disguise.

She was fireworks on a summer night. She had the power to hold the eye and the mind. Worse, she didn't seem all that aware of her allure. Of course, he hadn't heard her scream just now. What a lame excuse to go to her room. But he had to know, and she'd given him her answer without saying a word.

She was not a figment of his imagination and neither was their sexual chemistry. That night two years ago had affected him more than he wanted to admit. It had etched itself into his soul, and it was all real. So, where did he go from here?

He ducked his head under the spray, soaked his hair and shook off the excess water. There was a nook in the marble wall with several choices of shampoo. He took the only one that sounded vaguely masculine—Autumn Orchard—and worked it into billowing suds. By the time he was ready to rinse, he had begun to get his thinking back in line.

He wasn't here to win her back. He wasn't even here to pick up where they'd left off, although, God, he'd like to. All of his dark urges aside, he'd put Melissa and their marriage behind him and get on with his plans for the future. He had responsibilities to uphold and promises to keep that went beyond business obligations. They were personal and private. Jeanie Trent, the publicist, had promised a quick and quiet annulment if he went along with the happy-husband charade, and he'd agreed to it. They'd also mutually agreed to keep his real reasons a secret, even from Melissa. Why? Because Jeanie was afraid that Melissa might have backed out if she knew the truth.

For everyone's sake he needed to keep it a game, never let it get real. He had to pretend to be the passionate, sexually satisfied husband—and do it well enough to convince a national-TV audience. But it could never be anything but a charade, even temporarily. That's why he was in the shower. And why he might never get out of the shower again.

He turned in the spray, facing the vertical line of showerheads. One of the jets pummeled his shoulders, another his abs, and the third, his pelvis. As he looked down, he was reminded of a well-known Bible story, only in this case, it was an erection parting the seas. The lowest jet ricocheted off his hardened shaft like a wave crashing against the rocks. That was the impact she had on him.

Maybe if he turned the tap to cold?

Better yet, he would wash up, get the hell out of this steam bath, get some clothes on and find a way to occupy himself. Of course, what he should be doing was reading her book and preparing himself for their upcoming performances. But somehow he didn't think that was going to help his current condition.

He grabbed a container of liquid soap, also Autumn Orchard, squirted some of it on his chest and began to scrub. Foam rose from his amber skin and filled the stall with the scent of ripening apples. His hormone-weakened mind conjured up images of a man and woman romping in an orchard, hiding behind the fruit-laden trees, and falling onto the grass into each other's arms to make love. Particularly riveting was the skirt she wore and the way he slid it up her thighs to reveal a dark delta of succulent, apple-scented curls.

Eyes closed, Tony soaped himself with determination. The feel of his heaving pecs made him move down to his abdomen, but the tight muscles there offered little comfort as he massaged them. When his hands came into contact with his own engorged organ, it was like megavolts of electricity rocketing through him.

This was hell, and he had two more intensive weeks of it. After that the torture would become intermittent, but he would still have his thoughts to contend with. Of course, there was an easy way out. He could give himself some quick relief. He'd done it before, but he wasn't going to take that route tonight. He'd pleasured himself while fantasizing about Melissa Sanders for the last time. Better to endure and keep his edge than bow to the secret pleasures of a woman he couldn't have.

It had rocked him to see that wedding band on her finger. She was clearly driven to succeed, but he hadn't expected her to take it that far. Jeanie had told him Melissa wanted the money to pay back her parents and make their lives easier. Apparently they were Midwestern farmers who'd sacrificed to send her to college and give her the opportunities they'd never had. He had a feeling her ambitions might not be as selfless as all that, but even if her hard-luck story was true, he still had a score to settle.

She'd married him, bedded him, and vanished without a word. He'd woken the next morning and gone into a full-blown panic, searching for her. When he hadn't found her, he'd called the hotel where she'd been staying. They had given him the news that his new bride had checked out and flown home.

That night he'd sat out the night in his darkened living room, deadened to everything but the heavy thud in his chest. If it was naive to feel betrayed over what was essentially a one-night stand, then call him naive. He'd lived with those feelings until very recently, and he wasn't going back there now. And bringing himself to orgasm with her sweet face in his mind would be another betrayal.

When he stepped out of the shower, he grabbed a terry bath sheet and began vigorously toweling himself. His blood had cooled by the time he was done. Good, he thought. Of course, he knew the heat would return, and he'd have to fight his response to Melissa again. He wasn't *that* naive, but he'd won the battle for now. And meanwhile, he would enjoy flushing out the real Melissa Sanders. Trembling leaf? Or shameless hussy in disguise? It was his sworn mission to find out.

5

One of my personal favorites is the Happy Gardener game. What could be more fun than having your flowers fertilized and your bush trimmed!

101 Ways To Make Your Man Beg

IF YOU HAD A NIGHTMARE twice, did that make it recurring? Once, when she was a child, Melissa had dreamed of being lost in a never-ending cornfield. The field seemed to circumnavigate the earth it was so big and so dark. She was eight years old, small for her age, and the rustling cornstalks looked as tall as trees. Her mother called from somewhere in the distance, but her voice grew fainter. Melissa was going the wrong way, but no matter which way she turned, her mother's voice receded until it faded to nothing.

Now she was dreaming again, lost again in a forestlike maze that could have been cornstalks, and someone was calling her name.

"Melissa!"

She stirred. That didn't sound like her mother.

"Melissa, wake up!"

It felt as if something was shaking, as if everything was shaking. Now she was dreaming about earthquakes. She opened her eyes, and through a haze of sleep, she saw her publicist. Jeanie was at the foot of the bed, gripping the bedpost like a furniture mover.

"What are you doing?" Melissa asked.

"Trying to wake you up!" Jeanie gave the post another sharp tug. "Let's go, let's go! I have a car waiting out front, and you're going to be late for the book signing."

Moments later, maybe seconds, Melissa was in the bathroom, washing her face and wishing she hadn't taken that over-the-counter sleeping pill. She did look rested, though. In fact, she looked positively healthy. There was a glow to her skin she hadn't noticed before and didn't know how to explain. It couldn't have had anything to do with *him*, of course. You didn't glow over a man when the attraction was purely physical. And it was. Even he would have agreed to that. Lust could keep you up all night with overstimulated nerves. It could drive you to sleeping pills. But it couldn't make you glow.

And then there was that incredibly overdramatic thing he'd said about having to know if it was a dream. He had come up behind her in the bathroom, caught her off guard and blown her mind—again. He was good at that. For a moment he'd had her thinking they might have shared something deep and moving, that he'd been touched the way she had. But how much wishful thinking was that? It certainly wasn't reality. There wasn't any reality where they were concerned, and she had to remember that. He was so damn persuasive, so damn Latin…if he was Latin.

With men like Tony, it was the grand gesture. They were the knights in shining armor, appearing at the last minute to save the day. In her case it had been night, but she'd definitely needed saving. He'd probably pitied her, and she couldn't tolerate that. She was no one's fixer-upper, thank you.

She peered into the mirror as she patted her face dry

and checked the whites of her eyes. They were clear, too. She would have to make a note of the sleeping-pill brand. They were great.

Teeth next. She loaded her toothbrush with whitening paste. A total makeover would have been her first choice, but there hadn't been time. She was doing the best she could with what she had. Jeanie had just gone to round up Tony, which gave Melissa a chance to think about the book signing as she began to work on brightening her smile.

She'd been asked to do a short lecture first. They would probably want Tony to sit right next to her at the signing, looking like a stud in perpetual heat. Apparently the two of them were supposed to strike sparks off each other every time they spoke or touched. That shouldn't be too tough. They were combustible in each other's company. A touch from Tony came with sound effects. She could hear the hiss of a match being struck, and then *whoooosh*. Fire.

No, no. No touching. There was not going to be *any* touching. With him, touching was a gateway to other things.

Melissa was just about to rinse, when she heard a cry of alarm that sounded like Jeanie.

"Melissa! Come here!"

That *was* Jeanie. Melissa dashed out of the room, the toothbrush still in her mouth and foamy bubbles coating her lips. She found Jeanie in the living-room area, turning in a circle, her hand on her forehead.

"What's wrong?" Melissa asked.

"What's wrong? We're going to be late for the signing, and one of my authors is missing. It's every publicist's nightmare."

Melissa blotted her face with the sleeve of her bathrobe. It was gross, but not as bad as foaming at the mouth. "Are you talking about Tony? He's not an author. *I* wrote the book."

"The point is, Melissa, he's *missing*. He's not in his room. He's not anywhere in the suite."

Melissa's hopes soared. "Missing? Are you sure? Jeanie, that's fabulous!"

Jeanie's glare threatened bodily harm.

"Of course he's not missing," Melissa rushed to assure her. "He probably went down to get a cup of coffee. He'll be back in a jiff."

Then again, he might be on a plane to London or somewhere even farther away. He could have been kidnapped or comatose in some emergency room, mowed down by the same bus driver who'd splashed her. Fantasies were better when there was a little poetic justice involved.

Jeanie went to search the hotel while Melissa finished getting ready. Twenty minutes later, she was dressed in the powder-pink linen skirt and twinset she'd put out, but Tony still had not appeared. Jeanie had been down to the lobby. She'd checked the hotel's restaurants and its lounge, gift shops and health spa, but he was nowhere to be found.

"Okay, we go without him," Jeanie said. "You'll have to make some excuse."

"Like maybe he got exhausted from all the begging?" Melissa grinned and Jeanie gave her another warning look.

"Do you want to sell this book or not? And what's with that outfit? This is not afternoon tea, girl!"

Melissa checked herself out. "What do you want, a femme fatale? This outfit is lightweight, it's within my budget *and* my comfort zone."

Jeanie's sniff was audible. "I'll settle for a woman who looks like she could have written a book about hot sex."

"Excuse me? Have you heard of Dr. Ruth? I'd like to

say that I more than hold my own on that playing field, thank you.''

Jeanie directed Melissa to the door. ''Let's make a deal,'' she said as they left the suite and walked toward the bank of elevators. ''You expand your comfort zone, and Searchlight will expand your clothing budget.''

Melissa brightened. ''Deal.''

On the ride down, she fussed with her outfit, wondering if a shorter skirt might do the trick. What wasn't within her comfort zone was Tony's disappearance, now that she'd had time to think about it. The focus would be totally on her now, but maybe that wasn't an altogether good thing. The book might suffer for it. Still, it was a trade-off. Her life would be infinitely less complicated without him around. How could that not be good?

''STOP!'' Melissa shouted. The town car lurched to a halt, sending both Melissa and Jeanie into a forward slide.

Jeanie clutched the hand grip, juggling an enormous disposable cup of coffee. ''What is it? We're late!''

Melissa pointed out the car window. ''I think I see him! Look over there at the entrance to the park.'' As they were pulling away, she'd noticed a man across the street in Central Park. He had Tony's height and dark hair, and he was huddled with a slender young woman and two uniformed officers. He seemed to be arguing with the policemen.

''That's him, isn't it?'' Melissa tapped the windowpane. ''I'm sure that's Tony. I'm going over.''

''No, Melissa! You'll get killed.''

''I'll be right back.'' Melissa let herself out of the car, dodging cabs as she made her way across the street. She could hear Jeanie shouting at her, but she didn't stop. She had to know if it was Tony with the police, and what had happened. Some crazy reasons ran through her mind, including the possibility that they were trying to arrest him. With mixed feelings, she realized she might be about to discover the truth about what kind of person Tony Bond really was.

As Melissa approached, she heard the woman speaking in a language she didn't recognize. It sounded a little like Spanish.

"Por favore, ajude-me encontrar minha crianca!" the woman cried, clutching a shawl around her shoulders as if she was freezing.

Both the officers shook their heads. "No comprendez," one of them said.

But Tony did seem to understand. He spoke to the woman in her language, and Melissa realized he was trying to interpret for her and convey her concerns to the police.

"She's asking you to help her find her child." Tony spoke to the larger of the officers, a burly redhead with a round, ruddy face. "She says her little girl is lost."

"Did she see anyone approach the child?" the officer asked

Tony asked the woman that question, and she shook her head. *"Ajude-me encontrar minha crianca!"*

She'd begun to sob, which made understanding her even harder.

Melissa hesitated a few feet away, not wanting to interfere, and yet wishing she could help ease the mother's anguish. She could only imagine the horror of losing a child. The woman attempted to explain what had happened in badly broken English, and Tony continued to interpret.

"She says they were down by the lake," he told the officers. "She was sitting on a blanket, reading, while her daughter fed the ducks. But she dozed off—only for a minute, she says. When she opened her eyes, the child was gone."

"Per favore!" the woman keened.

The ruddy-faced officer shook his head as he spoke to Tony. "Sorry, but we're not down here on lost-kid detail. We're after a robbery suspect. You need to find one of the park cops."

Tony's voice was hard-edged. "Sorry, but I found *you,* and as I understand your job, it's to protect the vulnerable. What's more vulnerable than a lost child, especially in a park like this?"

Jeanie dashed up at that moment. "Tony, Melissa, we have to go. We're late for the signing."

Melissa grabbed Jeanie and hushed her. By now the terrified mother was in tears and begging anyone who would listen to help her. An elderly couple had stopped and overheard some of the conversation, and the older woman exhorted the police to find the child, shaking her cane at them. A few other passersby stopped, too, apparently out of curiosity. Melissa wanted to speak out, too, but she sensed that this wasn't the time.

Tony was involved in a stare-down with the two men. "I'm asking you to find the little girl," he repeated.

The redheaded officer took a look around, seeming to realize for the first time that they'd attracted some attention. The young mother wailed out her grief.

"All right," he conceded. "We'll start a search, and when the park detail gets here, we'll turn it over to them."

"I'm coming with you," Tony told him. "You'll need me to interpret."

"Tony, you are not!" Jeanie stepped into the fray.

One of the passersby spoke up. "I'm an interpreter with the U.N., the woman is speaking Portuguese and I speak it also. Can I help?"

Jeanie didn't give anyone time to respond. She turned to the redheaded officer. "Now, can we go? These are my authors and they're late for a book signing over on Madison.''

"We'll handle it," he told her. Turning to Tony, he said, "We'll find the little girl, and everything will be fine.''

Tony reluctantly agreed. He explained to the grateful mother that the two policemen would help her find her little girl, and he would check back to see that they did. Meanwhile, he pulled out a card, jotted down the name of the bookstore where the signing was to be held and gave it to the officers, asking them to keep in touch.

"Good work," Jeanie said. She hooked Tony by the arm, and at the same time, gripped Melissa's hand. The message was clear. They either went willingly or they would be dragged back through the traffic.

Once they were safely in the car again, Jeanie gave Tony a verbal pat on the back. "What you did was wonderful," she said. "Don't you think so, Melissa?''

"Wonderful, yes.'' Melissa couldn't disagree. He was always doing wonderful things. More proof of a complex, as far as she was concerned, that Don Quixote thing.

She leaned around Jeanie. "I didn't know you spoke Portuguese, Tony.''

"I speak several languages,'' was all he said. "It comes in handy.''

She could imagine. Multilingual. Why did that word sound so naughty? Or was that just the way her mind worked these days. When you wrote sex manuals, everything began to take on lurid connotations.

"English will be fine for the book signing.'' Jeanie was already pushing buttons on her cell phone. "I'm calling to tell them we're on the way. Melissa, do me a favor and burn that twinset when you get back to the hotel. And Tony, the dark shirt and slacks might be a little dramatic.

You two are supposed to be sexual dynamos, not Donnie and Marie."

Apparently someone came on the line, because Jeanie began explaining and making apologies. Melissa glanced over to see Tony checking out her twinset. He mouthed the words, "I like it."

Melissa blushed foolishly and looked away. She'd never had a chance to sit down and talk to him about her rules of engagement. There certainly wasn't time now. She should be rehearsing what she was going to say at the signing, but as it turned out, Jeanie wasn't done with them. As soon as she clicked off the phone, she began lecturing them on their relationship.

"The public is expecting a man and woman who can't keep their hands off each other," she told them. "Most of them can't remember what that's like, if they ever knew. They're counting on you to remind them—and may I be candid?—you're reminding me of a couple of cyborgs. Please, please, *please*, crank up the heat. Hold hands, cop a feel, steal a kiss."

She swiveled back and forth between Melissa and Tony, giving them instructions like a referee in the ring. "Melissa, when you and Tony are sitting next to each other, I want your hand on his thigh at all times, and don't let those fingers lie idle. Stroke him!

"Tony, if even half of what she's written about you in the book is true, you know what to do.

"Melissa, unlash that corset and give up the goods, girl. This is your man, your stud muffin, your tiger lover. I want to see some squirming. I want you and Tony to give this crowd the impression that you can hardly wait to get back to the limo and have sex, okay?"

She continued her swiveling until one of them spoke.

And it wasn't Melissa, whose lips twitched nervously when she tried to smile. Tony managed a husky "Sure."

"Good," Jeanie said. "We're going to wow this crowd, and do you know why? Because tomorrow morning, you two are booked on *Nice Girls Do*. Yes, I can see that you're dumbstruck, but I'm serious. It's only the biggest morning show in the country right now. Their ratings are unbelievable, their demographics perfect. The audience is made up of married women, ranging from their twenties to their fifties, and they're going to make everyone connected with this book filthy rich!"

Melissa was dumbstruck all right. Her publicist had no idea what she was asking of them. Fortunately, Melissa had picked up on the word *rich,* and it had reached out and grabbed her like a lifeline. Rich was good. Rich could make all the difference, and she needed the money for so many reasons. Of course, she wanted financial independence and security. She also wanted the chance to make something of herself after laboring in obscurity for so long. But her first obligation had always been to pay her parents back.

She'd been diagnosed with rheumatic fever in grade school and suffered a damaged heart valve. The valve had been surgically repaired, but her parents had no health insurance, and the cost had been staggering. Melissa had lost a year of her life, and her parents had lost their financial security. They'd been struggling ever since, but it hadn't stopped them from mortgaging their home so that she could go to a good college.

Melissa owed them everything, including her life. There wasn't anything she wouldn't do to ease their financial worries—and this was her chance.

She'd also written the book to empower women and to make them understand how vital and potent and in control they were when it came to their relationships with men. In many ways, it had been a defensive maneuver because she'd never felt more out of control than with Tony Bond. She'd left their hotel room shaken, confused and running for her life. Thrilled to her core, yes, but running from the bewildering feelings like a madwoman. She didn't want other women to have to run. She wanted them to accept their feelings, celebrate them.

She crossed her fingers, and glanced over at Tony, who surprised her by giving her a wink that actually made her smile.

"Prepare to be wowed," she murmured, hoping she could do it.

"Ms. SANDERS, have you and your husband always had a good sex life?"

Melissa tilted an eyebrow, trying to look coy and provocative. Not for the benefit of the woman who'd just asked the question. Melissa wanted the audience to think that she was choosing from such an array of answers, she couldn't make up her mind which delicious tidbit to share. But, in fact, she was scrambling to come up with anything that wasn't an outright lie.

"Good doesn't begin to cover it," Melissa said. "Crazy, wild, impulsive, erotic, romantic, even dangerous. And that was just the first night."

The woman blinked, possibly in surprise, and sat down. Other hands flew up.

This was only going to get worse, Melissa realized. Given what she'd written, these people felt as if they could ask her anything. The turnout was amazing by booksigning standards, according to Jeanie, and there were several reporters in the crowd, including one from *The New York Times*.

The store's events director had arranged twenty rows of chairs in a large semicircle with a podium at the front, where Melissa stood. Tony sat at a table next to the podium, where stacks of Melissa's book waited to be signed. She'd spoken briefly about *101 Ways* and read an excerpt, and just now she'd opened up the floor to questions. The crowd had filled every seat and spilled over to the back of the room, where people stood three deep, her publicist among them.

Melissa watched Jeanie make a log-rolling gesture with her fingers, as if to say, "More, more! Spill every juicy detail, even if you have to make it up as you go."

Hands flew up. Lots of hands. Too many for Melissa to ignore.

She nodded at a woman in a straw hat with a big flower on it, mostly because the woman looked safe.

"Are you and your husband as kinky as the book makes you sound?" she asked, peering out from under the flower. "Did you really do that thing with the pearl necklace, and does Antonio do gardening work like it says in the book?"

So much for safe.

"Gardening work?"

"Trim your bush?" the woman asked innocently. "Isn't that what it says?"

Antonio made a choking sound, which Melissa ignored. Some of the audience members gasped, some howled. Melissa forced herself to laugh along with them. However, she wanted to tell the questioner that she'd just ruined it for women wearing straw hats. Melissa wouldn't be calling on another one soon.

She held up her hands to restore order. "Just some fun suggestions," she explained. "They're in the chapter on 'Things Your Mother Didn't Want You to Know!'

A young Generation Xer jumped up next, giggling. "Do you have Antonio's name tattooed somewhere?"

Jeanie waved frantically, trying to get Melissa's attention. She cupped her hands and mouthed the word *yes*.

"No," Melissa said firmly. She waited for the next question, but the crowd clearly expected her to continue. Finally, she relented with a sigh. "That doesn't mean I don't have a spot reserved—but don't ask me to show you where it is."

Jeanie grinned and gave her a thumbs-up.

A man at the back who'd been scribbling on a spiral pad raised his hand. "Your book tells women to watch their men undress," he said. "It also tells them to switch underwear with their mates because of the sensory turn-on."

"That's true," she said. "It has to do with the softness next to your skin, the scents of perfume or musk."

"Are you wearing Antonio's shorts today?"

Melissa's smile was swift. "I'm delighted to know that you read the book."

"Was that a no?" the man asked.

"We have matching thongs. Does that make it a yes?"

Antonio glanced up at her, and Melissa blushed. Okay, so that was a fib. Occasionally you had to stoop to conquer. After all, newspaper space was worth something, wasn't it?

"Could we see them?" the man asked.

"I don't think we want to get arrested." Antonio spoke up before Melissa had a chance to respond, and his quelling look seemed to back the guy off.

A tabloid reporter, obviously. More hands waved, but Melissa had answered all the personal questions she was going to. "Enough about Antonio and me," she said.

"We're here to talk about your men, ladies. You must have some questions."

The woman in the straw hat raised her hand again. "Should a woman ever say no to a man?"

"Of course. Regularly. Make him wait for it. Make yourself wait. The anticipation that builds will have you hot as a firecracker when you do say yes."

"Do you have an example?"

Melissa had a beaut. Unfortunately, she couldn't share it. Antonio had been a master at making her wait on their wedding night. She didn't even want to think about how he'd had her body thrumming with anticipation. Certain parts had been screaming, but he hadn't given in to her demands. He'd lightened the kisses to nothing and slowed the touches until she was writhing. He'd actually told her to hold back her climax as he whispered every wicked thing he was going to do to her. But she couldn't, and his dark smile had told her that was exactly what he'd intended.

She glanced over at him and saw a shadow of that smile now. He was reading her mind. *He knew.* Melissa's breath turned to fire in her throat, and she actually thought she felt a strange sound rising up. Thank God, Jeanie chose that moment to speak up.

"How about some questions for the man who inspired the book?" she said.

Melissa didn't have a chance to agree before a sexy brunette popped out of her seat and smiled enticingly at Tony. "Would you come whisper in my ear?"

Everybody laughed at that one, except Melissa.

"Sorry," Tony said. "My mouth is already spoken for—and so is Melissa's ear."

Melissa wasn't sure she liked that answer, either, but her stomach certainly did. It was a butterfly farm.

A woman with a notebook and a very brisk voice spoke up. "What kind of work do you do, Mr. Bond?"

"I hang around the kitchen a bit."

"Really?" She cracked a grin. "You could hang around my kitchen anytime. Where's your favorite place to have sex?"

He laughed. "The kitchen, of course."

"How convenient," the woman quipped. "Do you also cook?"

"Cooking is foreplay," he said. "The sensual turn-ons are incomparable—the velvet of a sauce with real cream, the tart juices running from a bitten peach, the sizzle of prime meat on the grill. It's all very sensual."

"Mr. Bond, what nationality are you?"

She hadn't noticed who'd asked the question, but apparently Melissa wasn't the only curious soul.

"A bit of a mutt, I'm afraid," Tony said. "My mother was Hispanic, my father European." He tapped his chest. "There are too many nations in here to count."

Melissa glanced at her watch, hoping it was time for the questions to end and the signing to begin. But apparently the brunette hadn't given up. She jumped back into it with a question for Tony, uttered in a voice so breathy and laden with sexual possibilities that it could have steamed stamps off envelopes.

Melissa felt as if her blood pressure had just hit the high-normal range. At least.

"What makes a man like you so incredibly sexy?" the brunette asked.

Tony didn't seem to have a ready answer. In fact, he went so quiet that Melissa looked over at him, only to find that he was looking at her, too. The expression on his face made her breath stop. She didn't just feel it catch. This wasn't one of those situations where air was quivering in your throat, waiting to be expelled. She actually stopped breathing.

She wasn't at all sure she was going to like this.

What in the world was he going to say?

6

Nurture your inner vixen. Embrace her! She's been suppressed, repressed, oppressed and rejected. By you! It's her turn!

101 Ways To Make Your Man Beg

MELISSA TORE HER GAZE from Tony's and turned to the hushed crowd. The gallery of expectant faces left her searching for something fitting to say. Anything, for that matter. Jeanie made a throat-cutting gesture, which Melissa took as a signal to end the question period. Unfortunately, the clever sign-off she'd planned had vanished—along with the glass of ice water she could have sworn was sitting on the podium.

Hallucinations? That could be heatstroke, malnutrition, brain damage, and take your pick of mental problems.

She cleared her throat and thanked them all for coming. "If you'd like a personally autographed copy of *101 Ways,* I'll be happy to sign one for you, and even if you don't, come on up and say hi, please."

A crisis averted. Except that it wasn't.

Tony rose from his seat before anyone else could. "This lady asked me a question," he said, addressing the brunette, who beamed. "She wanted to know how a guy like me got to be—I think the word she used was *sexy.*"

Melissa stared at Tony, helpless. Now every eye was riveted on him.

"The answer is simple," he said. "If I'm sexy, she's the reason why."

"Who, the hot brunette?" a male called out.

Scattered laughter broke out in the audience. Melissa felt a burning pain just above her breastbone. She actually felt as if she'd been stabbed. Why was he doing this?

"Yes, the hot brunette." He turned to Melissa. "My wife."

He said it with enough edge to make Melissa narrow her gaze and peer at him. His dark eyes sparked with secrets, and her heart tilted. What was he doing now? She thought she saw his jaw muscle tighten, as if he'd quelled some errant emotion. But she couldn't be sure, and the next thing she knew, he was taking her hand.

He brought her fingers to his lips, and she could hear sighs coming from the audience. She understood the women's reaction. He could be romantic beyond belief. He turned her hand over, smoothed it flat and pressed his lips to the tender middle of her palm. Warm breath eddied and caressed her skin. Melissa almost sighed herself.

She could barely feel his mouth on her flesh, and yet it was a delicious sensation that brought back all the other delicious sensations his mouth could elicit.

When he turned back to the audience, he spoke to the brunette again, who wasn't looking quite so confident of her powers of seduction. Melissa didn't allow herself to feel smug, but, okay, it was a *nice* moment, and this man had provided her with more than a few of those.

"It has very little to do with me," he told the brunette. "What man is sexy without a woman to inspire those feelings in him? It's all about her, that special woman, the one whose smile can set fire to a man's heart."

The brunette shrugged, apparently conceding the battle, but not the war. "Okay, so what's your secret?" she asked Melissa.

Tony picked up one of Melissa's books. "All her secrets are in here."

Melissa laughed along with everyone else, but she wasn't quite sure how she felt about what Tony had just done. His grand gesture probably had every woman in the audience yearning for a man like him, one who would choose his woman over a femme fatale, and even put the seductress in her well-deserved place. Who wouldn't yearn for a man like that, if it was how he really felt? Melissa would have given anything to be so adored. But then, somehow he'd brought it all back to her book, and that had given her pause. It was a brilliant pitch—and probably nothing more.

Melissa's imagination churned, never a good thing in a situation like this. Tiny doubts exploded into big ones, and within seconds she had very nearly convinced herself that his vow was just another grand gesture. It wasn't all about her. It might have little or nothing to do with her. If anything, it was probably all about the book, which meant it was all about money. What had Jeanie said? That everyone involved with the book was going to get filthy rich?

With chilly politeness, Melissa removed her hand from Tony's and excused herself to go sign books. The ring he'd given her glinted in the bright lights like golden lace. Melissa resisted the urge to tug at it. She'd never been able to get the wedding band off before. Why should that change now? And it might look a little odd giving him back his ring at a book signing. Besides, she couldn't completely discount the possibility that she was overreacting. She'd been known to do that.

Jeanie pulled out two chairs at the signing table and

motioned for Melissa to sit down. Unfortunately, the publicist wanted Tony to inscribe the books as well.

"You know, as a husband-and-wife team?" Jeanie said. She flashed a smile that was probably meant to disorient Melissa with its brightness.

Melissa stepped around the table and reminded Jeanie under her breath that *101 Ways* was a hefty manuscript—one hundred and fifty thousand words—and Tony hadn't written so much as one comma.

"But he did provide the motivation, did he not?" Jeanie whispered back. In a louder voice, she added, "And I'll bet the ladies lining up for autographs might enjoy having Antonio's signature."

"Yes!" rose in a chorus from the waiting women.

"Of course," Melissa agreed with a tight smile. There were too many people around to say what she really thought—that Jeanie and Tony should go into the publicity business together. That they could have planned this entire campaign—and maybe they had.

The signing table had two chairs, and Jeanie came around to stand behind Melissa and Tony, apparently to help them get settled. "You do want to sell books, don't you?" she whispered as she poured Melissa a glass of water and began opening copies of *101 Ways* for her to sign.

Melissa had a ready answer, but she held her fire. The truth was, she did want to sell books. She had very good reasons for wanting to sell books, and it wasn't entirely clear to her why she wasn't thrilled that so many people were lining up to buy hers. Nearly everybody in the audience seemed to be there—and Antonio was undoubtedly a big part of the reason.

Okay, she thought as she signed the first copy and chatted with a bubbly young mother of three, who said she couldn't wait to read the chapter about all the things she wasn't supposed to do. Okay, this was why she, Melissa Sanders, was here. She was an author with a first book that she believed had something to say to women. What did she care why *he* was here? She hadn't seen the man in two years. What could it possibly matter what he did or why he did it? As long as he helped sell books, that was enough.

Right? *Right.*

"Embrace your inner vixen," she said as she signed the words in the woman's book. She passed the book to Tony, who wrote, "Happy gardening!" The young mother seemed to love it.

Melissa vowed to remember her priorities. She threw her energies into the signing, laughing and joking with the crowd and reminding herself what a miracle it was that they'd actually given up precious hours of their lives to listen to her speak and to purchase a book she'd written. She even joked with Tony and the women who attempted to flirt with him, which was most of them. See, she was a mature adult. If she had any hang-ups where he was concerned, they were now insignificant to the point of being inconsequential. It had been one night of her life. One night. Two years ago. How much could that have meant to either one of them?

Things picked up from that point on. She and Tony signed steadily, and they'd gone through two stacks of books, when Melissa heard a commotion and looked up. A small crowd had gathered at the entrance of the store. As she craned to see around the line of customers, a police officer appeared.

Melissa gave Tony's foot a kick under the table.

"It's the officer from the park," she told him, pointing out the tall redheaded man who was headed their way. A woman trailed behind him, tears streaming down her cheeks. She looked like the mother who'd lost her child.

Melissa had a bad feeling. The officer had a look of grim determination on his face, but when he reached them, he presented the woman to Tony with a good-natured grin. The woman had a little girl in tow behind her, hanging on to her skirts.

"She insisted on coming here to thank you," the officer said.

Tony immediately got up and went to the woman. He hugged her gently, letting her cry to her heart's content and thank him for helping to save her daughter. The room seemed to have been hit by a tidal wave of emotion, and even Melissa felt a tug on her heart. When the mother was more composed, Tony released her and knelt to talk to the child, whose big dark eyes lit up with surprise. He was speaking her language?

A shy smile slowly replaced the child's pensive expression, and by the time Tony had finished brushing her curls from her face and telling her how beautiful she was, the little girl was beaming and telling him the story of her great adventure. The mother smiled through her tears, and even the policeman looked misty.

Tony interpreted the little girl's chatter. "She says her balloon got away from her, and it could run faster than she could."

Who *was* this man? Don Quixote? Don Juan? Or some sort of gold digger? He couldn't just be after money, could he?

The whole room was smitten with him, Melissa realized. She took a visual poll of the women waiting in line. If she read their expressions correctly, they didn't have any question about who he was: a white knight in a world very low on courage and chivalry. Several of them gazed at him with wistful eyes, as if they'd love to take him home to meet the parents, or in some cases, the children.

Melissa felt a little twinge in the area of her rib cage and acknowledged that it could be the irrational jealousy that was no longer bothering her. Then again, she might be coming down with something, in which case, the diagnosis was pretty much a no-brainer. What she needed was an Antonio vaccination. On the other hand, if she'd already been bitten, shouldn't she be immune?

INCREDIBLE AROMAS brought Melissa out of her bedroom to sniff the air. That afternoon's radio interviews had been long, and Jeanie had suggested dinner afterward, but Melissa could think of nothing but the hotel suite and its beautiful bathtub. Tony had come back with her, and he'd suggested room service, but Melissa had pleaded exhaustion, and they'd gone to their separate rooms.

Now, bathed and ready for bed, Melissa was rethinking room service. But then the savory scent of onions and mushrooms, sizzling in hot butter, had seeped under the double doors and filled her bedroom, so she'd decided to follow her nose and investigate. The tantalizing smells had to be coming from the suite's kitchen.

Her silk gown and kimono rustled against her legs as she walked, and her bare soles were chilly against the marble tiles. She should have put on some clothes, but those smells were irresistible, and she was hungry. Her empty stomach would not be denied.

The suite had a full kitchen in its media room, with a built-in barbecue and spit for grilling, brushed-chrome appliances, copper accents and gleaming granite countertops. Subtle recessed lighting softened the modern, dramatic design. The room was worthy of a magazine spread, but the first thing Melissa noticed as she entered the room was the tiered plate of appetizers and the generous glass of red wine that had been set out.

She spotted Tony behind the counter, working at a chopping block. The wine was probably for him, although he seemed completely engrossed in what he was doing.

Another woman might assume that she was expected, even that this production was for her benefit. But not Melissa. She never assumed anything of the kind when it came to men. And besides, he had said he liked to cook. Maybe this was how he entertained himself.

"What smells so good?" she asked.

He turned immediately, surprising her. Maybe she was expected. His eyes seemed to light with pleasure at the sight of her, and that alone could make a girl's footsteps falter. But this girl was driven by hunger, a physical imperative. It encouraged her to cross the large room and sit down at the counter, despite that the man on the other side was achingly handsome in nothing more than casual slacks and an open dress shirt. He had a white ribbed tee on underneath, snug enough to reveal the muscle definition in his abs, although she didn't know why she was looking. She wasn't *that* hungry.

"Have some wine," he said, abandoning his chopping block to join her. He brought a half-filled glass and came around the counter.

"It's a very nice cabernet." He held up his own wine. "Medium-bodied, smooth and a bit fruity."

She picked up her glass, and they touched rims with a musical clink.

"But also saucy and impertinent," he added as she took a sip, "like the woman who's about to drink it."

It was all Melissa could do to hold in the wine. Her snick of laugher had a gurgling sound, and she waved a finger at him when she finally managed to swallow the cabernet. "That's not fair. You're not supposed to make someone laugh when they're taking a drink."

"Bad timing," he admitted, sliding the appetizers toward her. "Please, help yourself to some chow. I promise not to crack any jokes."

Greedily, Melissa surveyed a tantalizing array of Spanish tapas. There were empanadas, roasted poblano chiles that Tony explained were stuffed with three kinds of cheese, and some other scrumptious-looking tidbits that she couldn't immediately identify.

"Thanks," she said, helping herself to a bulging, golden-brown empanada. "You just whipped these up, right?"

She was kidding, of course, but he wasn't.

"They're still warm from the oven," he explained. "I called the concierge this morning and told her what ingredients I needed. They were in the fridge when we got back tonight."

"Wow," Melissa said, honestly impressed as she bit into the oozing meat pie. She'd had empanadas before, but these were spectacular. They were stuffed with finely ground pork, onions, green peppers and raisins, and lightly seasoned with cumin.

"Delicious," she said. "And so is the wine."

They clinked glasses again, and this time he made a toast. "To getting to know each other," he said, "two years later."

"And you thought we'd start tonight?"

"If you're willing."

She looked up and purposefully met his gaze. Maybe it was time to stop the avoidance behavior. After all, he couldn't hypnotize her with a look...although with very little effort, he did seem able to create that sensation in her stomach like a cork bobbing on the ocean.

She drank deeply, uncomfortably aware of his lips against the edge of his wineglass. Such a mouth he had. Beautiful. It should be against the law, that mouth.

He'd thought of everything. She hadn't even noticed the appetizer plates, forks and napkins on the counter. He took a plate, speared himself a chile and cut a large wedge out of it with a fork. She continued to eat her empanada with her fingers. It was too late for manners.

She nearly finished her wine and was pleasantly relaxed by the time he refilled her glass. Amazing how a little alcohol expanded her comfort zone with this man. He was on the bar stool next to her now, but it seemed to her that they were really very far apart, although their knees did bump occasionally.

"I have a crucial question," he said.

She glanced at the ring, anticipating him. "If I could get it off, I would give it back to you."

"What?"

"The ring, of course."

He frowned. "The ring is yours. I gave it to you."

"But it looks valuable, like an heirloom." She fingered the gold latticework. "You must be curious why I'm wearing it."

"I *know* why you're wearing it. What has me curious is why a woman would want to wear a man's underwear."

She gave him a look. "That's the crucial question?"

"Humor me, I'm going somewhere with this."

"Okay…but can't you imagine why she would?"

The tines of his fork tapped against the plate. "Well, normally I would say because it allows her to be intimate without even touching. She can feel the fabric against her skin and that tells her how it must feel against his. She can't *not* think about him while she's wearing his briefs."

"Even his T-shirt," she said, trying not to glance too

obviously at the one he wore under his shirt. "A woman can tell by the scent whether or not a T-shirt was worn by her mate. Her senses can identify him, even when she can't. They've done scientific studies. Intimacy changes our brains. It makes us bond."

"Hey, I believe you," he said. "I do."

With that he got up from the counter and went to the dining-room table where a small gift bag overflowed with sparkly strips of tissue paper. Melissa had completely missed seeing it when she came in the room.

"This is for you," he said.

Surprised, she took the bag and thanked him. She felt around inside and pulled out a glossy red cylinder imprinted with the brand name Brief Encounters. Two slinky black thongs were inside the package of men's underwear.

He leaned over and whispered, "Now you don't have to lie about the matching thongs."

"I'll wear mine if you wear mine." Her voice sparkled with challenge.

He took one of the thongs from the package and stretched it this way and that. "Couldn't we just use them as slingshots?"

"Chicken," she murmured.

His eyebrow tilted with interest, and suddenly the skimpiness of her kimono seemed to hold some appeal. "So...she really is a shameless hussy?"

Melissa gave him some chin. "Did you ever doubt it?"

"Several times, like when you wouldn't come out from under the covers, and when you fainted."

"I didn't *faint.* I swooned a little. All good hussies know how to swoon."

"Now you're going to tell me it was all an act?"

She snapped the thong he held, and smiled. "I guess

you'll never know, will you? And speaking of chicken, how's dinner coming?''

"Let's check it out." He rolled off the stool, and she followed him into the kitchen, aware that the wine had gone straight to her head. Her cheeks felt warm and her tongue fuzzy. Not much chance she'd pulled off the hussy imitation, though. He was no dummy—and she was no hussy, except in her dreams.

"We're taking a detour to northern Italy for the entrée," he told her. "It's a pasta dish made with raviolis stuffed with chicken, porcini mushrooms and pears in a white sauce. I use sauterne wine for the sauce and the finishing touch is pear nectar."

"Pears?" she said. "In ravioli?"

"You're going to love it, trust me."

Trust him. Just the thought gave her shivers. But they were rather nice shivers, she realized, surprised at the awareness. She was enjoying being this close to him without feeling the need to have her guard up. If the situation had been different, and they hadn't had so much crazy history between them, they might have been friends.

As well as lovers. No matter what the circumstances, they would have been lovers. Melissa couldn't imagine it not being sexual with him.

"Now I have a question for you," she said. It occurred to her that she might already have her answer as she watched him palm each one of the pears, apparently trying to decide which one was ripe enough. "What's so sexy about cooking?"

"What's not sexy? Have you ever peeled and sectioned a peach? Felt that juice running through your fingers?"

He looked up at her. "A wok makes some of the most sensual noises I've ever heard. The oil crackles and hisses as it hits the pan. Those are like the sounds of a female in heat.''

"A female animal?''

"A female anything. When you're hot, you're hot. How about the spitting fire of a grill as it seals the flavors into an aged cut of meat? Or the delicate work of filleting and boning the tender flesh of freshly caught fish?''

She didn't dare speak. Her voice wouldn't have sounded in any way natural. The way his hands caressed those pears was positively obscene.

"There are tactile sensations, too,'' he said. "The springy feel of al dente pasta. And smells, like the simmering richness and mystery of a good soup stock.''

They should be discussing business, Melissa realized. How to handle the tour, the interviews and the media. Her rules of engagement. Those things had all seemed so crucially important to her this morning. Now they barely seemed to matter. What mattered was knowing more about him, anything she could find out, and this might be her only opportunity. Was she crazy? Was it the wine? Or was this more of the spontaneous combustion that had set her life afire two years ago?

Lord, how her heart raced. Despite what he'd said today, it wasn't she who inspired him to be sexy. It was the other way around. His mind was as sensual and ripe and succulent as the pears he was sectioning. And his body was as hard and steely as the knife blade. In a terrifying moment of awareness she realized that they were going to make love again. Possibly even tonight, although he didn't know that. He wasn't intentionally trying to seduce her. He was merely cooking.

He wasn't planning it. She was.

7

Seduction is a lost art, and a man should be seduced with every wicked wile in a woman's arsenal.

101 Ways To Make Your Man Beg

EMBRACE YOUR INNER VIXEN. Melissa was dangerously close to taking her own advice. She urged her readers to use their God-given sensuality, but she'd only done so once in her life—and even though the experience had been wildly sexy, it hadn't been wildly successful, or she wouldn't have fled the scene like a criminal. Maybe that's why she was thinking about trying it again, *if* that's what she was thinking about.

It could be the booze talking. Spirits and Antonio Bond seemed to be a lethal combination for her. But what a way to go.

Oh, shit, it *was* the booze talking. She wasn't this gutsy, and she never said shit.

He had his back to her now. He did little more than rinse various pieces of fruit in the stainless-steel sink, but she could see all kinds of intriguing movement beneath his shirt. The muscles fanning across his shoulders were the most noticeable—and the most sensual by far. They rippled like running water, leaving an indelible impression of the natural power in this man's body.

Melissa wasn't sure she'd ever seen a man as comfortable in the kitchen. He moved around as if he owned the place. His confidence could have been intimidating, but other qualities became apparent as she watched him. Patience, for one.

He didn't rush at anything, even removing the annoying sticky label from the apple. He peeled the paper slowly, coaxing it with his thumb and forefinger until it lifted like a leaf in a breeze. Afterward, he took his time rinsing the fruit, and seemed to enjoy the feel of it in his hands. Water sluiced through his fingers and pooled in his palms until it overflowed. The man seemed to have a powerful thing for apples.

That was how he moved in bed, too, she remembered. Confident, knowing, and yet always patient, always lingering long enough for her to respond, as if he had absolutely nothing else to do in this world other than make her shudder with pleasure.

"I've been meaning to ask you something." She toyed with a napkin corner.

"What's that?" He didn't bother to turn around, which was fine with her. She'd just as soon he didn't notice that she'd turned the napkin into origami. He might think her nervous.

"I was just wondering why you used that word today at the bookstore. Remember, when you called me your wife?"

"You *are* my wife." He glanced over his shoulder at her, a possessive edge to his voice. "Besides, it felt right at the time."

"Right in what way?"

She saw his shoulders rise, as if he'd taken a breath. "It made me feel close to you, I suppose." He went quiet. "If that makes you uncomfortable, I won't use the word again."

Melissa smiled. Those were some pretty good reasons. "I don't mind."

"I've been meaning to ask you something as well." His voice rose above the splash of the water.

She stopped torturing the napkin. "What's that?"

"Why did you write the book?"

Melissa shrugged. She'd been asked this question many times. "I wanted to empower women to explore their own sexual needs. Believe it or not, many women still need permission to feel pleasure, and I want them to be able to give it to themselves. Permission, not pleasure, although there's no reason they shouldn't do both."

He turned off the water and dried his hands on a fluffy towel. A stainless-steel colander filled with fruit sat in the sink. He picked it up and brought it back to the counter. "Is that what you did the night we were together, give yourself permission?"

"In a way, yes, I suppose I did."

"All by yourself? Is that the idea? Or does the man have something to do with it?"

Melissa had to grin. Men and their egos. "Of course you had something to do with it." She wasn't sure it could have happened with any other man, but that much of a boost he didn't need.

Her book was actually lying open on the counter. "You were reading *101 Ways?*"

"It covers a lot of ground." He pulled a cutting board from beneath the counter and then selected a sectioning knife from the butcher block nearest him. "Especially to have been inspired by just one night."

She was beginning to see where this was going. "It's true we had only one night together. And granted, what we did was—hmm, what's the word?"

"Extraordinary? Radiant? An out-of-body experience?"

A smile quirked. "Yes, all of that. But it was still just one night. We did a lot, but not enough to fill a whole book."

Tony set the freshly washed fruit on the counter and began lining up the peaches, pears, apples and plums, as if they were beauty contestants. "So where did the rest of it come from?"

She'd been watching his hands. Now she looked at his face. He stared down at the fruit as if he'd just seen a spoiled spot, his forehead tightly knit. She was right about where this was going. The ever-confident man in the kitchen—and the bedroom—was feeling a little insecure, perhaps?

"Why do you ask?"

Tony shrugged as if it was no big deal. "A woman as beautiful as you, she must have many lovers, of course."

It was the first time she'd heard his perfect English slip—and for some reason, she laughed out loud. He raised an eyebrow.

"It's nothing," she said, shaking her head. "I watch too much television. I just had a flashback of Ricky telling Lucy she had some 'splaining to do."

He didn't seem to know what she was talking about. Maybe they didn't have Lucy where he lived. Where *did* he live?

"There haven't been any other lovers." She wasn't counting the one disastrous experience before him, even though, technically, it did count. "I haven't been with anyone since you."

His countenance softened a bit.

"My readers would probably be terribly disappointed if they found out that I'm not the wild woman that they— and apparently, you—think I am."

"And all those games and techniques in the book?" he

asked. "There are one hundred and one of them, according to the title."

"I made most of them up." She wasn't about to tell him that he had been at the center of her lurid imagination the entire time she'd written the book. There was no good reason for him to know that each kiss, nibble, tickle and touch described in her book had been performed by him in the deep recesses of her mind.

"I am a little curious about some of those games." He retrieved an enormous orange from a bowl nearby and rolled it under his palm, releasing some of the citrus essence. At the same time, he tipped his head toward the far end of the counter, apparently indicating the book.

Melissa picked it up and read the chapter heading. "Ah, yes," she said, "'Nooks and Crannies.' Now, *that* I didn't make up. Well, not exactly, anyway. I may have embellished a tad."

"The book needs a glossary." He pretended to be perplexed. "I know what nooks are, but I'm not sure about crannies."

Something emboldened Melissa, perhaps the subtle invitation in his voice. Whatever the reason, she slid off the stool and took the book with her as she walked around to the opposite side of the counter, where he was working.

"Maybe I should teach you a lesson or two." Her smile carried a flirtatious invitation of its own. "Think of it as a rehearsal," she said. "You'll need to know these things when we're making public appearances."

Tony regarded her with obvious interest. "Is that right?" His voice deepened to something very close to a sensual growl. "Be my guest."

Melissa set the book down and picked up a paring knife. With one easy stroke, she cut the orange he had been rolling in half. Its fresh, pungent aroma wafted between them as she settled one of the halves in her hand.

"'Nooks and Crannies' is about learning the most intimate details of your lover's body," she explained, using her best talk-show voice. "It's about exploring those sensual places we usually ignore."

"That sounds deliciously…dirty," he said.

She took his hand and held it, palm up. "It can be," she replied softly as she squeezed some orange juice into his cupped palm. "Now, watch and learn. You'll be tested on this later."

Tony's grin was slow in coming, but lovely and sensual. The heat of his hand set loose a flurry of erotic shivers that headed straight for her depths.

She lifted his hand to her lips. "This is about fingertips and tongues," she said, her voice dropping to a whisper. Feeling like a kitten at its saucer, she slowly licked the juice from his palm, using only the tip of her tongue. There was no liquor involved, but there could have been, given the sharp head rush she experienced. The sensation of her soft tongue against his textured flesh, combined with the tangy flavor of orange, was intoxicating.

What was she doing? What *was* she doing?

Her heart quickened, but she got no answer to her question—and probably wouldn't have listened anyway. Apparently she wanted to do this more than she wanted to stop, no matter how risky—and despite knowing what had happened before. That might be why she had to do it, because she *had* messed things up so badly before.

As with so many of the fantasies in her book, Tony had been the genesis for this one as well. Somewhere in the darkest hours of that one night together, she had drizzled papaya juice on his naked, reclined body and licked up every last drop. Even where it trailed into his belly button and then lower still.

The memory of how she had pleasured him with her tongue and lips was excruciatingly sensual. Melissa closed her eyes and took his fingers, one by one, into her mouth. She sealed her lips greedily around each as she slid it in and out, her tongue flicking teasingly. From above, she heard Tony's breath as it snagged in his throat. She was no mind reader, but she had a pretty good idea what he must be thinking, imagining. And it wasn't his finger she was lathing.

He touched her jaw, urging her head back up. "My turn," he said. His gaze burned her tender skin.

Melissa wet her lips, his taste still on them, as Tony chose a ripened plum from the cutting board. He slit it in half and gently squeezed it, bringing a flood of juice to the surface. "Tilt your head back," he said, cradling her neck as he held the dripping fruit to her mouth. Without saying a word, he ran the fleshy part of plum along her lips, painting them with sweet red juice.

When her lips were covered, he leaned forward and whispered, "This doesn't mean anything, you understand?"

"Of course not. We're just rehearsing." Had her voice been any softer it couldn't have been heard at all.

The tip of his tongue was feathery light as he brushed it along the fullness of her lips. She could feel a sound forming in her throat, and keeping it there was one of the hardest things she'd ever had to do. He wasn't actually kissing her. It was more like tasting, she told herself. But it was enough to make her shudder in the sweetest places, shudder like wheat fields in the wind—and to remember in detail all the unspeakably sexy things they'd done.

She wanted him to pull her close and kiss her as succulently as he had in their honeymoon suite. How wonderful to be pressed to the hardness of his body and enveloped in his strong arms. Couldn't he feel the desire burning through her? She must be hot to the touch. But if he'd picked up on her vibes, he was doing a remarkable job of restraining himself.

He stopped tasting her, and Melissa sighed. She wanted more of that, more of anything even close to that, but apparently he had other plans. He eased her hair away from her ear, and she felt coolness brush her skin as he again painted her flesh with the juice. This time it was her earlobe and the curve of her neck. The sensation was maddening and thrilling at once, followed by a more deeply erotic pull as his warm breath tickled the sensitive flesh along her lobe.

His lips moved along the delicate curves, suckling. "This must be a cranny," he murmured.

Melissa was too breathless to protest. To her it was definitely a nook, but as long as he kept doing what he was doing, he could call it whatever he wanted. Her breasts ached to be touched. They were hot and swollen against the rustling silk of her kimono. She closed her eyes and imagined the robe was his thumb pads caressing her nipples, teasing them, occasionally pinching them. He had done all that to her, and not just in the book.

With exquisitely slow strokes, Tony began lapping the juice from her neck. The plummy fragrance was rich in her nostrils, and Melissa had begun to identify with the pulpy fruit in more ways than one. It felt as though she could dissolve into juice herself.

She didn't want him to know how crazy she was to be with him, not unless he was crazy to be with her, too. These things had to be equal, or it could be too embarrassing to live. Asking him was out of the question, and she couldn't see him with his head nuzzled in the hollow of her throat. But her arm hung between them.

She moved slightly. Her hand brushed his thigh and came into contact with all the evidence she needed. He was plenty crazy. If he got any crazier, the zipper of his pants would be an endangered species.

Tony groaned when her hand "accidentally" grazed his shaft.

She could feel his fingers curling into a fist, capturing her hair, and suddenly everything was real and immediate. He drew her head back, exposing the full length of her neck. When Melissa opened her eyes, she saw the desire burning in his. There was no mistaking what he intended to do.

She reached for him, already lost in the power of his kiss. She could feel it all through her, sizzling on her lips and radiating in the echo chamber of her senses. When his mouth closed on hers, she would fall into him, giving in to all the strange and wonderful hungers she felt. In the swirl of her thoughts, she also understood that she wouldn't stop him if he swept her up, spread her out on the counter like a sumptuous gourmet meal and ate her alive.

But his mouth didn't close on hers, and eventually Melissa realized that he was looking at her in a different way. Passion shimmered in his eyes like night fires, but there was a different quality to it. He was in control again.

"We are just practicing, right?" he said.

His question had officially put an end to their rehearsal, and they both knew it. "Yes, of course," she said, smiling too brightly. "I think Jeanie's going to be proud of us, don't you? Maybe we could put in a request for fresh fruit at our next talk show."

She hoped her voice was steadier than it sounded. She could barely talk. She was shaking all over.

Very quickly they were back to code again, side by side. The fruit was on the cutting board, and Tony had picked up the towel. While he went to the sink to wash his hands, Melissa tried desperately to collect herself. Despite her intentions, it had turned into one of those embarrassing moments, and she didn't know when or why.

Was he as affected by this as she was? He seemed to be doing almost as good a job of avoiding her as she was him. But even though she'd just been rudely rejected, it felt as if something else was going on here. That in itself was progress. She had spent most of her life imagining men rejecting her because she wasn't attractive enough or wasn't something enough, but Tony had never acted as if he didn't find her attractive. Quite the opposite, to her continual surprise.

Maybe he was being noble, taking it upon himself to prevent a repeat performance of what had gotten them into this mess in the first place. She liked that a little better than the idea of rejection, but not much. She didn't have the answer, but a couple of things seemed reasonably certain as she headed back to the other side of the counter, where it was safe. One—she wasn't nearly as devastated by his withdrawal as she would have expected. And two— if she couldn't make her own man beg for sex, what right did she have to tell others how to do it?

TONY STOOD in his darkened room, gazing down at the city. Under the streetlights, a row of horse-drawn carriages stood, waiting for customers. Not much business tonight, except for the occasional tourists. Manhattan's well-heeled natives either cabbed it or walked to their glamorous destinations.

A walk to the State of Maine wouldn't have cooled him down, unfortunately. Payback wasn't everything it was cracked up to be. Just his luck that he had a hard-on that wouldn't go away. And he wasn't much closer to accomplishing his sworn mission than the day he'd sworn it. She might be a born trembling leaf—and he suspected she was—but she could do a damn convincing hussy when she put her mind to it.

Still, it wasn't a fair fight. He had a big advantage.

Jeanie had convinced him the tour would be a disaster if Melissa knew the truth about his situation, and he'd accepted the publicist's assessment. She'd told him Melissa had a chance at some sorely deserved success—and he didn't want to be the one to ruin that for her. He had some skin in the game, too, but it was different for him. He knew what was going on. He knew why he'd had to put the brakes on their relationship, and she had no idea. He probably shouldn't have let it go as far as he did tonight, but the woman was delectable, sweeter than any plum juice. Those wild little noises she made in her throat had *him* wild.

Still, he shouldn't have. When he'd come back to his room from their book signing, he'd discovered a dozen messages on his cell phone, some of them tagged as urgent. People were counting on him, waiting for him. He couldn't let them down. And yet, he'd had no desire to answer any of the calls, only a nagging sense of obligation.

That should have told him something—and it did. He had a problem. Still. After Melissa had disappeared from Cancún, he'd spent considerable time trying to convince himself that she'd run off because she was a flight risk— a love-'em-and-leave-'em kind of woman. The type who had no interest in attachments or commitments. That was the easiest way to explain why she'd left so suddenly and mysteriously—and it had allowed him to blame it on her.

But a part of him had known all along it wasn't the truth. She was frightened. She'd never done anything like that before, except maybe in her head. She had unlocked a part of herself that longed for expression that night. That was the only way to explain her unbelievably erotic behavior—and she probably felt ashamed afterward, maybe even dirty. What a tragedy.

Tony had treasured every sigh she'd surrendered to him, every rule she'd broken and vulnerability she'd exposed.

He'd wanted her back for years. Maybe he still did.

And now, with his lips afire from their broken kiss, he was coming to grips with another truth. Melissa Sanders wasn't just trying to empower other women to accept their sexuality. She was still trying to empower herself. She had something to prove, and that alone meant he had better avoid her like Samson should have avoided Delilah. The stronger she got, the weaker his will power became—and neither of them needed the chaos that could cause.

"Is THAT what you're wearing?" Jeanie tilted her head as she entered the greenroom and got a look at Melissa's outfit.

"What's wrong with it?" Melissa had spent hours this morning trying on one outfit after another, hoping to find something sexy, but not too sexy. It was no piece of cake trying to look like a hooker and Betty Crocker at the same time. She'd finally chosen the silk jersey wraparound, which, granted, would have been sexier if it had fit. It was a smidge too big, and she'd attempted to fix that by sewing in some extra snaps at the bust and skirt opening.

"Pardon the expression," Jeanie said, "but you look frumpy. What's with all these snaps? You look like you climbed inside a burlap bag and tied the top shut. Show a little skin, hon.''

Jeanie undid two of the snaps at the bust and two at the skirt opening. She stepped back and nodded. ''That will have to do, I suppose. Make sure you cross your legs and dangle your high heels from your toes. Tony likes that.''

''How do you know?''

''Well, duh. All you have to do is watch him. You dangle and zoom, he's there, all eyes. I think our boy has a foot fetish.''

Melissa laughed. ''You think so, huh?'' Interesting that Jeanie was giving her advice on how to attract Tony. If she'd known they were licking fruit juice off each other last night, she might not be so concerned.

''Dangle anyway. Speaking of Tony, where is he?'' Jeanie asked. ''We're up next.''

Melissa checked her watch. ''He said something about having to make a call. That was nearly ten minutes ago. He should be back anytime.''

They hadn't come in with Jeanie this morning. The publicist had an early appointment, so she'd taken a taxi. Melissa and Tony had been driven to the studio in a town car provided by the publisher. She'd felt too embarrassed to be chatty, and Tony had offered little more than a goodmorning. He'd concentrated on his morning cup of Starbucks coffee, seeming moody and distracted. She had a feeling he might not have slept well. Or maybe it was the phone call he'd made this morning. At any rate, it was a long, quiet ride.

''I hope he's not late,'' Jeanie said. ''We don't want to have to raise another search party.'' She plucked at Melissa's dress again, undoing another snap on the skirt.

''Did you kids go through the book last night?'' she

asked. "Did you practice fielding questions? Do you think you're ready? This has to sizzle, you know."

"We practiced," Melissa assured her. "It sizzled."

The guest-wrangler stuck her head in. "It's time. Ready?"

Melissa headed for the door, followed by Jeanie. As they entered the wide hallway that led to the set for the *Nice Girls Do* morning show, Tony joined them. He was dressed in a light, single-breasted linen suit that looked as if it could have had a designer label in the collar. His shoes looked expensive, too. How did he afford such pricey clothing on a waiter's salary? Of course, it was none of her business. He might very well have gone into hock to get some decent clothes for the tour—and for that, she should be grateful. Or he might have blackmailed Jeanie out of a few bucks.

As she passed a full-length mirror at the very end of the hall, she stole a look at herself. She *did* look frumpy.

Nice Girls Do was in the middle of a commercial break, and Dr. Darlene Love, a sex therapist and the show's host, hurried over to welcome them. She was well into her sixties, but with the kind of bubbling energy that made Melissa want to ask her what vitamins she took.

"Melissa and Tony? *Sooooo* nice to meet you two," Dr. Love said, giving both their hands a shake at once. "Listen, just relax and have fun, kids, the more fun the better. I'll be announcing you as soon as we're back on air."

With that she hurried back to the set, completely ignoring an adoring gaggle of audience members who vied for her attention. And they called her Dr. Love?

A voice-over announcer could be heard, and the host's round beaming face flashed on the studio monitor. She was holding up Melissa's book to a chorus of applause.

As they walked onto the set, Tony said under his breath, "No tricks today."

He could have saved his voice. Tricks were the last thing on her mind, right after sex, which didn't bode very well for this show, which was supposed to sizzle. Somehow they had to make America believe they were the world's horniest couple, an honor they'd just been given in the promo for the show, when they didn't even want to be in the same room. Tony was acting as if she had a contagious disease. Maybe she did. Her breath was a little short.

They took their seats on a crushed-velvet sofa the color of the plum juice that had been all over Melissa's face last night. Not a reminder she needed, thanks. Apparently Tony did think she was contagious. He sat at the opposite end of the couch, the big dope. What was wrong with him? Maybe she'd just go plunk herself in his lap and tickle him.

"Well, let's get right to it." Dr. Love graced them with a slightly loopy smile. "What do we women have to do to get our men to beg for sex?"

"Bite them," Melissa said, remembering the host's remark about fun. "A little nip on the neck or the earlobe is a sure sign that a woman's in the mood, right, Tony?"

"Teeth marks all over me," he said, deadpan.

"Oh, my," Dr. Love murmured. "Could we see them?"

Tony didn't answer, and the doctor's smile faded. "Do you two always sit so far apart?" she asked. "Is that in the book?"

With a glance at Tony's dark countenance, Melissa hastened to explain. "See, this is a little game we play. He gets grumpy, and I coax him out of his mood, no matter what it takes. There's nothing a man loves more than a persistent woman. Right, Tony Baby? Hmm, Tiger Lover?"

"Bite me," Tony said in a low voice.

"See—he loves it. They all do."

"Really?" The doctor sounded unconvinced. "That's the secret to your white-hot relationship? Grumpiness? Biting?"

The audience tittered.

"Just kidding, of course. Communication is the key." All too true, but not nearly exciting enough for the *Nice Girls Do* show. She searched her brain for some way to spice things up, and finally tossed it to Tony. "Wouldn't you agree?"

Say something provocative, Tony, please. Tell me I'm crazy. Naked vacuuming is the key.

"Communication," he echoed with all the enthusiasm of a performing parrot. "It's *all* about communication."

The smile on Dr. Love's face drooped noticeably, and Melissa knew they were doomed. This wasn't going badly. It was the turnpike at rush hour. It wasn't going at all.

Dr. Love stole a glance at her blue note card. "Oh, it's time for the call-in segment! Goody, right after this break, we'll take some exciting questions from our viewers." Her tone said please, God.

As the show went off the air, Darlene Love's smile turned into bared teeth. "What's going on?" she asked Melissa and Tony. "Is this some crazy publicity stunt? How do you two manage to have sex at all? You barely look at each other."

Poor Jeanie was jumping up and down in the wings, trying to get their attention, and Melissa knew she had to do something.

"My fault. It's the game." Melissa sprang from the couch and plunked herself in Tony's lap, much to his moody surprise. "He just needs some coaxing."

Under her breath, she warned him, "If you let me down

now, I'll push you over the hotel balcony when we get back.''

"I'm taking you with me," he said.

Steam hissed through Melissa's nostrils. He really was impossible. If only she had another glass of ice water. Anything would be better than sitting on his lap, goo-gooing and playing kissy-face. But when the stage manager began the countdown to airtime, Melissa did exactly that.

"Isn't that sweet?" Dr. Love cooed. "Our guests are demonstrating techniques for make-up sex. Let's hope they can break away from each other long enough to talk to our first callers—a Mr. and Mrs. Earnest Sanders. Have I got that right? Melissa, I think you may know these lovely folks from the State of Kansas."

Melissa had been blowing little puffs of air in Tony's face. One of them got stuck in her throat. Caught like a fish bone. This couldn't be.

"Mr. and Mrs. Sanders, is there anything you'd like to say to your naughty daughter and son-in-law?"

"Melissa, is that really you? Your father and I heard about your book at church last Sunday. The minister held it up and told the whole congregation what a great help a book like yours could be to married folk. We went out and bought it, and I must say—"

"Mom?" Melissa would have recognized her mother's prim-and-proper voice anywhere. But she didn't know what to do. Her brain had frozen solid, so her body decided for her. Melissa's respiratory system reacted to crises like a blow-dryer did to overheating. It shut down the plant. She stopped breathing altogether. No air, either way. She couldn't inhale or exhale.

She clutched her throat and waved her hand, trying to get someone's attention. But no one seemed to understand that she was in danger of suffocating. She could die right there onstage. And finally, Dr. Love let forth with a peal of laughter.

"Would you look at that!" she said. "Our outspoken author is speechless. Isn't that cute?"

8

___

As aphrodisiacs go, the mind is the most potent, but never underestimate a great tush on a guy.

101 Ways To Make Your Man Beg

MELISSA FIGURED she must be several shades of blue by now. She could hear her mother's voice droning in her head, which meant she wasn't dead yet, but she still couldn't make herself breathe. It felt as if her lungs were caught in a vise.

"Melissa, your dad and I tried that crazy game in chapter five. What was it called, Ern? Ride the Wild Pony? He had to see the doctor for his sacroiliac, but we're very proud of you, dear. When do we get to meet your handsome Tony?"

Dr. Love's eyebrows shot up. "Your parents haven't met your husband?"

Melissa let out a strangled gasp, and finally people began to realize that she was in trouble. Tony scooped her up in his arms and put her on her feet.

Dr. Love jumped up, too. "What should we do?"

"Give me some room," Tony said, waving the host away. "We've been through this before. It's her breathing."

Melissa fell against Tony as he clamped a hand over her mouth and pinched her nose shut. Not this again! She struggled, but couldn't break his hold. God, he was strong. She was smothering, and he was going to finish her off! Was that his plan?

Let go of me. Let go already! She couldn't scream at him, except mentally.

She tried to step on his toe and missed. Desperate, she kicked back with her high heel, meaning to hit his shin. She hadn't intended to hurt him, but she aimed too high.

"Oof!" Tony released her, doubling over in pain, and Melissa stumbled forward, sucking air into her lungs.

"These kids play rough," Dr. Love said. "Time for a break, folks. When we come back, we'll bring out our next guests—and hear this! It's the entire cast of *Girls Behaving Badly.*"

FORTUNATELY, Melissa's breathing made a rapid recovery. She was fine by the time she and Tony got backstage. And he was only limping slightly, but his mood didn't seem to have improved at all.

"It was an accident," she said, hazarding a glance at him. "I swear it was."

"One more accident like that, and I'll never have children."

"I'm *sorry.* Is there anything I can do?"

"Please, no! I can still walk."

Melissa decided she was only making it worse and went quiet, but by the time they reached the hallway to the exit, Tony seemed to have rallied. She checked with him again.

"I'll live," he said, shrugging it off. "How about you? How's the breathing?"

"Oh, I'm fine." On second thought, she added, "I really would appreciate it if you'd stop trying to smother me."

"Deal, if you'll quit going for my crotch."

They both managed wan smiles, which quickly faded

when they got a look at their devoted publicist. Jeanie stood stock-still in the middle of the hallway they'd just entered. Her mouth hung open like a sprung garage door. Her eyes seemed distant and remote. Melissa wondered if she was in shock.

The guest-wrangler flew by them as if they were invisible. On her way to pick up the badly behaving girls, no doubt.

"Jeanie, it wasn't that bad," Melissa said, speaking low so as not to jar her.

Jeanie blinked. She looked at them as if she'd been in a hypnotic trance and someone had snapped their fingers. "Not that bad?" she said. "Not that bad? It was a *disaster.*" She focused on Melissa. "You didn't tell your parents you were married? You didn't even tell them you'd written a book? How did you expect to get away with that?"

"The same way you expected to get away with passing me off as her husband?" Tony ventured.

Jeanie glared at both of them. "I think you need another publicist."

"Jeanie, no! My parents will be fine." Melissa couldn't swear that was true, but Jeanie obviously needed humoring. Melissa was just grateful her parents weren't too upset. She hadn't expected them to become a part of her fan base, but it shouldn't have surprised her. They'd always supported her in everything she'd done.

"They would never do anything to hurt me," she assured Jeanie. "They just didn't know. I'll speak to them. I'll ask them not to call any more shows."

"They probably sold more books than we did," Tony offered. "That Wild Pony business will make a great story."

Jeanie huffed. "Damn right they sold more books than

you two bozos did. You acted like you couldn't bear the sight of each other. And by the way, I didn't buy that make-up-sex game for one minute. I'm sure no one else did, either. You two have to get some chemistry going. You're duds in the fireworks department!''

Jeanie had her purse open, already searching through it for something, most likely her cell phone, which meant she was probably out of danger, as far as shock went.

''Go back to the hotel and wait for me,'' she told them, an ominous edge to her voice. ''This calls for drastic action, and I have some thinking to do.''

With that she turned on her heel and marched for the exit, leaving Melissa and Tony to stare after her with some trepidation.

LATER THAT EVENING, Tony answered a brisk knock at the suite's door. He knew before opening it that Jeanie would be on the other side. She knocked the way she walked and talked—with speed and determination.

''Where's the other lovebird?'' she asked as she brushed past him.

Tony closed the door and followed her into the living room. ''She's on the phone with her parents, assuring them that I saved her life on the show today. Nice folks. She put me on the line, and we all had a good chat. They've agreed not to call the police.''

''You must have made quite an impression,'' Jeanie said, setting a loaded shopping bag on the living-room coffee table. ''Did they really like the book?''

''They've already started an online fan club.'' He grinned, indicating the bag she'd brought. ''What do you have there?''

''Salvation…I hope.'' She marched to Melissa's door

and called, "Come out of there, Ms. Sexpot. We have work to do."

"And just what are you trying to save?" Tony sank to the sofa and folded his arms. It was beginning to look like a very long evening.

"Our collective asses, if you must know. We have to turn you two into red-hot lovers." Jeanie rapped on Melissa's door. "Chop-chop. I'm serious."

Tony heard some kind of female grumbling and supposed Melissa was no more excited than he was about this apparent crusade of Jeanie's. A moment later Melissa appeared, casting a suspicious gaze upon the scene in the living room.

Slitty eyes flattered her, Tony realized. He had to be going nuts. Slitty eyes didn't flatter anyone but Clint Eastwood.

Melissa dropped into an overstuffed chair by the window.

"And I'm so happy to see you, too," Jeanie said with an overly bright smile. "Now, down to business. Tomorrow the two of you will be demonstrating some of Melissa's techniques, in person, on live television."

"Oh no we're not," Tony and Melissa said in near unison.

"Oh yes you are," Jeanie chirped. Tony wasn't sure but he thought he recognized a woman on the verge of hysteria. Her cutting sarcasm and sharp-edged smiles were her only defense.

"I've already taken care of everything," she said. "The venues have been notified as to what they'll need, and I have a list of what you'll be doing tomorrow."

She handed each of them a sheet of neatly typed paper, along with a copy of Melissa's book. "Go to the chapters I've marked and study them as if you were cramming for finals. I've highlighted each of your copies, so really I've done all the work for you. All you need to do is learn, memorize and practice. Practice, practice, practice. The entire key to this is practice. You need to look relaxed and natural as you're demonstrating. If you don't, I swear I *will* kill you both."

She flashed them another blinding smile and began rifling around in her bag of tricks. "There now, that wasn't so awful, was it? What have I done with the Ginseng Revitalizing Tonic in a Capsule?"

She produced a huge bottle of pills and plunked it down on the coffee table. "Two of these, three times a day, on an empty stomach. I can personally vouch for their effectiveness. They'll lift your spirits, sedate your nerves and focus your mind. These babies can take the edge off a razor and give you a lovely little buzz to boot. Go at it, kids, with my blessings."

With that, she pivoted like a drum major and headed for the door.

"You know, they have decaf," Tony said.

Jeanie spun around, that god-awful smile still plastered on her mouth. She waggled her index finger toward the book in his lap. "Practice, mister, and take your pills. Melissa, tomorrow, I will dress you myself. Good night, dearies."

After she left the suite, Tony considered locking the door. "She seems a little tense, you think?" he asked.

Melissa was looking over her sheet of paper. She appeared very pale now, as if she'd been bitten by a vampire and left to die. "I have a feeling we'll be joining her soon."

"Why?" Tony didn't wait for an answer. He skimmed his own sheet of instructions, and felt the blood draining from his face as well.

"We can't do this on television," Melissa said under her breath. "They'll arrest us!"

"SEXUAL PASTE? She wants us to pretend we're stuck together? *There?*"

Melissa was afraid to look up from her instruction sheet. She and Tony were on the sofa, surrounded by the contents of Jeanie's care package and, just like a man, Tony had already begun flipping through his copy of *101 Ways*, looking for the first warm-up exercise on Jeanie's list.

"This is like being joined at the…uh, hip," he said, looking over at her.

"Actually, it's worse—or better, depending on how you look at it."

Melissa had spent so many hours on her book she knew its contents inside out, an advantage Tony didn't have at this point. She also knew what to expect from the games and exercises on Jeanie's cheat sheet. There was no way to demonstrate them without some very suggestive touching and physical contact. It would be great for the talk-show circuit, but deadly for those nights alone in the hotel suite together.

Melissa was still a little shaken from the *Nice Girls Do* appearance, and her parents' call wasn't the only reason, although it had certainly cooled her jets. She'd also realized after last night that seduction was a tricky business, with ramifications beyond the bedroom. Playing games with a man you were legitimately married to was one thing. An unknown quantity like Tony, quite another.

"Maybe we should take our herbal supplements?" Melissa picked up the bottle Jeanie left. A pill that could energize, calm and tranquilize all at the same time sounded damn good to her, but her only interest at the moment was tranquillity.

"Maybe later," Tony said, eyeing the pills. "Are they safe?"

"Jeanie takes them and she hasn't keeled over yet." Melissa opened the lid and spilled out two of the capsules. "I'm starting now, *before* I require hospitalization. Come on, be brave."

But Tony declined when she offered him the bottle. With a sigh she put it back on the table. Jeanie wanted them to take the herbs, and she hoped Tony wouldn't be difficult. Men did tend to be difficult about taking pills. Maybe it was a macho thing. Then again, maybe he had the good sense not to trust what lurked inside the pungent-smelling brownish capsules.

"Tony, there's no way we're getting out of this," she said, telling him what he already knew. "I hate to admit it, but Jeanie's right. Today was a fiasco, and not just because of my parents. If we blow it again tomorrow, I'm afraid it'll be all over."

He laid his book and paper on the massive coffee table. "You don't think we came off as the world's horniest couple?"

She had to laugh at that. "Maybe the world's most hostile. But I suppose after last night, we were just trying to protect ourselves."

Tony rose and slipped his hands into his pockets. He'd taken off his suit jacket earlier and loosened his silk tie at the knot. Even in relaxed mode, he looked good. Hot, in fact. Too hot for her poor overworked circuits.

"Speaking of last night," he said. "That retreat on my part wasn't about you. I need you to know that."

"What was it then?"

He affected a shrug. "Maybe I don't want the kind of collision we had before. One car wreck in a lifetime is enough."

"That's how you think of it, as a car wreck?"

"It did some damage," he said.

His somber expression made her think it was a lot more damage than he was willing to say. She wasn't the one who'd been left, but it had never occurred to her that he would want her to stay. And when it appeared that he'd made no attempt to find her, she'd assumed the worst.

Melissa eyed the pills again, wondering when they would kick in, if ever. Everything was moving too fast, especially her thoughts. But as she stared at the bottle, an idea came to her that made her think the pills might be working.

"Do you think if we practice enough we might desensitize ourselves to the point that the games wouldn't get to us? You know, like when someone says a bad word so often it loses its shock value."

"I don't think it's quite the same thing," he said.

She blew out a long breath and rose from the chair. "In that case, I think we need to agree in advance of any practicing we might do that there won't be any sex. In fact, let's not even think about sex. Let's just suck it up and do what we have to, you know, like performers and prostitutes and politicians."

"No thoughts of sex? I can't guarantee that."

"Okay, we can think about it, but we *can't* do it."

"Agreed. However—" His gaze traveled down the length of her body, lingering on the openings of the wrap dress she hadn't yet changed out of. "If we're going to try the Sexual Paste game, you might want to put some pants on."

The rules of engagement at long last. Ten minutes later they were back in the living room. Tony had changed from suit and tie into jeans and a blue cotton T-shirt. Melissa wore a pair of workout shorts and a racer-back sports bra.

Like two dancers about to rehearse their routine for the first time, they met in the center of the room.

"I'm all yours," Tony said. He placed his hands on his hips, one of his many mundane gestures Melissa found downright erotic.

"The Sexual Paste game is actually very easy." She forced herself to sound detached and professional. "It's supposed to be played in the shower, but we'll have to pretend that part. But do keep in mind that this would normally be done in the nude."

Tony's eyes glinted with interest. "I can do that."

She chose to ignore that. "Here's how this works. If we were really in the shower, the first thing we would do is lather each other with soap. Tonight, we'll have to fake it. You do yourself and I'll do myself."

The glint became a frown. "That's no fun."

Melissa shot him a warning look. "Hey, this can be sexy. It's the anticipation phase, like foreplay."

"If you insist."

And Melissa did. Insist. "Now, after we're both wet and slippery, we take turns touching each other, but we're not allowed to touch, you know, the goods. You can touch fronts and behinds, but no primary sexual zones."

"Which are?"

"Well, technically, nipples, labia and vagina on a woman. I'm not allowed to touch your—" She had it in mind to be subtle, but her gaze dropped like a rock to his crotch. "Manhood."

"I don't think I like this game." Tony pretended to grumble.

"You will, trust me. It requires some patience, but you're good at that. This is about getting to know your lover's body in a slow, tactile way."

"So I'm going to put my hands on you?"

"Yes, but it's more than that." Melissa sighed. "It might be better if I just showed you. Whatever part of my body I place against yours has to stay where it is until the game is finished. That's where the paste part comes in. Like this."

She stepped close to him, close enough to catch the light woodsy scent of his cologne, and gave him the once-over. She took her time looking him up and down, demonstrating correct procedure. He was a sexy guy. She was a sexy chick, getting an eyeful, and so on and so on. No big deal. They could do this.

Actually, Melissa knew he expected her to place one of her hands on him, but she decided to try something else. Instead, she pressed the inside of her right calf against the outside of his left calf.

"See? Now I'm stuck to you."

Tony gazed down at their conjoined legs. "This could get very interesting," he said. "So I don't actually have to use my hands yet? I can use any part of my body I want?"

Melissa nodded, her heart already pounding. It was now her turn to be shamelessly surveyed from head to toe, and Tony took his own sweet time with it, too.

"Maybe I'll do this." He pressed his right thigh to her left thigh. They both had to spread their legs a bit to keep their balance, but they remained joined through the process.

"What about the soap part?" Tony asked. "Why are we all slippery if we can't rub each other?"

"In a sec." Her voice was beginning to fade on her. There didn't seem to be enough air when she got this close to him. Melissa's next move was a rather bold one. Maybe those pills really had started to work. She reached around and placed her hand on his right butt cheek. It was a hard, rounded muscle, and she could feel it flexing under her touch. Unfortunately, her brain wanted her to see the action, too, and she had a rather intense flashback of another time she'd curved her hand to his beautiful bronze behind—and watched muscles rippling wildly from the effort to gain control.

The things she'd done to this man. The things he'd done to her!

She had to give him some credit, though. Until now she had only seen flashes of the deeply sensual nature that she knew was hidden in his gaze. That seemed to be changing. His chest rose and fell more slowly than it had just seconds ago. And his eyes had narrowed and focused as if he, too, was imagining the forbidden.

"I can touch you anywhere?" he asked. The thickness in his voice betrayed him.

"Anywhere except those primary sexual zones I mentioned." If she didn't find her breath soon she'd be reduced to sign language.

Apparently Tony decided one bold move deserved another. He moved his hand upward and cupped the fullness of her left breast. He lifted it gently and squeezed its softness. Her sports top was a bra in itself, and only the thin cotton material separated his flesh from hers. Melissa nearly whimpered under his touch, but the resistance her mind threw up was futile. There were too many sensory reminders! There'd actually been a time that night in Cancún when all he'd had to do was brush his tongue over her nipple, and she'd come close to peaking. That was how wildly responsive she'd become as the hours wore on, and their honeymoon suite became a fantasy realm. She wondered what would happen now if he were to brush his fingers over her tender nipples.

It didn't take long before they were as intricately pressed

together as they were going to get. All that remained was their lips. "It's your turn," Melissa said. "You should probably kiss me now."

"Where?"

"Wherever you can reach."

She knew his options were limited. He had access to her forehead, cheeks and lips. Maybe her neck, too. She hoped he stayed away from her neck. His kisses there made her insane.

Tony had made his decision. He pressed his lips to hers and began nibbling, teasing her. She wasn't sure if that was fair or not. It seemed he was breaking the rules, but she wasn't able to correct him. Her own mouth had decided to play along.

She broke the kiss enough to speak, which was probably against the rules, too. She couldn't quite seem to remember what the rules were. "This is where the soap comes in," she said, her lips murmuring against his. "We're supposed to slide ever so gently against each other. Only a fraction of an inch, no more than that. Okay?"

Every nerve ending in her body lit up as Tony began to move. His palm rolled her breast with light pressure, and she moved against him, creating a riot of pleasure. Such wild sensations. Holding the position made her thighs tremble. He teased her budded nipples with the pad of his thumb. Slow and deliberate. Back and forth, making her nerve endings sing. Lord, so sweet. *So intense.*

They had to be breaking some rules, right?

His hipbone nudged hers, causing her legs to sway. He turned in to her and caught her back against his chest, reestablishing his hold. His body made contact with hers in several startling places. His groin nestled her derriere, the hardness between his legs was unmistakable. She didn't need to see it to know it was there. She could feel it sliding toward the crack of her other cheek. Now, *that* would be breaking a rule!

"You're not moving," Tony whispered.

She rolled her breast against the heat of his hand, and a sharp thrill rewarded her. Tony groaned into her mouth as she toyed with his knotted glute. Even their calves created friction sparks. Whether by accident or design, his hands curled tighter, forcing her closer. One wrong move, and they would be on the floor.

It didn't help that Melissa felt tipsy. She tingled everywhere. Her face was flushed, her head muzzy and light. Was it the herbs or him?

"Don't forget to breathe," he said.

"Breathe? What's that?" She broke away from him with a soft gasp. She could only take so much of this, and Tony seemed to have the same problem. They both backed off a good foot. Melissa avoided looking at him as she tried to catch her breath.

"There's a problem," he said.

"Only one?"

"Well, one big one."

Melissa glanced up and right back down as she saw what he meant. The protrusion in his jeans pressed firmly against his fly. It was a good size, big enough to hang a hat on, as she'd once quipped in an article called "Ten Signals He's Interested."

A sound squeaked out of her. Laughter? Where had that come from?

"Well, if that happens," she said, "at least Jeanie won't be able to say we're not turning up the heat. In fact, I think you should do everything you can to have an erection on the air just to keep the woman quiet. Think of the reaction."

"You mean *after* they take me to jail? Or before?"

More squeaky laughter. She sounded like a bicycle with bad breaks. Still, this was fun. She couldn't remember the last time she'd enjoyed anything as much, not since the tour started, for sure. And if Jeanie's pills had anything to do with it, she might decide to take them on a regular basis.

"Want to try another game?" she asked him.

"And risk a blowout? I think my erection and I are heading for the showers, thanks just the same."

"Chicken!" she called after him as he adjusted his jeans and made his exit. At least she had a front-row seat to catch a view of his retreating derriere.

THE LUMINOUS DIAL of Tony's watch told him he wasn't going to get any sleep that night anyway. Still fully dressed, he let himself out of the bedroom and walked the entire length of the living room, coming to a stop at her bedroom door. Was she wandering around in the dark, too? He hoped so. Insomnia should be mutual.

For several seconds, he stood there, breathing, feeling what she'd done to his body and his mind. Breasts weren't supposed to burn a man's hand with their softness. The pressure of her rounded bottom against his manhood wasn't supposed to leave him engorged. Not all night. Hard. Ready. Aching to be inside her. Aching for some relief from this madness. Even his thighs burned from the tension.

What the hell was he going to do about Melissa Sanders Bond? His wife. The woman who couldn't get her wedding ring off or catch her breath half the time. He'd had no doubt about his intentions when he'd gotten here—and they hadn't included a 24/7 erection. Or standing in front of her door obsessed with the thought of spreading her legs and tasting the apple sweetness of her sex.

This was ridiculous. Pathetic.

He took a step back, turned...and stopped. A flash of light had caught his eye. Moonlight streamed through the windows, bouncing off the gigantic bottle of pills. Jeanie's pills, the ones that could take the edge off a razor.

He rubbed the roughness of his unshaven jaw as he debated.

They couldn't hurt him. They were herbs.

And his edges were sharp enough to cut paper, for Christ's sake.

A moment later, he had the bottle in his hand. He poured out a handful, stared at the pile of brown capsules for all of sixty seconds—and downed them like candy. There, that was done. One of the more sensible decisions in his relationship with her. They tasted like shit, so they had to be good for him, right? At least maybe he'd sleep.

"NOW *THERE'S* A SEXY OUTFIT," Jeanie said as she stepped back to appraise Melissa's ensemble. They were alone in a large, sumptuous dressing room, and, true to her word, Jeanie had picked out Melissa's clothes for the late-night talk show that would start taping in less than twenty minutes. Melissa stepped carefully—and rather awkwardly—to a ceiling-to-floor mirror to survey the damage. The heels of her sexy black stilettos felt six inches high.

Lord, her reflection would have made an underwear model blush. Jeanie had insisted that she shimmy into a clingy black skirt that wasn't quite a mini, but short enough. What put it in the sexpot category was the center seam. An alarmingly deep slit pointed north, taking your glance—and your imagination—along with it.

Melissa took a test step and noticed how provocatively the slit opened up. Her top was a cropped jacket with some detail stitching on the hem and sleeves. Under the jacket was a low-cut black camisole.

"I can't wear this out there," she said, her voice a low moan.

"Yes, you can, and yes, you will," Jeanie said. "You look great. If this doesn't get Tony's attention, nothing will."

"It isn't Tony's attention I'm worried about. Look at this slit, Jeanie! One wrong move, and I'll be facing obscenity charges."

"You have panty hose on. What are you worried about?"

"Indecent exposure, maybe?"

"Here, take a pill," Jeanie said, searching through her tote. She produced a smaller bottle than the one she'd left at the suite, but the capsules were the same. "Take two."

Melissa took two and popped a third for good measure. She'd been taking them regularly, and they left her pleasantly relaxed yet energized. At times, her blood rushed and she felt a little giddy. But it was a lovely sensation, actually. She didn't mind it at all. Maybe another one? Four? Mmm, no. She was mellow enough.

Eighteen minutes later, she and Tony were sitting side by side on a leather sofa stationed next to the talk-show host's desk. A former stand-up comic, Larry Gunderson had a rather breathtaking overbite and slightly crossed eyes with pupils that roamed freely, even when he looked straight at you. Melissa was reminded of Groucho Marx from old clips she'd seen on the Comedy Channel.

Larry had asked all the usual questions, and either Tony or Melissa had answered with more than enough sexual innuendo to elicit giggles and gasps from the audience. Everyone seemed pleased, even Jeanie, who for the first five minutes of their interview had stood in the wings, wringing her hands. Now she was smiling, laughing along.

Larry leaned toward the two of them as if he was about to whisper something. "I've been told," he intoned, "that you've agreed to demonstrate one of your games." He gave the audience a wry glance. "Waddaya think, folks? Want to see a man beg for sex on national television?"

Hoots and howls brought Larry out of his chair. He waved extravagantly toward a curtain that opened to reveal the frame of a shower stall in the middle of a bathroom set.

"My stage is your loo," he told Melissa and Tony. Turning to the cameras, he said, "We do things right here on the *Larry Gunderson Show*. We even have flesh-colored bodysuits for our sex experts to wear. Can't wait to see that, folks? Stick with us. We'll be back right after this commercial break."

The bodysuits came as a surprise to Melissa, and naturally there was only one screen for her and Tony to change behind. Why would a married couple need separate screens? Melissa's resembled a two-piece tankini, and behind the screen she turned away from Tony, planning to put on as much of it as she could before taking off her clothing. She managed the bottoms easily, but as she began to work on the top, she felt some air on her backside, and a sharp sensation.

"Hey!" She shot Tony a look over her shoulder. He'd snapped her spandex tankini bottoms, and she couldn't retaliate. Her arms were tangled in the camisole she was trying to take off inside her jacket. But she didn't miss the dark and dangerous sparkle in his eyes. This was nothing like the *Nice Girls Do* show. He looked ready for anything. His rakish smile made her knees weak, and she needed her wits about her to get the tankini top on. Thank God, the suit fit. Someone must have given the producers their sizes. Jeanie, the woman who would barter her soul to sell a book? Who else.

Tony already had his Speedo-style suit on, and he seemed more than interested in Melissa's predicament. As she shed her jacket and camisole, he nuzzled her neck, his warm breath caressing her ear. "Need some help?"

"I'm fine."

"Yes, you are," he whispered.

"Tony, what are you doing?"

"I'm whispering in your ear—and making plans to molest you."

"On national television?"

"Anywhere, Melissa, anywhere. I'd like to drag you into the nearest closet, lock the door and never let you out."

Melissa didn't know what to make of him. Either he'd lost his mind or something wicked had taken possession of Tony Bond's soul. She wondered if it had anything to do with Jeanie's pills. They'd certainly worked their magic on Melissa. Her heart raced pleasantly and she blushed for no good reason. All day she'd been smiling over nothing, and she wasn't the slightest bit worried about exotic illnesses.

But Tony wasn't taking the pills. It couldn't be that.

When the curtain came open moments later, Melissa was all set to explain the game to the audience. Her tankini strap had been carefully miked. She only needed to speak clearly. But try making sense while a man was looking at you as if he wanted to devour you, starting with your trembling lips.

"Everyplace we touch, we stick," she managed to get out.

Tony pasted the outside of his calf to the outside of hers,

and when she cupped his behind, the audience roared with approval. The two of them had agreed to go with most of the routine they rehearsed last night, except for his hand on her breast. No doubt the crowd would have loved it, but Melissa didn't think it was appropriate, even for late night.

She was also trying to avoid any possibility of another meltdown in front of God and everyone, although she wasn't certain God watched Larry Gunderson. She hoped not. Whimpering in front of the late-night audience would be embarrassing enough—and she didn't trust herself not to whimper if Tony touched her that intimately. He had a way of making her feel as if no one else existed, and that could only get them into trouble tonight.

"Your turn," she told him.

He leaned close. "I can't wait to get my hands on you," he said under his breath.

A gasp resounded as the mike picked up Tony's sexy warning and broadcast it to the room. Melissa barely heard the clamor. She was too startled at what he actually did with his hand. Her breast was supposed to have been off limits, but he touched it anyway, cupping her tenderly enough to elicit the whimper she feared. Her legs nearly gave way when she registered the searing heat of his skin. She was terribly weak. Was it because she hadn't expected this? Or because that's what he did best, make her terribly weak?

He was dangerous, out of control. *What had come over him?*

Somehow she swallowed back the sound in her throat. She even steadied her legs, but as his fingers closed over her flesh, she lost touch with everything else for a second. She knew this was wrong, against the rules, an infringement, but she couldn't seem to hold that thought. Or any thought. Every nerve ending was in shock, quivering. And she was engulfed with the sweetest kind of need. *How did he do that to her?*

She had no idea what came next. Anything? Oh, yes, the kiss. Was she supposed to say something, do something, or just be kissed to the brink of oblivion by this sexy, reckless man?

"Tony, don't kill me." She tilted her face up to him, and their mouths touched. Tony's soft moan resounded like thunder, but Melissa could only hear it in her mind. Nothing else existed but him. He lifted her off her feet and enfolded her in his arms, pasting their bodies together from lips to toes. They'd broken the rules, but Melissa couldn't remember what game they were playing anyway, so it didn't matter.

He was still whispering in her ear, vowing that he was going to have his way with her the minute they got back to the suite. Maybe in the limo.

"Have your way with me," she said. "Yes, *do*."

The curtain came down on their sizzling kiss, and Larry Gunderson could be heard saying, "I think that's all we need to know, folks. Show's over. Let's go buy the book."

"HOTSY-TOTSY! You two are barbecue starters."

Jeanie's excitement filled the town car. The show had been taped live, so it was late in the evening when the three of them returned to the hotel. Jeanie talked nonstop during the drive back, congratulating them on their astonishing performance. Melissa didn't say a word. She couldn't get past the noise of her soaring heart. Tony was quiet, too, but she could feel the tension pouring off him.

Jeanie wanted to celebrate. She offered to buy them a nightcap in the hotel's lobby bar, but Melissa begged off. Too tired, she said. Tony used the same excuse.

Their next ride was even more silent, just the two of them in an elevator all the way up to their suite. Silent. Tense. Vibrant. The air seemed to shimmer before Melissa's eyes, the way heat shimmers on a summer day.

Tony used his key to open the door, and Melissa stepped into the darkened room. She didn't bother to turn on the lights as Tony snapped the door shut. She dropped her bag to the floor and turned to face him. His embrace was quick and tight, his kiss immediate and desperate. And hot. Steaming hot.

Melissa kicked off her dreaded heels and pressed herself to him as intimately as she had on the talk show. No, that wasn't intimate. This was. She didn't even try to pretend that his touch didn't burn her flesh. Just being near him dragged her into a deep pool of desire.

Their hands created a frantic flurry as they began undressing each other. There wasn't time to speak. Words would only get in the way. They both seemed to understand that this was inevitable, preordained after their one night together two years earlier.

A sense of joy flooded Melissa. This time they would make love. He wouldn't change his mind. She couldn't bear that. How many times had she fantasized about the way he would find her again, sweep her into his arms and make love to her with wild abandon? She'd imagined it just like this, him taking her wherever they happened to be, without a word. He wouldn't change his mind. Not this time.

9

Don't think of it as rejection. Think of it as an invitation, a challenge, or better yet, a dare.

101 Ways To Make Your Man Beg

TONY WAS A MAN BESET by demons. Melissa's naked skin brought a thrill of pleasure as drugging as the most potent opiate. And just as illegal. He couldn't do this. Some part of his mind had been telling him to stop all night, but it didn't have a chance against the fires roaring in his blood. He was drunk, high, over the moon. Maybe he'd taken too many of those damn pills, he thought but at this same time knew it wasn't about pills. She was the drug.

Her nails ripped him sweetly. She kissed him like a kitten, with hungry, feeding bites of his lips. She sucked on his tongue. He shuddered and kissed her back. Brutally. A moan caught in his throat. This wasn't a conscious choice anymore. Maybe it never had been.

They dropped to the floor and sprawled in the deep nap of the carpet. Their heat-slicked bodies entwined like rope. Knotted like rope. God, it was beautiful. He wanted this heaven to last forever, just the naked wonder of her body sliding against his. But not as much as he wanted to feel her tighten with pleasure.

That was his drug of choice. His pleasure. Hers.

They rolled, and her cool hair brushed over him like a

breeze. She was on top of him and below him, rolling and touching, on top and below. Moonlight poured silver all over her liquid curves. She threw back her head, and he ran kisses down the ice-white slope of her neck. Her breasts were small, luminous moons. Her swollen pink nipples begged to be kissed.

He captured a rosy nub in his mouth and rolled his tongue around it. She bit back a cry of surprise. He drew on her gently to let her know how that felt, but it was the hard pull that she liked. She arched up, as if surrendering herself to the carnal delight. To the heat of the fires. To him.

Tony, don't kill me.

Those were her words. Could she actually die from this? He could. He could die.

They fell to their sides, and he searched her face, wondering how she made him feel powerful and vulnerable at the same time. A God and a beggar. He wanted his power back, all of it. But he wanted her, too, and for some reason, he couldn't get near her without experiencing every damn emotion known to humankind. Why was that?

Melissa sensed the change in him. She moved over him and braved the fire that lit his eyes. An emotion flared within him that she'd never seen before, and for a second, it frightened her. Passion or anger? She never got her answer. A more urgent concern took hold as she straddled him. The width of his hips forced her to open her legs wide, sending dark thrills spiraling through her.

All she could think about was this wild beauty she felt when she was with him, if beauty could be felt. She gloried in being on top, on all fours, and letting her breasts swell like ripening fruit. Not since their last time together had her body been this sensitive and needy. His erection brushed against her inner thigh, unleashing the years of frustrated longing.

She was instantly wet. He was hard enough to break.

The ache to be joined with him was enough to make her cry.

"Take me," she whispered.

A roll of her hips, a rock of his and he was deep inside, exactly where she needed him to be. He let out a moan, the sound muffled by the nipple he was suckling. Melissa felt it vibrate through her breasts like a low-voltage current. Nerve endings tingled that she didn't know existed.

He lifted her with his arms, laid her out on her back and sheathed himself all over again in her writhing body. Melissa cried out in surprise and delight. She reached out blindly, found his rocking hips and dug her fingers into the firm flesh. She pressed him into her, greedy, unable to get enough, until suddenly, it was enough. *It was too much.* Too sweet and sharp. Too wild. Her climax was unexpected and urgent. Pleasure broke like a cloudburst. For minutes she ceased breathing and existed on nothing but bliss. And then all at once she was gasping.

Don't forget to breathe.

Tony reared back, and a growl of sweet anguish ripped through him. He was magnificent above her, his body rippling with the deep feelings of completion. His jaw spasmed, and the constriction in his throat sounded like a cry. As he collapsed, he pulled her into his arms and held her as if she were his only source of sustenance.

They rolled again, this time landing on their sides, still joined and throbbing with feeling. Melissa clutched him with every muscle in her body. She never wanted him to withdraw, but her legs ached from the strain of squeezing him.

"My God," Tony breathed, "what just happened?"

"I don't know." She couldn't have explained it either, but she understood his astonishment. Their coupling had the force of a breathtaking accident. One moment they'd been separated by mute tension, and the next they were tearing at each other's clothing. Now they were naked on the floor and stunned from the collision. Still vibrating. Still rolling end over end.

She closed her eyes and had a silent conversation with her roaring heart, but nothing would quiet it. He pulled out, and then gathered her close again. She could hear the roar of his heart, too. It was oddly reassuring. She rested her face in the cradle of his shoulder, and his heart pulsed against her cheek. But as the mad rush of his blood gradually transformed into the long, steady rhythms of sleep, she was lulled into the depths with him.

Sometime later, she felt herself being lifted and carried to the bedroom. It was still dark, and she had no idea how late it was. Groggy, she clung to him as he settled her on the bed and drew the comforter over her. He stepped back as if he wasn't going to join her, and Melissa protested. How could they not spend the night together after they'd become a part of each other? They'd been as close as a man and woman could be.

"We'll talk in the morning," he said.

Even in her sleepy state, she picked up the finality in his tone. "What's wrong?" she asked.

"It can wait until tomorrow. Go back to sleep."

"No!" She couldn't see his expression in the dark. "Are you sorry we made love?"

"I'm not sorry about anything. But I'm not sure what the hell happened, and I feel responsible. Sex should be a mutual decision, not a random impulse."

"I thought it was a lovely impulse." She reached for

him, but he wasn't there. "Tony, come back. You're not responsible for anything. I'm a consenting adult."

"Get some sleep."

His voice had gentled, but the click of the bedroom door told her that she was alone. She sank back on the pillow, overcome by a sense of despair. As an only child to older parents, she'd always felt alone in some ways, but never more so than at this moment. She could no longer question that Tony was attracted to her. He wanted her. He just didn't want to want her.

TONY STRETCHED OUT on the bed naked. He'd thought about putting on some pajama bottoms in case someone walked in, namely Melissa. But the room was dark, and he needed to cool down and think. He didn't like anything about the clumsy way he'd had to put her off, but there hadn't been much choice. What else could he have said under the circumstances? He still didn't know what the hell had happened tonight. It wasn't the first time he'd given in to a forbidden impulse, but this was different. He'd made a pact with himself not to take it that far—and he never broke vows. At least never before.

When had he lost control? It hadn't felt gradual, more like falling off a cliff into a pit of oblivion. Erotic oblivion. He'd been fine one minute—or reasonably so—and sinking with concrete tied to his ankles the next. He still didn't understand how she did it—and it had to be her. He wasn't like this with other women. He'd always had the control he needed when he needed it, even in his twenties. He made the moves, set the pace. But with her, he did insane things.

Like ask her to marry him.

Like break vows.

What was her secret? Why was she his Delilah?

He knew what had done him in this time. Crazy as it seemed, watching her struggle with the bodysuit had been the tipping point. He'd seen her naked from just about every possible angle, but her determination to sneak the spandex suit on under her clothing had confounded and enchanted him. Who did that?

He smiled. Couldn't help himself. All that tugging and wriggling? Much sexier than if she'd just stripped. Odd how that one incident had started a blaze that had whipped itself into a firestorm. Odder still how hot he still was now.

Could this really be a chronic case of sexual heat? He held the back of his hand to his forehead, wondering if he was coming down with something. Chills? Fever? Maybe a weakened condition could explain his lapse. Not to take anything away from Melissa. The woman was lethal. Few men would have put her in the category of femme fatale, but they would have been wrong. Mata Hari had nothing on her. Being around Melissa was like getting ambushed with one of those illegal date-rape drugs.

A sigh escaped him. This was bad. Now he was imagining illnesses, disasters and sabotage. He was turning into her!

He reached over to switch on the bedside light and knocked something to the floor. As he snapped the light on, he saw the bottle of pills Jeanie had insisted he and Melissa take. He'd downed a handful last night, and taken more during the day. He picked up the bottle and scrutinized the label. Ginseng, of course, but the rest of the ingredients were even more exotic. There was also red Korean ginseng, wild green oats, yohimbe, damiana, ylang-ylang, *Jasminum grandiflorum,* ginkgo biloba and zinc gluconate, to name just a few.

The list was long and every one of the ingredients sounded like an aphrodisiac to him. He knew yohimbe increased blood flow to the penis, which was the last thing he needed. Several European drug companies were competing to market the herb. What the hell had Jeanie been feeding him? It was a wonder he wasn't out accosting women on the street.

BY MORNING Melissa had decided that Tony was either a professional gigolo with a wealthy woman in every port or a secret agent for the publishing police, out to catch her and Jeanie in an act of consumer fraud. The latter made more sense. Gigolos didn't marry starving writers, which he'd done with great enthusiasm two years ago. Of course, maybe he'd spotted her creative potential and predicted their one night would inspire a bestseller. That would mean he was clairvoyant. Or a talent agent.

He'd told her they would talk today, and she already knew what he planned to tell her, unless she beat him to it, which she intended to do. Antonio Bond had rejected her for the last time.

She threw back the comforter and went straight to the bathroom, where she looked herself over in the mirror while she checked her pulse. Naturally, it was racing. Unfortunately, she wasn't ill. She looked in the pink of health, a woman in full bloom. No one would believe she was dying of some mysterious illness, for which the one symptom seemed to be horniness.

Dropsy. By the time she'd pick up her toothpaste tube for the third time, she'd diagnosed herself with the nervous disorder. Not dramatic enough, though. Or fatal, either. Horniness, now *there* was a fatal illness.

She wove her hair into a single fat braid, determined not to look in any way fetching. A little mascara, a little peony-pink lipstick. This was not the woman who just last night had fondled a gigolo's butt and offered him her breasts. Absolutely not.

The bedroom closet was the next step in the desensualization of Melissa. What to wear for a confrontation with the man with whom you'd had red-hot and very wet sex on the floor? Something that shrieked I'm not interested. A nun's robes? A burka?

She laid out several things and finally decided on a black linen sundress that was relatively prim and proper, if you didn't count the fact that it showed some cleavage and some leg. Once she had it on, and a matching pair of sandals, she checked herself out in the mirror. Actually, just the right amount of cleavage, she decided. Why not taunt the boy a little with what he would never have again? Not as long as he lived.

She took a turn in the dress, smoothing the fabric and adjusting zippers and bra straps, until finally she was satisfied. You would have thought she was getting ready for her first prom. That alone indicated the severity of her hang-up with him. She'd just spent forty-five minutes trying not to look sexy, yet make him drool with desire.

She bent a little to test the cleavage. Perfect. *Melissa, you look good enough to be the man's breakfast melons.* She was ready to go, but something held her back. Possibly the fear that she might be mistaken for a fruit cup and lustily consumed. Or slowly savored?

She looked longingly at the phone on the nightstand. Maybe she should call Kath to discuss this. No, she knew what her friend would say. *Have sex with him, Melissa! As often as you can. The rest of us would kill to be where you are—in a suite with Antonnnnio. His whispery voice gives me the shivers. Does it really make you orgasmic?*

At that point, Melissa would have hung up the phone.

Interesting that the so-called sex expert had nothing but sex maniacs for friends.

She mentally squared her shoulders and left the bedroom. As she walked into the living room, she felt the warmth of the morning sun beaming through the floor-to-ceiling windows. Just beyond the open French doors, she saw Tony out on the balcony. He sat at the table in his robe, reading the paper and absently caressing the coffee-cup handle. The view was spectacular. Not him, of course, Central Park. Nothing Melissa loved more than a panorama of leafy-green trees and sunny blue skies. The impossibly handsome gigolo added zero to the scenery as far as she was concerned.

The aroma of freshly brewed coffee drifted from the kitchen, but she decided against it. Her nerves were alert enough. Since the French doors were already open, she made shuffling noises to alert Tony that he had company.

He didn't look up as she walked out onto the spacious deck. She waited a moment, taking in the veranda's bright contrasts. Bright red poppies and lush white orchids abounded in glossy black pots. The teak patio furniture had blue-and-white-striped cushions and a fringed umbrella that looked like an enormous sun hat. On the table, a large silver tray overflowed with goodies. Apparently he'd ordered up a continental breakfast. There was a thermal urn of coffee, pitchers of juice, a basketful of crusty rolls and pastries, and tiny crocks of honeys and jams.

She shuffled again, waited some more. Still he didn't look up.

Well, isn't this a cozy setting? she thought. The man at breakfast, reading his paper and drinking his coffee. The little woman waiting to be acknowledged.

Finally he peered at her over the sports section of *The New York Times,* and she forgot she was annoyed. Just for an instant she marveled that his eyes could be so dark on a sunny day. It would be possible to lose your way in the black of his pupils...and she had.

"Last night," she informed him. "That can't happen again."

He went back to the paper, muttering, "You're darn right it can't. You can't be trusted."

"Excuse me?" She stared in shock at the newsprint that hid him. When he didn't respond, she walked over and pushed the paper down. She was already shaking her head. "*I* can't be trusted?"

"That's what I said."

"I wasn't rolling around on the floor all by myself, Mr. Tiger Lover. *We* can't be trusted."

The paper hit the deck. He held up the bottle of herbal supplements that Jeanie had given them. "You think these sex pills might have had anything to do with it? They're loaded with ginseng and Chinese aphrodisiacs."

"Sex pills?"

"As in aphrodisiac."

She folded her arms. "What are you saying? That we were drugged?"

"We've been guzzling sex pills. You can draw your own conclusions."

Melissa picked up the nearly empty bottle and skimmed the list of ingredients. "They're herbal supplements, just like Jeanie said, and if anyone's been guzzling them, it's you. I never took more than the prescribed dosage." She studied him through narrowed eyes. "You have been acting oddly. How many of them did you take? Maybe we should go to an emergency room and have you detoxed."

"No emergency rooms. I was trying to make a point about the pills and what we did last night."

Ah, yes, last night. She set the bottle down in front of

him. "Nice try, but I don't think it had anything to do with a few pills. I think it's us, you and me. We're like a lit match and a gasoline leak."

"With a wild green oats chaser." He rose and pulled out a chair for her to sit down. It was all very gentlemanly, but she liked being taller than he was. He offered coffee and rolls, but she couldn't be bought off with bribes, either. He helped himself to a warm French roll from the basket, broke off a crusty chunk and buttered it generously. Polite to a fault, she waited until he'd refilled his cup and was settled again before she continued.

"Just for the sake of argument," she said, "let's say the pills are having an effect. We can stop taking them. That's easy. How do we stop our—"

"Ourselves?"

"Our glands. This attraction we have is a physical thing, like a drippy faucet. Once the water's turned off, the leak is gone."

As she talked, Melissa watched the butter melt into the steaming roll and run over the side. Equally fascinating was the way several drops clung to one of his fingers, and he caught them with his tongue. His lids drooped for a second, as if he was savoring the sensuality as much as the flavor.

A breeze fluttered the flowers, and Melissa's stomach felt as flimsy as the poppy petals. She knew the sandy softness of his tongue.

"You think our attraction's just physical?" He took a bite of the roll, revealing a flash of white teeth as he began to chew. His jaw muscles made slow, beautiful work of the crunchy roll. It was like watching a dance.

"I do," she said. "Absolutely."

His tongue darted in search of buttery crumbs. "And how do you propose we turn off the water?"

God, he was sexy. Those eyes. That mouth and velvet tongue. Maybe she could just wade in the water for a while. Dip in a toe?

"I don't know," she said. "That's why I'm here, watching you lick butter off your lips. Maybe for starters, you could stop doing that? You could also stop doing that thing with the handle of your coffee cup?"

That produced a frown. "I can't eat or drink?"

"It's not the eating or drinking. It's the sexy stuff you do with your lips and hands. A grown man is not supposed to put his fingers in his mouth, okay? And you don't hold things, you caress them. I'm not saying you do it on purpose, or that you know I'm watching, although sometimes I wonder…like when you adjust yourself."

He held her gaze, daring her to look as he reached down at that very moment and rearranged things. Naturally her mind conjured up lewd images of what was happening beneath his robe. Those tan fingers moving dark and dangerous parts. He'd probably planned it that way. Maybe it was all a carefully constructed plot to drench her brain in hormones and impair her thinking. Maybe he wasn't Tony at all. Maybe he was an impostor, a saboteur sent from a rival publisher to drive her mad with wanting and ruin the entire tour.

Honking drifted up from the street below. The breezes lifted, the flowers fluttered, and Melissa's stomach joined the dance.

"Well, now I don't have to wonder," she said. "You are doing it on purpose."

"Like you're playing with your bra strap on purpose? I'm not the only one who adjusts things. You're always fiddling and fussing."

Damn, she was worrying her bra strap again. She didn't

know whether to stop—or defy him and boldly continue. "It's a nervous habit. Not sexy at all."

"It's the sexiest thing I've ever seen. I'm insanely jealous of your bra right now."

She stopped. He didn't. He gave her low-cut sundress a lingering inspection with what could only have been called a smoldering gaze. Her face flushed. Her nipples burned.

"Listen here," she reminded him, "I don't whisper erotic things in your ear. Do you remember what you said to me last night? It was indecent, and that was on the *Larry Gunderson Show*."

"But I wasn't the one wearing a skirt up to my ying yang, now, was I?"

"I didn't know you had a ying yang. Darn, I could have put that in the book."

He lifted the coffee urn. "Are you going to sit down and have some breakfast?"

"No, but if I did, I wouldn't play with my coffee cup."

A dark eyebrow arched. "And I don't play with my pearls or dangle my high heels from the tip of my toes."

"You wear pearls and high heels, too? This may be all the information I need to plug the leak."

His voice faked a husky tone. "I can plug any leak you've got, baby."

"See, that's what I mean. You shouldn't say things like that. You shouldn't even think things like that. You have to stop nibbling on my ear and touching me—especially those barely there touches, they're the worst—" She shivered as she experienced a flashback of those touches. "And this is big," she told him. "You have to stop looking at me like you want to drag me into the nearest closet and lock the door."

"Then maybe you should stop licking fruit juice off my palm."

"I was demonstrating something! And as far as my clothing goes, Jeanie ordered me to tart it up."

"So you haven't been flirting with me?"

Flirting? He thought that was flirting? She'd been flat out trying to seduce him. Her skirt swished as she walked past him to the wrought-iron railing and looked down on the city. When she turned back, his gaze was locked on her like radar.

"Okay, here's the bottom line," she said. "I'm setting some boundaries, and if either of us crosses them, there will be terrible consequences."

"Like what?"

"I don't know, but they will be terrible. I'll start, but feel free to jump in."

"Shoot."

She made a face. "Don't say 'shoot,' okay? That's a dirty word when it comes out of your mouth."

"That's one of your boundaries?"

"No, it's a polite request. I may have several more of them over the next few days. Meanwhile, boundary number one—No more smoldering, peel-me-like-a grape looks from those bedroom eyes of yours."

"Agreed. No more high heel dangling from those slutty toes of yours."

"No more whispering smut in my ear, thank you!"

"Fine, but you're not allowed to call me Tony Baby or Tiger Lover—and no more checking out my equipment."

"That was two, and I have never checked out your equipment."

She crossed her arms, and he rose from the chair, mirroring her. She squared her shoulders. He did, too. It was a standoff, but she had the last bullet.

"No more touching, kissing or sex, except in public. Do you agree?"

Melissa barely got it out before Jeanie breezed onto the patio, all decked out in a bright metallic pantsuit.

She gave them both a quizzical look. "What's going on out here? Why didn't anyone answer the door? I've been knocking and knocking."

Melissa turned away, arms still crossed. She didn't want Jeanie to see how upset she was.

Tony tried to ply the publicist with coffee and rolls, but Jeanie wasn't to be diverted. Melissa could hear it in her voice.

"What's going on with you two?"

"Nothing," Tony insisted.

Melissa turned at the same time, aware that her face must be flushed. She certainly felt hot and bothered. "Everything's fine, Jeanie."

Jeanie's eyes narrowed with suspicion as she looked from one to the other. "Okay then, you'll be excited about my good news. Your autographing's been canceled, so you have a free morning."

"That's the good news?" Tony asked.

"No, no, I have a much bigger surprise. We're going to crack Nielsen ratings records with this one." She stopped short, looking them both over. "Okay, what is going on with you two? Something's different. Have you been fighting?"

Melissa started to protest, but Jeanie was already shaking her head. She looked from one to the other, taking in their rigid posture, their folded arms and red faces. But it was probably the deep denial and profound guilt that gave them away. Body language was hard to hide, and Jeanie was a human lie detector.

"Oh my God," she whispered. "You two had sex! You did, didn't you? You had *sex*."

10

If you're smitten, kitten, let him hear you purr.

101 Ways To Make Your Man Beg

"HOW DO YOU KNOW we had sex?" Tony asked Jeanie. "Do we glow?"

Melissa gave him a warning look. "Stop talking like that or Jeanie will think she's right about us having sex."

Jeanie's *tsk* dismissed any hope of plausible deniability. "Oh, of course I'm right," she said. "Anyone would see it. Just look at the two of you. You're giving off enough heat to melt the polar caps. Global warming is *all* your fault."

"It was an accident," Melissa said. "It wasn't supposed to happen, and it never will again."

"Global warming?"

"No, the sex!"

Jeanie winked, and Melissa knew enough to throw in the towel. No sense prolonging the agony. Jeanie would have figured it out anyway—and not given up until she had a confession. Still, Melissa couldn't believe they were as bad as Jeanie claimed. She made them sound about as subtle as two wildebeests in heat.

Jeanie helped herself to a croissant and began to pick at it, popping feathery bits into her mouth. She'd dressed for spring in a striped slacks outfit that made her look like a pink-and-gold rainbow. Bright and pretty, but a little out of character for Jeanie, who usually wore black. Melissa had noticed something subtly different about her lately, but couldn't put her finger on what it might be. Was Jeanie glowing, too?

"You don't have to justify anything to me," Jeanie said. "You're adults and can do as you please in private. And it might not be the worst thing that could have happened, considering my news."

"Oh, God, the surprise," Tony said with a groan. Melissa groaned. Everyone groaned but Jeanie.

"Now, don't get negative," she warned. "I can honestly say that I've never come across a hotter promotional opportunity than this one, and it wasn't even my idea."

She peeled off another strip of croissant and nibbled it, making them wait.

"Well?" Melissa helped herself to a hard roll from the basket on the table and began to pick at it out of nervousness. The crumbs dropped to the balcony floor. In the blue skies above, a small flock of birds began to circle.

Jeanie finally relented. "Okay, you've both heard of reality TV, right?"

Melissa had. "That's where people get paid to be under surveillance around the clock. Cameras watch you floss your teeth and drool on your pillow while you sleep. They have no shame. They'll even record the gross stuff guys do, like scratching their privates and breaking wind."

"Sounds like fun."

Tony's comment elicited sharp looks from both women. He bowed out with a shrug and returned to his chair. Wise man, Melissa thought.

Jeanie addressed herself to Melissa. "You've been watching the wrong shows. The reality television I'm talking about is where *the* top-rated network chooses an absolutely fascinating couple and documents their absolutely fascinating relationship for a short period of time.''

"How short?'' A small mountain of crumbs had accumulated at Melissa's feet, and several eager birds were perched on the patio umbrella.

"Twenty-four hours.''

"Hours? Did you say *hours?*''

"That's a nanosecond in the great scheme of things,'' Jeanie argued. "You wouldn't trade twenty-four hours for a lifetime of fame and fortune, would you?''

"Twenty-four hours of humiliation can feel like a lifetime.''

"Oh, pooh.'' Jeanie dismissed her with a head shake and went to work on Tony. "Care to guess who the chosen couple is?''

"Are you looking at them?''

"That I am.'' She beamed, apparently charmed by his sense of humor. "You guys were so incredible on Larry Gunderson's show that the network is in a dither. They want you for your own reality show.''

"Our schedule is booked solid,'' Melissa said.

"I've cleared the way,'' Jeanie assured her.

"How? When's this supposed to happen? Is there time to rehearse? We'll never be ready.'' Melissa threw out everything she could think of, but Jeanie was unflappable.

"The producers want to start this afternoon—and what's to rehearse? Their goal is to capture your relationship.''

"We don't have a relationship!'' Now Melissa was worried. "We're faking it, or did you forget?''

"Who was faking last night?'' Jeanie asked in a superior tone.

Melissa threw up her hands, accidentally lobbing what was left of her roll over the balcony ledge. The birds dive-bombed in formation, and some poor passerby on the street below whooped in surprise.

"Tony, speak to her," Melissa pleaded. "Tell her we can't do this. Tell her why."

Tony tilted back in his chair and rubbed his unshaven jaw with one hand. "Sure, as soon as I find out what it is we can't do. Jeanie, what's the deal? What kind of show is this?"

"There won't be a camera focused on the throne, if that's what you're thinking, but there will be cameras in every room of the suite, including parts of the bathroom. For example, there'll be one trained on the shower stall, so you should let it steam up before you go inside."

She pressed on, clearly excited. "The network is betting millions of viewers will tune in to watch American's hottest couple behind closed doors. Viewers want to know how you keep it passionate, and secretly they're hoping they can do the same.

"Tony, tell her no. Tell her *why*."

Melissa wasn't giving up, and neither were the birds. Some of them had already returned and were eyeing Jeanie's croissant. She popped the last of it in her mouth and washed it down with a glass of orange juice. Melissa could have sworn the birds looked crestfallen. She knew how they felt.

"What's with you two?" Jeanie said. "It's not like you'll have to fake anything. You're human torches. Just be yourselves, and the rug will catch fire. Fight if you have to. The American public will love it when you make up."

How did she know about the rug? Was the suite bugged? Melissa struggled to quell her paranoia. Jeanie obviously didn't get it. They didn't want to be human torches, or at least Tony didn't.

"Maybe this isn't such a good idea," Tony said.

See. She was right. He didn't.

"It's a fabulous idea," Jeanie insisted. "The producers plan to organize the footage into episodes and air them on consecutive nights. They're predicting a forty share for the first show. That's twenty million people. If they pull even half that, we would reach more people with this gig than the rest of the tour put together."

The numbers gave Melissa a twinge. She'd written the book to break out of the negative spiral she was in. She barely made the rent with her magazine articles. This one show could turn the tide. It could be her ticket out.

"Did you hear me, Melissa? Did you hear those numbers?"

Tony tried again. "Jeanie, Melissa and I have been working out some ground rules for our *relationship,* and they don't include setting rugs on fire."

Jeanie picked up another roll and began to pace, apparently unaware of how much danger she was in. "All right, how about this?" she said. "You do this show, and your obligation to the tour is over. I'll cancel the rest of the schedule."

Tony looked intrigued.

He glanced over at Melissa, and her stomach dipped. She felt as if she'd been sitting in a rocking rowboat too long. He wanted to do it. He wanted to be free of his obligation—and of her. She'd been leaning toward doing the show, too, but Jeanie's deal meant everything would be over in twenty-four hours.

"We'd both be free to go our own way?" Melissa asked in a faint voice. "Will Searchlight let you do that?"

"They may not like it, but what can they do? I've already made a verbal offer to both of you. Will you do it?"

Jeanie waited, oblivious to the birds circling her head.

Melissa stayed silent and so did Tony. Apparently no one was going to crack first.

"I guess we need some time to talk it over?" Jeanie bestowed a motherly smile upon them. "That's fine. I have plenty of things to do. I'll call you in fifteen minutes for your decision. Deal?"

"Deal," Tony said, coming out of his chair. "I'll show you to the door."

"Not necessary." Jeanie was already on her way back inside. "You talk her into it, Tiger Lover. I'm counting on you."

The front door slammed, and the two accidental lovers were alone again.

Melissa closed her eyes and wished the rowboat would stop rocking and the birds would stop circling. Maybe she was ill. Or pregnant. Could you get morning sickness after being pregnant one night?

"Want some coffee now?"

Tony's voice coaxed her. Melissa shook her head and wished she hadn't. "The cameras are going to be on us every second," she said with an ominous tone worthy of the late Vincent Price. "They'll expect us to touch, kiss, dangle high heels and fondle pearls. Everything we said we wouldn't do."

"Melissa? Why are your eyes closed?"

"I can't deal with this."

"Open your eyes. It's all right, baby. It's going to be fine."

His velvety tones made her heart pound. They reminded her of that moment in Cancún when he'd dropped to one knee and proposed. He hadn't wanted to be free then. He'd wanted to be tied to her, a knot that could never be undone.

What a foolish girl she was, thinking these things.

She opened her eyes and looked into his accusingly.

"You promised you wouldn't look at me like you wanted to drag me into a closet, remember?"

"Right, I did—and I won't. It'll be hard because I want to drag you into every closet I see, but I won't."

Yeah, sure. "We agreed not to touch or kiss, either."

"That's true, *except* in public." He smiled at his own brilliance. "And what could be more public than television?"

"Or more fantastically awkward. Think about it, Tony." He really did want to do this, in front of God and everyone. She didn't understand that at all—unless it *was* about wrapping things up and going on his way. Well, let him, dammit. She was fine before he got here, and she would be fine again. She hadn't even wanted him here. Her life had been rolling along quite nicely. Like a parade.

Suddenly she was more angry than hurt. That made it easier.

"If you feel that strongly," he said. By his look he'd picked up the edge in her voice.

She felt like tearing up more bread, but the growing flock of birds could have been auditioning for a Hitchcock movie. "No, I'll do it," she snapped. "Let's just get it over with—and while we're at it, let's get this whole tour over with."

"Are you sure?"

"Yes." Twenty-four hours, and she'd be done with it. She would take the money and run. He would get his annulment. Jeanie would probably get her own publishing company, and everyone would be happy.

He was still studying her as if he didn't know whether or not to believe her. "How about this?" he suggested. "No cameras in the bathrooms or bedrooms. I'll make that a condition of our being on the show. Would that make you feel better?"

Not really, but she couldn't admit it. And he wouldn't get it anyway. He really had no idea what was bothering her. "I doubt if they'll go for that. These shows have cameras everywhere. They don't want to miss a thing."

"Fine, then we won't do the damn show. Sound like a deal?"

A phone rang, and Tony fished his cell out of his bathrobe pocket. It hadn't been fifteen minutes, but Melissa could tell it was Jeanie from the conversation. Tony told her they'd come to a tentative decision and glanced over at Melissa for confirmation. She bit her lip and nodded. She was still biting her lip when he hung up the phone.

"Jeanie's going back to the network brass with our conditions. If they can come to an agreement, the camera crew will be here at one," he said. "That gives us better than three hours. Jeanie suggested we come up with a game plan. She likes the idea of several different scenes, blocked out like a stage play."

"What happened to 'just be yourself'?" Melissa sniffed.

"It'll be all right," he said. "I know you're nervous, but we can do this. Only a flaming exhibitionist could get sexy under twenty-four hour surveillance."

"But we won't *be* under surveillance in the bedroom."

That gave him pause. "Maybe we shouldn't have insisted on those conditions."

"Maybe we shouldn't have agreed under *any* conditions," she muttered.

He scooped up the herbal supplements and shook the bottle. "If we do the show, these are history. No more drugs or alcohol in our systems, making us do crazy, impulsive things. We'll be sober as judges."

Melissa sank down in the chair next to him. It was true that all of their "accidents" had happened when they'd been under the influence. She'd been tipsy on Rum Mo-

cambos in Cancún, and she'd been drinking wine that night
in the kitchen when she'd had the bright idea of seducing
him. And then, of course, there was last night on those
ginseng things. She was still reverberating from that.

With a flick of Tony's wrist, the herbal supplements
went the way of Melissa's roll—over the side of the balcony. Just as quickly the circling birds were gone. They'd
formed another military formation, but no shouts came up
from the street this time. Instead, someone yelled, "Hey,
thanks, I could use a lift!"

Melissa wondered if anyone would catch her if she
dived over the railing.

"What's the verdict?" Tony asked. "I'll back whatever
you want to do."

*Whatever I want, Tony? Really? Let's forget the reality
show and bring some reality to this relationship. How
about admitting that it was about us last night and not
about some silly herbs? Or that you're still wildly attracted
to me and not here for some other sinister reason? How
about that, my pretend husband? Let's stop pretending.*

A tiny fire burned bright within Melissa. Her desire to
know the truth was almost as strong as her desire to protect
her heart. And for a second, she thought she might actually
say everything she was thinking. Let him answer those
charges. Let him speak up in his own defense. But of
course she didn't do it. She'd already put her hand out
there and had it slapped too many times. She'd learned her
lesson. Much smarter to laugh it off. Make some clever
comment and be done with it. This was all for the good
of the book, right? The network, the Neilsens and everyone
else concerned? It was what she'd always wanted, right?

The now-familiar pep talk ran through her head: *You
may never get another shot like this, Melissa. It's your
once-in-a-lifetime. You wanted to break out, and this is*

your chance. Besides, it isn't just about you. Imagine how many people you'll be letting down if you don't follow through.

She glanced over at Tony, managing a grin. "Think you could arrange for Jeanie to take a fall from this balcony? One of those freak accidents that will have New York talking for years to come? We could say we left her out here with the birds, but only for a moment."

"Me*lissa.*"

"Okay, okay. I said I'd do it, and I will." She sat up in her chair and figuratively dusted herself off, waiting for him to join her. They had some serious negotiating to do.

"Okay," she said, all business. "How are we going to play this, hot or cold? The audience is going to be expecting hot. Everyone's going to be expecting hot, for that matter. But I'm thinking we could fudge. Maybe we could get by with lots of sexy talk."

Tony nixed her idea immediately. "They'll want action, and if they don't get it, they may just keep shooting until they do. You said you wanted to get this over with, so let's give them what they want."

"Flip a coin," Melissa suggested. "Heads, we give them hot talk and lots of it. We scorch their earlobes with our double entendres. Tails, we give them—" She saw where that one was going and stopped.

"Tail?" Tony grinned, fished a quarter out of his pocket and tossed it high in the air.

Melissa watched the coin twist and turn and glint in the sunlight. She said a little prayer.

"BABY, oh, baby, you taste like every kind of delicious…"

"You like that, do you?"

"Mmm, I need more honey."

"Where would you like it this time, Pooh Bear?"

"Right here in my mouth."

"My, my, look at those big sharp teeth."

Melissa scooped up some crème brûlée on her finger and got most of it into Tony's open mouth. The rest she smooshed on his lower lip and promptly nibbled off with lusty smacking and slurping noises. She also put a dollop of crème on the end of his nose and licked it up with her tongue. The buttery-rich taste made her purr with pleasure.

Tony added to the noisiness with a satisfied growl or two. A very happy bear, that one. And a hungry one, too. He popped her finger in his mouth, as if it were a lollipop, and drank up every last drop of crème brûlée. Melissa's stomach floated like the weightless cork it was. This adventure in food had been his idea, and quite an adventure it turned out to be. He'd whipped up the crème brûlée and a chocolate mousse, and they'd ordered up pies, puddings and a jar of peanut butter from room service.

Where would the mousse taste best? She hadn't tried that yet. His eyelashes? Earlobes. Maybe his toes! She still hadn't finished the lemon meringue pie on his chin, and he'd left some butterscotch pudding on her elbow. Thank goodness she'd worn a washable teddy. His cotton briefs were headed for the hamper, too.

"Cut!"

The bellowing voice startled Melissa, and she sat up straight. She'd almost forgotten the camera crew was there. Maybe it was the frosting that had practically glued her lashes together. She would have to shower for hours to get the gunk off.

"We're taking a break," the show's young male director announced to his crew. Tall and lanky in designer-label jeans, he turned in a circle, addressing everyone. "Go get some fresh air, people. I need a word with our *stars*."

Melissa and Tony exchanged a look. The only star on the set was their director. Jeanie had introduced him as *the* Bat Bohanan and raved about his background directing music videos. Right now Bat didn't look happy, but Melissa had no idea why. Surely he wouldn't accuse them of holding back. They'd done everything but throw food at each other. What did he want? *Animal House?*

Melissa had lost the coin toss. It was probably a loaded quarter, but she was a woman of her word. Tony wanted action, and action he would get. He might even wish he hadn't been so lucky. Talk about pretending. If this had been an Olympic event, she could have taken the gold.

Bat sauntered over to them, his hands on his hips.

"Is there a problem?" Melissa asked, blotting meringue from Tony's chin.

"I thought cuts weren't allowed," Tony chimed in. "Isn't this reality TV?"

"That *is* the idea." Bat anchored his sunglasses in his dark blond hair, apparently to better scrutinize his stars. "Which is why I'm going to have to ask you two to stop hamming it up. Just relax, okay. Turn down the volume. This show is about who you are in your real life."

"Hamming it up?" Melissa batted her sticky eyelashes, pretending innocence. He probably wasn't going to buy this act, either. "But this *is* how we are in real life. We're all over each other all the time. Really."

One of Bat's eyebrows nearly went vertical. "You sit on each other's laps and smear food on each other?" He glanced at Tony for confirmation.

"Absolutely," Tony said. "She eats chunky peanut butter off my thighs. For breakfast," he added.

Melissa didn't dare smile. Both Bat's eyebrows were involved now.

"You don't think that might be laying it on a little thick?" he said. "And I don't mean the peanut butter."

Melissa concentrated on pulling a strip of drying crème brûlée from her cheek. Tony dipped up some of the chocolate mousse on his finger and ate it. Bat cleared his throat. Loudly.

"Okay, Tony was kidding about the thighs," Melissa admitted. "I am a peanut butter fanatic, though. I even put it on broccoli."

"That's sick," Tony murmured. "You're not getting near my thighs again."

"Are you sure you guys are married?" Bat squatted down, peering at the two of them like a high-school counselor with troubled students. "Wouldn't most husbands know their wife's weird little food quirks? I'm divorced, but my ex was a sushi nut, and nothing I could say would convince the woman that God put seaweed in the ocean for the fish. The point is, I *knew* her quirks. I could probably have finished her sentences if she'd stopped talking long enough. We had our own shorthand language, inside jokes, special looks."

Hard to argue with that, Melissa conceded. If Jeanie had been here, she would have had some clever answer up her sleeve, but Bat wouldn't let Jeanie on the set. He'd warned her several times to stop coaching his stars, but she hadn't listened. Of course, Jeanie wouldn't. And of course, she'd refused to leave the set. Bat had been surprisingly masterful, cupping her elbow and hustling her out the door. Melissa suspected this was the first time anybody had manhandled Jeanie and lived to talk about it.

Bat frowned at them. "To be perfectly honest, you two act like you're on a blind date."

"So would you if your eyes were glued shut with frosting."

Melissa chuckled merrily at Tony's quip. "Isn't he ador-able?" She smiled in the face of Bat's skepticism and gave it her best shot. "Actually, Tony and I have worked very hard to reestablish the crazy unpredictability of courtship. You know, when it's all brand-new, and you're a little off balance. That newness keeps things very…"

"Tense," Tony offered.

"And that's good?" Bat said.

"Oh, very good." Melissa and Tony spoke in unison.

Bat nodded, but he didn't look convinced. "So what's the story?" he said. "How did you guys meet?"

"It's a great story," Melissa assured him. "But could we take a shower first? If all this food dries, you'll have to put us through a car wash to get us clean."

"You guys want to take a shower?" Bat popped up and yanked his cell phone off his belt. "Hold on long enough for me to get the crew back here."

"No, I didn't mean that you should be involved," Melissa said. "Give us some time to get cleaned up, and we'll start all over again, the real deal this time. Tony and Melissa exposed, okay?"

But Bat was already on the phone, ordering his crew back. "No cameras in the bathroom," he told his assistant director, "but we can get a shot of them walking into the spa with their towels on. Once they're inside, they can toss the towels out. You won't see anything, but you'll get the idea. If any bits and pieces show, we can always blur them."

Naked in a tiny shower stall with Tony? Blurry bits and pieces?

Not what Melissa had in mind.

Tony had the decency to look uneasy, too. But nothing could be done to deter Bat, and he hadn't breached their agreement in any way. The director couldn't have known that he was testing this crazy married couple to their limits, possibly even breaking their will to resist. He probably thought he was giving them a chance to calm down and cool off. *Naked in a tiny shower stall with Tony?* Melissa could almost hear her resolve snapping like a twig.

Within moments the camera crew had descended on the suite like a swarm of locusts. Melissa and Tony were being ushered into her bedroom, told to undress behind a screen—another screen!—and given towels that looked as if they would barely cover the essentials.

MELISSA STILL HAD her towel wrapped tightly around her as she entered the shower stall. Tony had already tossed his, and she tried not to look at any of his bits and pieces, but she had a challenge on her hands. He took up more than his half of the stall and he stood boldly facing her. She could tell him to turn around, but then she'd be dealing with the rear view. A quarterback's shoulders and rock-hard glutes.

"Come on in," he said in his velvety rogue's voice.

"I am in," she said in her witchiest voice.

Melissa dealt with stimulating mental imagery for a living, and even though she had limited personal experience, she knew what she liked. Those ads of naked men with water streaming all over their bodies were like an electrical current to her nervous system. Here she was *in* the shower with one of them. A girl could get electrocuted.

"Melissa! Throw that towel out here."

Bat had opened the bathroom door and shouted at her. Melissa ignored him, gripping the soggy material tighter. The terry cloth grew heavier and heavier as the spray soaked her down.

"Turn around," she told Tony, mouthing the words and making circling gestures with her hand.

"I don't want to," he mouthed back.

Obviously he wasn't going to show her the same courtesy she had him. Staring hard into his eyes, she whipped off the towel and snapped it over the stall. Naked. Both of them. Naked and glistening like starlight. The water pricked her bare skin like needles and aroused her nipples to rosy peaks. She didn't have to see it happening, she could feel it. He could, too. His eyes on her were as physical as his hands would have been. He might as well have been molesting her…and she loved the very thought.

Despite everything, she did.

There it was, the shameful truth. She *was* a hussy, but only for him. She hadn't been pretending at all. Not ever. She was in heat for this man. Out-of-her-mind-in-heat. She would do anything, cry like a baby, purr like a kitten. No self-control at all. She was a lost cause, and for some reason that thrilled her. Now she just had to be sure he didn't know it. How about that for a mission impossible?

Tony took in her taut, dripping curves with a rueful smile. He seemed to understand that this was going to be a painful lesson in restraint. She glanced at herself and saw what he saw—a silvery gown flowing over pink and white flesh. She did love water on a naked body.

"You look beautiful," he said, not bothering to disguise the words.

Melissa put her finger to her lips, signaling Tony to keep his voice down. No microphones were allowed, either, but Melissa wasn't taking any chances on being overheard in any way, even by the naked ear.

He coaxed her closer with a crooked finger. He wanted to whisper in her ear, but she knew where that would take them. She edged closer, trying not to come into contact with his male protrusions.

"Bat is going to want us to talk about how we met,"

he said, half whispering, half mouthing the words. "Are you up for that?"

She nodded, absently aware of wonderful smells. Honeysuckle and clover. Had to be the soap. "Might as well tell them what happened. It's the truth."

"Except the part about you running out on me?"

"What?" She pretended not to hear him, and the crooked finger invited her closer.

Bat could just be heard muttering about uncooperative artists as he shut the bathroom door. Melissa breathed a little easier. She had been terribly nervous about being naked with Tony in the cold light of day—and sober at that. But maybe this wasn't so bad.

As fragrant steam rose around them, Tony pulled her into the circle of his arms and whispered in her ear, "We have to do this more often."

Their knees bumped and other parts touched. His arm brushed her breast, and she could feel him twitch and harden. Somewhere inside her a coiled spring of desire tightened.

"What?" she whispered back. "Play dodge the erection?"

He laughed. "No, meet in the shower. This is the only place they can't see or hear us."

He spoke the truth, and Melissa couldn't blame the whole situation on Jeanie. This was too diabolically inspired, even for her. The same fickle gods who'd put her and Tony together in the first place must be conspiring against her. Did they want her to make love with him again? Was it written in the Book of Life in the chapter on Melissa and Tony? They'd probably sent the birds, too.

Tony reached around her for something, and his erection teased her thigh. She had visions of stroking him, but knew that would invite disaster. The unintentional contact was bad enough. One deliberate touch, and Bat would be hearing some noises he wasn't supposed to hear.

Tony stretched even farther, and she locked her arms around him for balance. "What are you doing?"

"Getting this." He showed her the bottle of shampoo he'd taken from a nook in the shower wall. "There's whipped cream in your hair and I'm in a perfect position to get it out. Close your eyes."

She didn't even argue. She just gave herself over, knowing that having his hands in her hair might well send her to places she wouldn't be able to get back from. He squeezed a dollop of shampoo into his palm and drenched the stall with the sweetness of honeysuckle. Melissa felt as dizzy as a kid playing Spin the Bottle for the first time. She didn't want to slip on the shower tiles, so her only choice was to stay close to him and let him steady her against his body as he turned her around. He began to massage her scalp, working the rich shampoo into clouds of foam.

"You'll need to bend over to rinse," he whispered.

Melissa shuddered at the erotic image that flashed before her eyes. There was only one way to bend over in this stall, and that *would* be inviting disaster. Glorious, mindless disaster. If ever there'd been a moment when she had to stop herself with this man, it was now. This moment. *Stop.*

11

Don't believe the popular wisdom. Men *love* intimacy
rituals. Want his undivided attention? Let him shave
your legs, his way.

101 Ways To Make Your Man Beg

TONY FELT MELISSA SHIVER under his hands, and his body
zinged like a lightning rod. He grimaced at the pressure of
overengorged veins and tightly cinched skin. If the lightning rod got any bigger there wouldn't be room in the
shower for both of them, unless—

*No, no, no, don't go there, Bond. That's begging for
trouble. Kinky sex is the path to chaos and ruin.*

So, of course, he didn't want to walk the path, he wanted
to run.

Oh, the joys of sex from behind. Just the thought put
him in a state of pulsing carnal bliss. And it was all for a
good cause. Perfect way to save space. They would no
longer have an awkward encumbrance between them. She
was probably tired of bumping her butt against it anyway.
And he was damn tired of being a human battering ram.

"Bend over?" she said. "I'm not sure that's a good
idea."

"No, not a *good* idea." His voice was tellingly husky.
"It's an excellent one."

She craned around to look at him, her eyes wide and

questioning. A glob of shampoo melted onto her forehead and headed straight for that blinking gaze. Another slid to the bridge of her nose.

She winced and scrubbed at the suds. "Ouch, that stings!"

"See what I mean? Rinsing is a must."

"Okay, but I can do it." She waved him away, but there was nowhere for him to go unless they changed positions entirely. Which might be an interesting dance.

She nearly banged her head against the wall when she tried to tilt forward. The second try, her feet went skating on tiles slippery with shampoo. Fortunately, it was a tiny rink. The third was her last solo effort. Teamwork had its advantages, lucky for him.

"Hey," she called back to him, "hold on to me so I don't fall."

"No problem. I've got you." He slipped an arm around her waist and watched her bend like a ballerina. Her beautiful bottom tilted up at him invitingly, and the sheer sensuality of it made his jaws ache. He sucked in a breath, but it didn't help. Heat rocketed toward his already steaming groin. With one well-placed thrust, he would drive it home. A groan caught hard in his throat as the idea resonated in his mind. God, how many problems he could solve with just one hot, aching thrust. The way she was wriggling, he wasn't certain she didn't have the same thought.

"Are you doing anything back there?" she asked. "I don't feel you doing anything."

"Would you *like* me to do something back here?"

The beating water had already washed most of the suds from her hair, and he hadn't touched her yet. Not the way he wanted to.

"Am I too far away?" Her behind swayed, pressing

toward him. "Can you reach me now? Is that the problem?"

God, woman, don't press your luck. I'm about to launch the shuttle here. With all her wiggling and squirming, she'd nudged his penis up and back until it was pointed toward the ceiling. Soon it would be burning a hole in his belly. Men had died this way, as he recalled. The cause of death was blood loss, all of it from the brain.

He bent over her to rinse her hair, and the pressure wedged him gently in the slippery cleft of her cheeks. She let out a moan that sent pleasure knifing through him. Did she want him to take the path of chaos and disaster? Beautiful chaos. Sweet ruin. His mind was as tightly focused as his shaft, and he could think of no greater satisfaction than to be encased in her while they were both encased in this steaming waterfall.

Not going to happen, Bond. You made a vow. To yourself.

He wound her drenched hair into a long knot and drew her head back, letting the spray catch the last of the soapy residue on her forehead. Her sigh turned into a smile as she reached back to touch his clenched arm. She couldn't quite make contact, but it was a privilege watching her try. From his vantage point, he could see her breasts shiver as she moved. Was there any sexier position to a man than having a naked woman bent forward in front of him?

God, he was ready, so ready he ached. But the physical pain reminded him he was being tested, and he intended to pass this time.

"Do it," she whispered. "I want you to."

Had he heard her right? No, he must have been hallucinating. But just in case, he asked, "Do what?"

"You know *what.*"

"Do something else to your hair?"

"Tony, put it in, for heaven's sake. Do it!"

"What are you talking about? Sex?"

The frantic tension in her voice made him suspicious. Desperation was written into everything she said and did. She was throwing in the towel, giving up the battle with her good intentions. He'd lost that battle last night, and entered a world of pleasure and pain, heaven and hell.

Desire flashed like a match in the dark as he thought about making love to her again. Even his butt muscles clenched.

"Please," she said. "Let's just get it over with. You know we're going to do it anyway. We'll never last twenty-four hours. You're harder than the showerhead, and look at me! Naked and upside down in this tiny stall. Just do it, okay? Take me, dammit. I want you to."

Lord, was he being tested. "We can't—"

"Why not?" The pitch of her voice veered even higher, bordering on a cry of frustration. "Tony, why can't we? It's not like we're ever going to do it again. This will be our last time. The show wraps tomorrow afternoon, and we'll go our separate ways. Do you really want to be as hard as a plumbing fixture all night long?"

"It'll be all right. We can hold each other."

"Oh, don't be ridiculous. Do me and do me now!"

Okay, now he *was* hallucinating. Every drop of blood had evacuated his brain. "We agreed not to. We have ground rules."

Ground rules. How lame was that?

She gave him a sexy little bump with her butt, possibly unintentional. But at the same time, he heard a strange sound in the bathroom. It sounded like the click of the bathroom door. Bat and the crew must have heard her yelling, even over the noise of the shower. He hoped they didn't pick up what she'd said.

"Well?" she pressed. "Are you going to do it before or after I drown?"

"Shhhhhhhh." He placed his hand over her mouth and brought her back to a standing position. Half turning with her in his arms, he gestured toward the shower-stall door, letting her know that something was amiss.

"I forgot all about the crew," she whispered.

"That's what they're hoping you'll do."

She bowed her head, shaking it, as if in despair.

"Hey, it's all right," he said.

"No, it's not."

She could have been crying as she turned and gazed up at him through the spray. She looked embarrassed—inconsolable—and he felt as if his heart were going to twist out of his chest. He understood her frustration. He felt it, but as sympathetic as he was, he couldn't give in to it.

God, she *was* crying. Tears filled her eyes, and she tried not to let him see. She turned away, and he tugged her back, gathering her into his arms. She resisted him at first, but finally she rested her forehead in the curve of his shoulder and sighed.

The sound nearly broke him. It cut into him as nothing else could.

A moment later they were clinging to each other in the heart of the waterfall. He locked his arms around her, aware of the deep satisfaction it gave him to comfort her. But as the water crashed around them, and his head cleared, he asked himself the question that had rocked him last night. What the hell had happened? They were like two stars on a collision course. It was cosmic, and fatal. She was a total enigma to him, a mystery without a solution. Why had fate dropped her into his lap two years ago? And why again now? Apparently the first time had been impossible for her. This time was impossible for him.

But he wasn't going to think about that right now. He'd waited too long for this, for her.

"LOVE AT FIRST SIGHT. Do you believe in it?"

Bat directed his question to both Melissa and Tony. He'd been quizzing them with personal questions for the last fifteen minutes—with the cameras rolling. Most reality shows shot for extended periods and edited huge volumes of material into weekly episodes. This one was more like a newsmagazine with a looming air date and a tight production schedule. Interviews with Tony and Melissa would connect the candid segments.

"Well, not in the sense of Cupid shooting arrows." Melissa started to elaborate, but Tony spoke over her.

"We'd better believe in it," he said, "because that's how it happened, for me at least."

"Tell me more." Bat jumped in, forgetting for a moment to be cool.

Melissa was more than a little curious, too. She reached around the back of her neck, where perspiration slicked her fingertips. The air-conditioning ran at full blast but couldn't compete with the heat of the lights the crew had set up in the living room. The extraordinarily humid weather outside didn't help, either.

"Melissa doesn't know this," Tony said, "but I saw her first."

He rested his hand on her bare knee with a familiarity that startled her. Bat had wanted them to be interviewed on the living-room couch in the robes they'd put on after their infamous shower. Melissa wasn't certain how much of the shower activity the mikes had picked up, but she would have been uncomfortable anyway. She'd exposed far too much of herself, and not just physically.

"She was on vacation in Cancún with some girlfriends," he said, "but she used to take a walk every morning, alone, and she went past my restaurant."

"Your restaurant?" Bat motioned for one of the cameras to move in.

"The cantina where I worked," Tony said. "I started going in early because I didn't want to miss her. She looked so unhappy."

Melissa stared at the hand on her knee. "I looked unhappy?"

"You guys have never talked about this?" Bat hooked his sunglasses on the crew neck of his T-shirt.

"I didn't want to scare her off," Tony said, seeming caught up in the memory. "It felt as if I'd been given an opportunity, but I only had one shot. If I missed, she'd be gone, like a deer in the woods."

"And you were the hunter," Bat said.

"Corny, I guess, but true."

"I looked unhappy?" Melissa's heart had taken on a strange, erratic pattern. He'd been watching her for days before the morning they'd met?

Tony transferred his gaze to her, and she was struck by the length of his lashes, the depth of his expression. You could almost believe he meant what he was saying.

"I couldn't figure out how to approach you," he said. "I'm glad I did, though, because the night you showed up in my restaurant, I knew I was right."

"Right about what? My being unhappy?"

"About having fallen in love with you at first sight."

Melissa couldn't think what to say. She just stared at him, wide-eyed and stricken. Why was he doing this? He shouldn't make light about such things. No one should. You could get hurt joking about this stuff.

After what seemed like an eternity, Bat made a throat-cutting gesture, signaling a break.

"Okay," he said once the crew had shut everything down, "it's late, and the guys need a break. So do I, for that matter, but you two won't be alone. The cameras never sleep around here. How about some pillow talk right here on the couch? Tony and Melissa, why don't you keep your robes on—that way it'll look like you sleep nude— and continue this conversation."

"It's clothing that stimulates the imagination, not nudity."

Melissa's statement made every man in the room look at her as if she was certifiably crazy. She didn't have the energy to defend her statement. She didn't have the energy for anything at the moment, and especially not pillow talk with tripods and wall-mounted cameras directed at them.

"I have to go to the bathroom," she said. Bat and his crew were still watching her as if she might be a danger to society. With a measure of satisfaction, Melissa realized she'd picked the only room in the suite besides the bedroom where they couldn't follow her. Bat had tried to talk her into a wall-mounted camera in the bathroom, directed at her vanity so they could capture her cosmetics rituals, but she'd said no. She must have known she would need a refuge from all of them.

"IT'S ABOUT TIME you answered your phone! I've been leaving you messages for days. So? Are you having fun yet, just the two of you?"

The cheery question made Melissa wish she *hadn't* answered. Still, how could she not have? She was in the bathroom, taking off her makeup, and her cell phone had started playing the theme from *Last of the Mohicans*. Hard to ignore.

"Kath, I'm sorry. I haven't had a moment."

Melissa had no way of letting her friend know that she

and Tony were on a TV show, or that this conversation might be caught by the ultrasensitive sound system. The producers had expressly forbidden them from telling anyone about the show, even friends and relatives. If the conversation was caught on tape, Kath would be told afterward—and given a chance to have the footage involving her omitted if she didn't want to participate. Melissa just hoped Kathy wouldn't ask any awkward questions that would require Melissa to say more than she wanted the mikes to pick up.

"Melissa, you there?"

"Kath, I'd love to talk to you, but it's pretty late here."

"Oh, right, there's that time-zone thing! Sorry, am I interrupting anything?"

"No, it's not that."

"Melissa," Kath blurted, "I met a guy, and I used one of your role-playing exercises on him."

"Really? Which one?"

"Shameless Hussy."

"Oh, my goodness, Kath, what happened?"

"I created a stalker. The man won't leave me alone. He sends me flowers. He writes me love letters. He begs to give me pedicures!"

Melissa smiled. Shameless Hussy was inspired by her night with Antonio, and apparently it was a foolproof way to get yourself into trouble. She should have started the chapter with a disclaimer.

A knock on the bathroom door preceded Tony's husky voice. "Are you decent? I hope not." He waited a moment, then opened the door and looked in, just the way a curious husband would. He certainly had the role down.

"Can a guy get a little bathroom time?" he asked.

"Sure, I'm done here." Melissa began clearing the counter of her makeup remover, cleansing pads and alpha hydroxy moisturizer. "I can finish my phone call in the bedroom."

Tony loomed in the doorway, blocking it as she approached. "Where are you going?" he said. "We love to be in the bathroom together, remember? It's one of our intimacy rituals. Chapter eighteen, I think."

He raised an eyebrow, indicating the bathroom door, which probably meant the camera crew hadn't left yet.

"Oh, right, our intimacy rituals. How silly of me."

"Might as well hang around and finish your conversation," he said. "This won't take me long."

"*What* won't take you long?"

"What I'm about to do."

Apparently he wanted it to be a surprise. She watched him study his reflection in the mirror. He ran a hand over the stubble on his face as if he was going to shave. What a perfect idea that was. "Let me get your shaving balm," she said.

"I have it right here." He crouched to search the cabinet under the sink.

"Intimacy rituals?" Kath was saying, obviously having overhead. "Isn't that sweet? Is he going to whiz? And by the way, what category does he fall into? Power tools or lethal weapons?"

In her book, Melissa had created a section about pet names for the male organ, and encouraged her female readers to use them, swearing that men loved to have their penises given macho names. Power tools and lethal weapons were two of the name categories.

"Kath, I really should go."

"Probably lethal weapons. He looks like he'd have a pistol to me."

Melissa lowered her voice. "Tony can be found in your grocery store's produce section."

Kath gave out a little squeal. "He's a cucumber?"

"A plantain."

"Isn't that a great big ol' banana?"

"A great big ol' banana from south of the border."

"Oh my God, Melissa, I'm so jealous."

"As well you should be. G'night, Kath."

Tony gave Melissa an inquisitive look as she clicked off the phone. She smiled brightly, the picture of innocence. He had his secrets. She had hers. She was starting to wonder if he'd really just come in here to shave.

Intrigued, she watched him unzip his leather travel case and paw through it, looking for something. A brisk citrus essence teased her senses as he pulled out a dark green bottle of cologne, some nail clippers and a cuticle brush. A wicked-looking straight razor appeared next, and his smile told her that he had finally found what he wanted. Must be a Latin thing, she thought.

"There is no smoother shave," he said, catching her eye in the mirror.

Melissa couldn't help but notice his heavy five o'clock shadow—or think about what the texture of his skin would be like when he was done. Cool satin. But when men shaved before bed, it was usually in preparation for one thing. Sex.

"You're going to use that on your face?" she asked.

"No, I thought…your legs. Have you ever had the experience?"

Her stomach dipped wildly. "Tony, I don't think so. I'm still trying to recover from having my hair washed."

He nodded and began to lather his jaw with a creamy white meringue that looked good enough to eat. "Let me know if you change your mind."

Melissa drew her lower lip between her teeth and bit down, trying to contain her excitement. She already had.

"SOFT ENOUGH?"

"Like a baby's bottom," Melissa said, smoothing her hand over the satiny skin of her calf. She sat on the vanity seat, and Tony was cross-legged on the floor, cradling her foot in his lap as he put the finishing touches on her ankle. Apparently, some very delicate maneuvering was necessary down there to negotiate the anklebone and the various other subtle curves.

Melissa sat very still, enjoying the new feelings. His fingers were warm and firm, and the straight edge tickled rather than scraped, as she'd imagined it might.

The "experience" of having her legs shaved hadn't been bad at all once she'd gotten used to the idea. Tony had wielded the wicked-looking razor with great care and finesse. Most of the time she'd felt as if there were boa feathers gliding over her skin. She'd actually found it relaxing, an unusual feeling in her relationship with Tony.

He finished up with the razor, rinsed it in the sink and wiped the remaining cream from her skin with a steamy towel. She could almost feel her pores opening and sighing with happiness.

"Now what?" she asked.

"Whatever you'd like. Some lotion, maybe?"

Her ridiculously eager smile must have given her away. He snagged a porcelain bottle from the countertop behind him, poured some lotion in his palms to warm it, and began to massage her calves.

Melissa's eyelids fluttered. Now, that was nice. She could have slithered right off the vanity seat it was so nice. By the time he'd worked his way down to her toes, she was so relaxed, she was having trouble sitting up. This man's hands outperformed even Jeanie's pills. Even her mind was floating like a cork.

"How's that feel?" he asked.

"Mmm," was all she managed.

He rose from the floor and helped her to her feet, catching her as she swayed.

"What's next?" she asked, still floating. Such a lovely thing, floating.

"I think it's bedtime for baby."

MELISSA SNUGGLED deeper under the crimson silk sheet that she and Tony had pulled up over their heads. There were no cameras around, and the crew was gone, but they were both a little paranoid by now. And, anyway, having their own little tent created a feeling of safety and privacy they hadn't had since the show started.

Tony had propped a fist against his jaw, his head and drawn-up knee serving as tent poles. His dark features were bathed in rosy light, but his expression was one of confusion and tenderness. He seemed on the verge of asking Melissa a question, but she had to ask one first.

"You didn't mean any of that, right?" she said. "About love at first sight?"

"A big ol' banana?"

Apparently love would have to wait until they'd discussed produce. She'd lost the battle against nudity, so she was careful not to look anywhere but his eyes as she spoke. "Would you rather I'd said a string bean," she asked. "Could we talk about love now?"

"Sure, right after we finish talking about sex. Just for the record, string beans are a really unfortunate choice of side dish. They look bad, taste bad and sound bad. And while we're on the subject of sex, what did you mean by every damn day?"

"Every damn day?"

"That's what you said at the Plaza when the driver let

us out—that you thought about our wedding night every damn day.''

''I said *you* thought about it every damn day.''

''And I quote—'You've been thinking about it every damn day, just as I have.''' He lifted his head, fixing her with his sexy expression that said I'm gonna love you within an inch of your life. ''You included yourself, and you were furious at me.''

''Well, that's nothing new. I've been furious with you for two years.''

''Yeah? Well, it's mutual.''

Somehow that encouraged her. Must be a sign of her desperation. ''But you didn't mean that love-at-first-sight stuff, right? You just said that for the cameras.''

''Actually, I did.''

She punched her pillow, flopped her head down and sighed. ''That's what I thought.''

''I meant it, Melissa. I fell in love with you that first morning.''

She stayed flat on the pillow. ''You never told me.''

''I would have if you'd stayed.''

She shushed him without even thinking. It was habit by now. ''I couldn't stay,'' she told him, mouthing the words. ''I'm not a fixer-upper, and you're not Don Quixote, even if you think you are.''

He lowered his voice, too. ''Am I supposed to know what that means?''

''You said I looked unhappy. That's a weird thing to be attracted to. Are you sure it was love and not pity?''

''Melissa, are you angry at me for falling in love with you?''

''I just don't understand why.''

''Who knows why people fall in love? It's chemistry.

You were the most irresistible unhappy woman I've ever seen.''

"Um, sure,'' she said, wishing she could believe him. Obviously her self-esteem wasn't up to the challenge. But then why would it be, with him wanting her, rejecting her, wanting her again? If he had been so madly in love with her back then, why couldn't he make up his mind now? Of course, he might be protecting himself the way she was. Or protecting something or someone else. Whatever it was, she just knew he wasn't telling her everything.

She really didn't know which way to go with this. He was saying things she wanted to hear, and even that frightened her—that she *wanted* to hear them. Talk about thin ice. She could hear it splintering.

"Okay,'' she said at last, "let's say I buy this love-at-first-sight business. That was two years ago. How do you feel now?''

Of course, he didn't answer that question. And of course, the way he lifted his head and fixed her with his darkening gaze made her stomach float away—like a balloon on a string this time.

12

There's a reason they call it making love. Put your heart as well as your body into it, and the sex will soar.

101 Ways To Make Your Man Beg

IT WASN'T Melissa's question that left Tony momentarily speechless. It was the answer that had almost spilled out of his mouth. He couldn't believe the thoughts that were rolling through his head. They were crazy, *impossible*. He felt his chest squeeze tight as he tried to talk, and maybe it was just as well. He wouldn't have made any sense anyway.

Melissa looked ready to pop, too. If her eyes got any bigger, they would tip her over. God, she was lovely. Clothes on, clothes off, she was irresistible in a way that had nothing to do with her looks. All that trembling expectation that the next ship on the horizon would be hers, all that sweet despair when it wasn't.

"Love you?" He cleared his throat of its huskiness. "I'm out of my mind, Melissa. I'm not safe on the streets I love you so much. They should put crazies like me in straitjackets."

Suddenly her brown eyes crinkled, taking on an expression of suffering. "You really shouldn't make light of things like that," she said.

He jabbed a finger at the silk ceiling above their heads and mouthed the words, "The walls are paper, and the cameras are likely still running." She was born for reality TV. They loved it when people made fools of themselves for the entertainment of millions.

"I'm not making light," he said, enunciating in case she'd been overheard. "I've never been more serious, Melissa, I promise you. I adore you, I do."

She looked more stricken with every word, and worse, she seemed to be sinking into the mattress. Maybe he should have stayed with the speechlessness. What had he done now?

"This is all a joke to you, isn't it?" She turned away from him and curled up, apparently so that he couldn't see her beautiful naked ball of a body. "You're not in love with me and probably never were," she went on in muted tones. "It must be the money. That's why you're here. It's the only thing that makes sense."

"What? What are you talking about?"

"Shhhhhh! The walls are thin."

"I don't care about the walls, Melissa. To hell with the walls."

He gave her shoulder a gentle tug, hoping that she would roll over and open her arms to him. He could almost imagine her coming into his embrace and letting him make it all right. Now, *there* was a *serious* thought.

But it wasn't to be. She stubbornly kept her back to him.

"I don't give a damn about the money," he said, lowering his voice. "If you believe anything I say, believe that."

"Then why are you here?"

He couldn't tell her, and that angered him. He should never have made the promise to Jeanie, but it had made sense at the time. The payback he'd had in mind for Melissa was strictly personal. He'd never intended to harm her career. He knew how committed she was to doing something with her life—and to paying back her parents as well. He admired that.

A silence fell around them, broken only by the catch in her breathing.

He contemplated her hunched shoulders and made a decision.

"You," he said. "That's why I came back. All I thought about was you…every damn day."

"You don't mean that," she mumbled into her shoulder.

"If there's a Bible anywhere in this suite, I'll swear on it."

Her breath seemed to whistle in her throat. For a second nothing moved other than the blink of her eyelashes. He gave her another gentle tug, and this time she did turn, rolling toward him with grace and urgency. The anguish in her expression was the sweetest thing he'd ever seen. One bright tear slid down her cheek.

"Get over here," he said, collecting her like a bundle of perishables.

She held back at the last minute, her hand on his biceps. "You came back just for me? You don't have some kind of deal with Jeanie?"

"It's not the kind of deal you're thinking of. I'm here because I want to be." He stumbled over the words because they weren't what he wanted to say. He didn't know what he wanted to say, but right now she felt like the only thing in his life that mattered. He couldn't grasp all the ramifications of that for his future, but he knew it was huge. It would change everything.

His throat felt as if it were paved with sand. "There's

no reason in the world that I want to be here right now, except you, Melissa. You're my reason. Just you."

She fell into his arms, a heap of sighs and gooseflesh. "I think I'm falling in love with you," she said, struggling to control her voice. "Even if you don't love me, I think I am."

Her confession cut straight through him. He closed his eyes and worked on breathing normally. Only one of them should be losing control under these circumstances, and she was clearly already over the edge. He needed to be strong, but this was crazy. His temples throbbed, and his throat was on fire. The sensations made him profoundly uncomfortable, but if he stopped to figure out why, he might lose this feeling, this feeling that his heart was about to burst. And he hadn't felt this way in years, not since the morning he first saw her.

He brought up her chin and looked into her eyes.

Tenderness and lust consumed him in equal measure.

"This *isn't* for the cameras," he told her. "I love you, Melissa. I don't need to think about that. I know."

She made the strangest gurgling noise he'd ever heard. He had a hunch she was trying to say something but couldn't. He knew what that felt like, but never got the chance to tell her. Her fingers slid over his mouth, touching him in ways that made her needs known. The delicate pressure brought every one of his nerve endings alive. Her warm breath riffled his hair, but it was the dreamy softness of her breasts that ripped a sigh out of him.

He kissed her lightly and all hell broke loose. Desire sizzled between them. Tony's jaw clenched with how sweet it was. Heat jetted through his nostrils. She arched her back, and he pulled her under him, capturing her with the weight of his leg. She couldn't move, nor did she seem to want to.

Another sexy sound purred in her throat as she touched him intimately. Her fingers trailed softly along the inside of his thigh until she reached his sac. She cupped his testicles, lifting their weight in her palm, and blood flowed like a river into his already hard shaft. That was all the encouragement Tony needed.

He reached down to gauge her readiness and found her warm and wet. Her petals quivered under his touch.

"Tell me what you want," he said. "A velvet tongue, a wild pony, a very happy gardener? Your wish is my command."

"No games," she whispered. "All I want is you, and I can't wait another moment."

The thought of stopping may have entered his brain for a nanosecond. But he couldn't stop. He had a million reasons—imperative reasons—and none of them mattered. Only one imperative existed in Tony Bond's mind—making love with her. Now, in this suite, under these sheets, and stone cold sober.

"We can't make any noise," she whispered as he moved between her legs.

"The hell we can't. I'll get up and disable every damn camera."

"No!" She clutched at him. "Don't go anywhere."

A sharp sensation made him realize that she'd sunk her nails into his flanks. Every muscle fiber knotted in wild anticipation. She pulled him into her, and they both groaned with the savage joy of it. One thrust of his hips, and he was engulfed in the tight, slick heat of her. This was right. This was what they were made for.

He sank his fingers into her hips and locked the two of them in sensual combat. Heaven couldn't be better than this. Nothing could. He was sheathed in her luscious flesh and the desire to go slowly was the only thought that existed, the only reason he existed. She curled her legs around him, urging him into the rhythm of deep, mindless thrusting, and he surrendered with a hungry shudder. Pleasure moaned through him.

"Tony, it's love," she murmured. "Not liquor or aphrodisiacs. It's love that makes us so crazy."

Something wrenched deep inside him. She'd written a book full of erotic tips to make men beg, but there was no way to capture this in a book, this wildness she called love. You had to feel it. If he was begging for anything, it was to take her back into his life, into his heart.

He could feel her cresting. Her entire body tightened, especially the muscles that caressed his shaft, and she didn't intend to let go of him. A powerful urgency built inside him. He slowed his thrusting to delay his release, and she cried out, cursing him softly. She twisted frantically, urging him to pump, to bring her to completion.

"I feel it coming," she whispered. "Deeper, faster."

"I will do neither," he said, kissing her passionately. He kept his thrusting slow as she screamed into his mouth and came apart in his arms. Somehow, he held out against the terrible pressure building inside him, but when she raked his back with her nails, he lost the fight for control. Their bodies bucked and pounded, his climbing toward a release that felt as if it could rip him apart when it came.

She sobbed his name and a sensation more intense than pleasure flooded him. Something hot and wet stung his eyes. Tears? No, impossible.

When their breathing had quieted, he pulled her close. Almost immediately, she dozed off with her head in the crook of his shoulder and her leg draped over him. He listened to her rhythmic breathing deep into the night, never closing his eyes. He was glad that she trusted him enough to sleep easily. Knowing she felt safe gave him the sense that he might have done something worthwhile, despite this crazy mess of a book tour. But she didn't know what was coming, and he couldn't tell her. He could only pray that everything went well.

The crew would probably be back by the time they woke up, but Tony had a news flash for Bat Bohanan, and he didn't care whether the director liked it or not. In fact, Tony had a news flash for several people, and he sincerely doubted whether any of them would like it, starting with Jeanie.

The sense of relief he felt had been a long time coming. He took a deep breath and let it go. He could hardly wait to put his plan into motion.

MELISSA AWOKE to a sunlit chamber. Surrounded by a rich golden haze, she wondered for a moment where she was. Gradually, she realized two things. She was no longer hiding under a canopy of silk sheets, and she wasn't in Kansas anymore. She'd also misplaced a bed partner. Or should she say husband?

"Tony?" She rolled over and checked out the bedroom, but didn't see him anywhere. She had no idea who might be around, so she didn't want to yell, and she didn't want to jump out of bed, either. Not nude anyway. Odd that the suite was so quiet. She couldn't hear the crew at work, and the bedside clock said 9:00 a.m. They should have been here long ago.

Another feeling crept into her awareness, but this one she couldn't put into words. Just a tingle of dread beneath her breastbone.

She shivered and sat up, covering herself with the sheet. Even the spring sun couldn't warm her up, but she wasn't going to let a fleeting mood bring her down. Last night had been wonderful. Shockingly wonderful. She was in love. Correction, *they* were in love. Who would have guessed? Apparently it had surprised him, too.

She smiled, remembering the look on his face when he'd admitted his feelings. Confession looked good on him. The only time he'd been even more uneasy was when she'd blurted out her feelings.

Time to find him and shock him again.

Inspired, she slipped on her robe and made a dash for the bathroom. She took a quick shower, toweled off and hurried to get dressed behind the screen. Having no idea what was on the shooting schedule for that day, she chose a khaki skirt and a red sleeveless turtleneck top in a lightweight cotton knit. For underwear, she slipped on one of the matching thongs Tony had bought for them. And nothing else. Breezy, to say the least.

Her butt did not fall into the category of thong-worthy, and she had no intention of a permanent switch from her one hundred percent cotton bikinis, but it would be fun to see Tony's reaction when she revealed her fashion secret. She would show him at some appropriate time—or better yet, inappropriate. She loved surprising him. That could have been why she was born.

The suite appeared deserted as Melissa walked through it. For a second, dread skittered back, tapping her with cold fingers, and then she saw Tony out on the patio. His white Polo shirt gleamed in the sunlight, and a pair of khaki shorts showed off his long bronzed legs as he sat at the table. Bent over a legal-size tablet, he seemed completely absorbed in whatever he was writing, but he closed the notebook when she called his name.

"I missed you," she said, her voice breathy as she joined him.

He was already on his feet, and she marveled at how fit and robust he looked this morning. His black hair was as rich and lustrous as onyx. His dark eyes were dangerously bright, and his mouth was curved in a sensual smile. Love must agree with him. As for her, love did crazy things to her heart.

He opened his arms, and she wrapped herself around him like a ribbon on a birthday gift. "Last night was wonderful," she said. "Did you miss me this morning?"

"Fiercely, but I didn't want to wake you."

"What are you writing?" She gazed up at him. "The sequel to my book, maybe? *101 More Ways* or *How To Make Your Woman Beg*?"

"Neither, but that last one's a good idea." He laughed and released her. Too quickly, in her opinion.

"Here, sit down," he said, pulling out a chair for her. "I'll get you some coffee. We need to talk."

He poured her amaretto-scented coffee and set about slicing her some coffee cake laced with cinnamon and walnuts. Melissa sipped the coffee, but she was too nervous to eat anything, no matter how delicious the cake smelled. She assumed their talk would have something to do with the lovemaking—or maybe the missing camera crew.

Despite her nerves, her stomach rumbled at the sight of food, and she tried to remember how long it had been since she'd eaten. "Where's Bat this morning?"

Tony poured himself a cup of coffee and sat next to her. "When I got up, there was a voice mail from him saying he'd reviewed last night's tape, and they have everything they need for now."

"They have everything they need?" Melissa mouthed the words. "What does that mean?"

"You don't need to whisper anymore," Tony pointed out. "There's no one here but us."

"Were we noisy, do you think?"

"Even if we were, no one's going to know. I'm going

to have a look at the footage and veto anything that's embarrassing. They had plenty of material without including last night.''

''Do you think they'll agree with that?''

''They will if they don't want a hot-blooded Latin on their hands, threatening to block the show's release. I suspect I could find some publicity-hungry lawyer to take our case, and that's not the kind of buzz they're looking for.''

He sounded serious, and Melissa didn't imagine Bat would want the show held up. She relaxed a little and broke off a bit of her cake, then looked up at the sky to see if the birds were back. No sign of them. A good omen, she hoped.

''You said you wanted to talk. Was it about the meeting with Bat?''

''Actually, no. I have a meeting set up with Jeanie this morning. In fact, I need to get going. With the traffic, it will probably take twenty minutes to get to the Searchlight offices.''

''You need to talk to Jeanie? Why can't you talk to her here?''

Tony leaned over and took her hand, cradling it in both of his. He kissed her fingertips. ''It has to do with my agreement with Jeanie and Searchlight. There may be forms involved, but it won't take long, I promise.''

''What's going on, Tony? You're not going to tell me?''

''I'll tell you everything. In fact, I'll tell you my life story, right *after* I've talked with Jeanie.''

He rose from the table and Melissa got up with him to walk him to the door. It didn't seem that she had any choice. ''Am I going to get any clues?'' she asked. ''How about a game of Twenty Questions? Does this have anything to do with that secret you've been keeping?''

He angled her a quizzical look that told her she'd hit a

nerve. But the man could cover well. His enigmatic smile gave nothing away.

"Aha," she said. *"Aha."*

"Everything to do with it," he admitted.

"Aha!"

He laughed and pulled her into his arms for a goodbye kiss. "It will be all right, I promise."

His lips brushed hers fleetingly, but his main interest seemed to be in finding her left hand. Melissa presented it to him, and he fingered the ring she wore.

"Here's a secret," he said. "This band won't come off because it's not supposed to. It means our love was never meant to end."

Melissa gazed at the ring's woven braids of gold. "Did you just make that up to make me feel better?"

"No, I didn't make it up. The ring has been in my family for years. My mother gave it to me before she died, and she told me what her mother told her—that the ring means unending love. Of course, I didn't believe it at the time."

"Of course not."

"But then you couldn't get it off your finger, and I began to wonder."

She resisted the impulse to laugh. Maybe it was nerves. "This is silly, but I actually wondered if the ring brought us back together."

"I did, too," he admitted, kissing her again. "Now go have your breakfast and relax. Our obligations to Jeanie and the tour are over. You have nothing to do today but wait for me to come back and explain everything."

"I'd rather you made love to me."

"I'll do that, too."

Giddiness brought a lilt to her voice. "I think you talked me into it."

"WELCOME TO MY humble abode." Jeanie called to Tony from her desk, beckoning him into her small office. "I'm just finishing up here."

A phone pressed to her ear, she waved him to an over-stuffed chocolate-brown and white couch. Tony remained standing, and she nodded at him, smiling brightly. Perfectly okay with her, she seemed to be saying.

He'd called at the last minute and she'd had to squeeze him in between her other commitments, so he hadn't expected her to be waiting for him. He hadn't expected her to be so cheerful, either.

Her office intrigued him. The small rectangular space had been made larger by the artful use of mirrors and false windows depicting the city skyline. A vividly blue aquarium set into the wall was, in fact, a screen saver for some kind of flat-screen monitor. *Nothing is what it seems,* Tony thought. Life was a series of charades, and his life might be the greatest charade of all. Maybe it was fitting that he end all that right here.

"That was one of the reality show producers," Jeanie said as she hung up the phone. "He's excited about the footage, says it's going to be a ratings blockbuster."

"Is that right, a blockbuster?" Tony made no attempt to disguise his irony. "Will we get our own talk show?"

Jeanie shrugged. "Stranger things have happened. And by the way, I told him you'd asked to see a rough cut of the show before it airs. He said it could be arranged."

"Fast work, I appreciate it." He'd only asked her that morning when he'd set up the appointment with her.

"We aim to please. What else can I help you with?"

Jeanie wasn't one to equivocate, and Tony decided to come straight to the point. "I want out of our agreement," he said. "Melissa has a right to know what's going on, and I want to tell her. The tour's over, so it shouldn't have any effect on the promotion of the book.''

Jeanie settled back in her chair, appearing to reflect. Finally, she said, ''You're in love with her, aren't you?''

He didn't confirm or deny it, but Jeanie had obviously made up her mind.

''Melissa knows virtually nothing about you, Tony. Are you going to tell her that you aren't a waiter? That you own restaurants around the world and—''

''And maintain quality control by anonymously waiting on tables? Of course, I'm going to tell her that. I'm going to tell her everything.''

She arched an eyebrow. ''Everything? She won't react well.''

''I have to take that chance.''

''I can see that, but I don't want her hurt, Tony. This has nothing to do with the book or with Searchlight. I like Melissa. I care about her welfare.''

''For God's sake, Jeanie, so do I.''

''Then wouldn't it be easier if you just left, went back to your life and let her go back to hers. Do you really want to entangle her in your affairs?''

''I want her with me, and whatever that takes, I'll do it.'' He had conviction enough for ten men, but Jeanie had made a good point. His situation was messy, and Melissa could be hurt no matter how hard he tried to shield her.

''I know what you're thinking, Jeanie,'' he said, ''and I won't let that happen. I'll do anything to protect her.''

''I hope so.'' She scrutinized him like the mother of a budding teenage girl. At last she rose to shake his hand. ''You take good care of her, hear? Any complaints and you'll have me to deal with.''

Jeanie obviously had more to say, but their handshake got interrupted by a rap on her office door. Tony turned around to see Bat Bohanan himself loitering in the hallway. He had on his usual jeans and cotton Polo shirt, sunglasses hanging in the open neck.

"Bat, what a surprise," Jeanie said, blushing hotly.

The director jammed his hands into the pockets of his jeans. "I was in the area," he explained.

The awkward silence told Tony that he was the one interrupting. "Me, too," he said. "Just leaving."

He slapped Bat on the arm, and they briefly gripped hands. Tony glanced back at Jeanie to say goodbye, and noticed the red mark on her neck. Maybe it was her flushed skin, but the mark looked suspiciously like a love bite.

On his way out the door, Tony shot the director a grin. Now he knew why they called him Bat. He also knew why Jeanie was so cheerful.

A CLOCK CHIMED throughout the suite, and Melissa looked up from the suitcases lying open on the bed. She'd been trying to decide whether or not to pack while she waited for Tony to return. She had no idea where she would go once she did pack, but she needed something to do that would make her less anxious about his news. He'd said he loved her and everything would be all right, but she couldn't seem to make herself believe that.

If one was packed, one could always go. It was a rule of life.

More chimes. They rang and rang. Maybe that wasn't a clock.

The doorbell! She headed for the living room on a run. Tony must have lost his key card.

Puffing from exertion, she flung open the door. "That was quick," she said. "Oh, sorry, I thought you were—"

It was a woman at the door, not Tony. Melissa didn't know what to say for a moment, especially since this particular woman looked as if she was about to cry. She'd folded her arms, tilted her chin high, and her lush dark lashes blinked furiously.

Beautiful, exotic, defiant, hurt. All those thoughts flashed through Melissa's mind as she realized she hadn't said anything. "Can I help you?"

"Please, may I speak to Antonio?"

"Do you mean Tony? He's out. Is there anything I can do?"

The woman's almond-shaped eyes flashed angrily. "I think you have done quite enough. I want to talk to Antonio, please."

Odd that she called him Antonio. Melissa had begun to wonder if she was dealing with an overzealous fan. That happened when people became public personas, and Tony had proven to be extremely popular with the ladies on the tour. On the other hand, the woman had a Latin accent, and maybe this was all a mistake. She wanted some other Antonio.

"Are you sure you have the right room?" Melissa asked. "It's a big hotel. Could I call the desk for you and check?"

"Are you Melissa Sanders and did you write a book called *How To Make Your Man Beg*?"

"Yes, I did, but I still don't know what you're talking about."

"I'm talking about your husband." Her chin trembled violently, and she seemed on the brink of tears again. "He h-happens to be my fiancé."

"Your fiancé?" Melissa's first impulse was to shake her head. She'd never heard anything so ridiculous. Either the woman was out of touch with reality, or this was some kind of joke. On the other hand, maybe she *was* an obsessed fan. She was highly agitated and making wild claims. Both were red flags from what Melissa knew.

Stay calm, Melissa told herself. *If you're calm, she will be. If you don't panic, she won't.* She nodded at the woman reassuringly, trying to assess how dangerous the situation might be. At the moment, she appeared more hurt than angry. Now all Melissa had to do was get to the phone and call security without alerting her that anything was wrong. That shouldn't have felt so overwhelming, but she could hardly hear herself think. The sense of dread had returned, and it wasn't quiet anymore. It was screaming in her ears that something was terribly wrong here.

13

A sensual massage, role playing, sex toys…all of these are secondary. If you want to reach the heights of ecstasy, your heart is all that really matters. It gives meaning to all the rest.

101 Ways To Make Your Man Beg

MELISSA CONSIDERED her options. She could slam the door and lock it, but if the woman tried to block her, Melissa would have a fight on her hands. Right now she looked too distraught to put up much of a struggle, but anything could trigger her, and delusional fans could be violent. Melissa decided to try something she hoped was less risky.

"If you'll wait here a minute," she told the woman, "I'll try and reach Tony by phone. Who shall I say dropped by?"

"Tell him it's Natalie de la Cruz, his *fiancée*. Ask him what I'm supposed to do about the wedding? *Our* wedding. We were to be married next month."

Her batting eyelashes couldn't stop the tears that welled and spilled over. She fished a delicate lace hankie from what looked like a Gucci bag and tried to stem the flow, but failed miserably. Her lovely face was awash. Even her shoulders shook as she battled with her emotions.

Melissa shouldn't have been sympathetic, but suffering in any form was difficult for her to witness. As a child on the farm, she would mourn for weeks when one of the animals had to be butchered. She never got used to it, and finally her worried parents stopped altogether and bought what little meat they could afford at the market.

"Miss de la Cruz," she said, "would you like to come in and sit down while I call him? Perhaps that would be easier for you."

The woman peeked over the lace of her handkerchief, studying Melissa as if uncertain she could be trusted. Finally, she nodded, but her expression changed when Melissa touched her elbow to guide her inside.

"Where did you get that ring?"

Melissa glanced at the wedding band. Her visitor's horrified gaze was fixed on the delicate gold lace, and Melissa's first impulse was to say it was a friendship ring or something left to her by a relative, anything but the truth. Instead she remained silent.

Tear-stained and defiant, Natalie de la Cruz presented her hand in the way of engaged women everywhere. A huge emerald-cut diamond sparkled on her ring finger, left hand.

"Tony asked me to marry him on Valentine's Day," she said. "The ceremony will be at Tattershall Castle in Lincolnshire."

"How nice for you." Melissa wished she'd slammed the door.

Natalie sniffled and brushed right past her, her high-heel sandals echoing on the marble tiles of the foyer. Her ebony tresses fluttered with the breeze she created, and she didn't bother hiding that she was casing the place, apparently intent on finding someone lurking behind a doorway.

Melissa followed her into the room. "There's no one here but me."

"Are you going to call Antonio?" Natalie's elegant white silk pantsuit rustled as she turned to Melissa.

Noisy creature. "Yes, of course. I'll do that now." Melissa had never intended to call Tony. Her original plan had been to call hotel security and have them deal with Miss de la Cruz. Now that seemed like a very good idea.

Melissa casually walked to the wet bar and lifted the wall phone receiver. "Why don't you have a seat there by the window and make yourself comfortable. It'll just take me a minute."

Natalie hovered, watching as Melissa's finger dropped to the red button on the panel.

"What are you doing?" She rushed over, sandals tapping, hair fluttering. "If you're calling security, go right ahead. They'll come and escort me out, but you won't be rid of me, Ms. Sanders, because I'm telling you the truth."

Okay, Plan B. Melissa hung up the phone without dialing. "Miss de la Cruz, would you like some tea? If you'd just sit down somewhere, anywhere you'd like, I'll go fix some."

"Nothing, thank you."

"Are you sure? Biscuits? Tea and some lovely English biscuits? No?" *Plan C.* Melissa could feel the strain in her smile. "Let's try this. Since I don't know when Tony's coming back, why don't I have him call you? You could write him a note and leave your number."

Melissa indicated the hotel stationery near the phone. She was inviting Miss de la Cruz to sit and compose—the note, as well as herself.

"I'm not writing any notes, and I'm not leaving."

Now the woman's behavior was simply rude. Melissa couldn't help but wonder if someone had put her up to this. A practical joke? More reality TV? Whatever was going on, Melissa had run out of plans. "I wish I could help you, but—"

"Help me?" Natalie de la Cruz's dark eyes sparkled with anger. She clenched her tiny fists. "This is how you help? By trying to steal my fiancé? I saw the two of you on CNN in London. My whole family saw it. Now everyone's consoling me to my face and making jokes behind my back. I'm a laughingstock!"

Out of patience, Melissa marched straight to the door. "I'm going to have to ask you to leave," she said. "If you don't, I *will* call hotel security."

Melissa braced herself for an explosion. But Natalie began to cry again. This time she sank to the sofa and broke down in convulsive sobs. The lace hankie couldn't begin to contain her anguish. When she tried to speak, her voice wobbled and cracked.

"I'm not going until I—I see him," she said. "He hasn't called or written in days. I won't be treated like this."

Melissa had thought the woman was faking, but no one except a consummate actress could have faked this display of emotion. Her pain was palpable. That didn't mean she wasn't delusional, however.

"Please do sit down," Melissa said, "and I'll make us some tea. I don't know when Tony's going to be back, but if it's that important, you can stay. I'm sure he'll clear this up."

Natalie seated herself on the large sectional sofa, still blotting her tears. If she was a kook, she was a wealthy one. Her pantsuit was almost certainly an Armani creation, and she carried herself like a woman accustomed to the finer things. Her legs were crossed at the ankle, her posture impeccable.

Melissa left to get the tea. It only took her a few minutes

to put together a tray, but that was more than enough time for unwanted doubts to creep in. She didn't want to think about whether or not her visitor was telling the truth, but the nagging concerns wouldn't go away. Tony had been harboring some kind of secret since he arrived. They'd even talked about it, and he'd promised that everything would be explained when he got back from his meeting with Jeanie.

Melissa returned to the living room with the tray of tea and various goodies that she knew wouldn't be eaten. Sometimes just the presence of comfort food was enough.

She poured a cup and offered it to Natalie. "How did you and Tony meet?"

Natalie balanced the saucer on her knees and took a sip of her tea. She let out a quick sigh of appreciation. "It wasn't nearly as interesting as his whirlwind encounter with you." Bitterness tinged her voice. "But I did meet him at a restaurant, just as you did."

Melissa nearly dropped the bone-china cup she was holding. "How did you know we met at a restaurant?"

"Tony told me, of course."

Melissa just managed to get the china safely to the table. Natalie could only have known about that through Tony. Melissa had never revealed publicly how she and Tony had met until yesterday on the reality TV show, which hadn't aired yet.

Could she be telling the truth?

The door lock clicked before Melissa could ask the question. Both women looked up as Tony entered, a smile wreathing his handsome face. His gaze was locked on Melissa as he came through the foyer and entered the living room. He didn't seem to see Natalie at all.

"Tony?"

He stopped, confused. He glanced from Melissa to the woman who'd spoken.

"Natalie," he said. Disbelief swept over his face, and his entire countenance changed. The room seemed to go dark, as if the sunshine had been snuffed out by clouds.

Melissa thought she was going to be ill. He knew this woman.

Natalie's cup and saucer clattered to the table. She rose, wobbling on her heels. "I'm sorry, Tony, but I had to come. Are you angry with me?"

His face clearly asked, *What the hell are you doing here?* Instead, in a calm voice, he said, "I started a letter to you this morning."

Natalie gestured toward Melissa. "She doesn't seem to know anything about me, Tony. Why didn't you tell her?"

"I had good reasons, Natalie. The same reasons that you and I agreed not to tell anyone why I had to come here. We did agree, Natalie."

Her cheeks turned an angry red. "I didn't tell anyone. You did. You showed up on CNN with that woman, playing some game called Sexual Paste."

Tony registered surprise. "CNN in London? Since when do they air American talk shows?"

"Apparently marriages around the world are in need of some hot sex. See what a wonderful public service you provided? You and *her*." She jabbed a finger toward Melissa.

"You knew I would be posing as Melissa's husband. I explained the situation before I left."

Posing? Melissa felt as if he'd slapped her.

Natalie's reaction seemed almost as strong as Melissa's. She glowered at Tony as if she wanted to slap him. "Tell her how much I mean to you, Tony."

"Natalie, why are you here? Why are you doing this?"

"Tell her how you proposed to me." She thrust out her hand. "How you bought me this ring."

Tony's jaw flexed. "The ring is a family heirloom, Natalie. *Your* family. I didn't buy it."

"But we're engaged to be married! Tell her that, dammit!"

"Tony?" Melissa could hardly get his name out.

The edges of Tony's mouth had turned white. Finally, he spoke to Melissa. "It's true," he said. "Natalie and I are engaged, but this is not how I wanted you to find out. I just spoke with Jeanie, and I was coming back to tell you everything."

Natalie wasted no time vindicating herself. "You see. It's all true, everything I said. His marriage to you may be a fake, but his engagement to me is real."

Melissa couldn't make herself believe it, even now. "Is this for real, Tony? There aren't any cameras running, recording this?"

He heaved a sigh. "I almost wish there was."

"You're going to marry her? That's why you wanted the annulment?"

"Give me an opportunity and I'll explain how all this happened, Melissa. But not this way. Let me take Natalie back to wherever she's staying first—"

Natalie swooped like one of the birds on the patio and linked her arm in his. "Come on, darling, let's go. There's a car waiting for us." Her fingers curled around his wrist.

Tony pried her hand free and turned to Melissa. His voice grated like car wheels on gravel. "Will you hear me out, please, before you decide that I've been intentionally deceiving you? There's so much you don't know."

Melissa couldn't even nod. "Does she know about us?"

"She knows about our past...but not about our future.

I'm going to need some time with her. Is that all right? It's only fair that she understands what's happened."

"Of course," Melissa said. "But there's no need to take her anywhere. I'll leave. I'll go right now."

She started for the door with no thought except to get out of the suite. Why hadn't she packed those suitcases?

Tony caught her arm and drew her back. "Where are you going?"

"Why didn't you tell me?" she asked him, her throat burning with pain.

"That was Jeanie's condition. It was the only way she would agree to a quick annulment of the marriage once the tour was over. She said you wouldn't go through with the tour if you knew I was engaged."

Laughing wasn't possible. Otherwise, Melissa would have been hysterical.

"I'm sorry it happened this way," he said, "but I'm not sorry it happened. I wanted to tell you. I wanted you to know everything."

She nodded, although in truth she couldn't hear anything but street traffic and screaming birds. Had someone left the balcony door open? The next thing she knew she was in Tony's arms, and he was talking to her, only to her.

"It will be all right," he whispered. "Melissa, I promise it will."

She wasn't able to cling to him the way she wanted to. Her arms wouldn't work. Nothing would work. "Tony, I'm afraid."

He held her against his chest, cradling her head with his hand. Natalie's toe-tapping could be heard, her impatient mutterings.

"I have to tell her about us," he said. "And I have to do that now. I should never have let it go this long."

"Go," she said. "Talk to Natalie. I'm all right."

"Stay here while I'm gone. Do you hear me, Melissa? *Don't go anywhere.*"

He released her, and she sank into the chair behind her. Her legs wouldn't hold her. Tony hesitated, but she waved him away.

"Please, just go," she said. "I'll be all right."

Reluctantly, he took Natalie by the elbow. Melissa couldn't watch them leave. She was heartsick. Quite a secret he had. His fiancée was one of the most beautiful women she'd ever seen, and she obviously loved him madly. Why would a man ever want anyone but her?

She had just begun to berate herself for being a gullible idiot, when the door to the suite banged open and Tony strode back in.

"What is it?" she asked him.

"I love you," he said, hesitating halfway across the room from her. "No matter what happens, don't ever doubt that. I *love* you."

Melissa was instantly terrified. "What's wrong?"

"Nothing, I just couldn't leave that way, without telling you."

She rose from the chaise. "Tony, what is it? Please, tell me. Oh, God—"

He stepped back, and she realized he wasn't going to tell her. Something had made him come back inside, and either he couldn't or wouldn't explain it. Reflexively, she began to pry the wedding ring from her finger. If she could get it off maybe the pain would stop ripping at her heart. Her knuckle burned as she forced the band over it. Blinded by a grief she barely understood, she held the ring out to him.

His face drained of blood. His cheeks sucked in with a ragged breath.

"Keep it," he said. "This is as close to begging as I will ever come, Melissa. Please, I want you to keep it."

She didn't have the energy to argue. The room seemed to spin, and she closed her eyes. Only for a second, but she thought she felt his lips on her forehead and his voice whispering that he would be back. The only thing that registered in her mind was the resounding click of the door as he left.

The ring fell through her fingers to the floor. It was an accident. One moment it lay cradled in her palm, a symbol of something precious and permanent, and the next, it was swallowed up in a white sea of carpeting. Lost.

She dropped to her knees, searching for it in the rug, fiber by fiber. *It was an accident. She hadn't meant to drop it.*

"ANTONIO, before you say anything, let me speak. There's something I need to tell you, and it can't wait."

Tony didn't like the sound of Natalie's pronouncement, but he felt an obligation to let her have her say. He was about to do something he would have given anything to avoid. It would change the course of both their lives, and he already knew the pain that could cause. Natalie deserved his undivided attention now, as well as his understanding.

"Glenlivet on the rocks?" She walked over to him with the drink she'd prepared, an ice-filled highball glass brimming with his favorite scotch. She'd even turned on the soft jazz he loved. Her hotel room was actually a spacious suite with expensive furnishings and a beautiful view of the city. The French antiques and fresh-cut flowers were all very much Natalie's thing.

"Thanks." Tony sampled the amber liquor, wondering why he couldn't taste it—and why he had never been able to feel what he should have for this woman. Her beauty defied description. Men turned in their tracks when she walked by. Traffic came to a halt. All the usual clichés. But none of that had ever moved him. Natalie had been a friend since their childhood days in Cancún. They'd grown up together, and their families had been pushing them at each other since they were teenagers. Tony had resisted until his mother's death last year made him realize it was time to stop drifting and make a decision about the direction of his life. He'd needed to let go of the past.

But he'd made the wrong decision, and for the wrong reasons.

Natalie held up her glass and clinked it against his. "To us," she said.

The back of his neck tightened. Was she saying goodbye or toasting to their future? He couldn't tell by the odd edge in her voice. Her smile seemed distorted, too.

"Natalie, there isn't an us," he said softly.

"What do you mean?"

"That's what I came here to tell you. Things have changed. Everything's changed."

"What the hell do you mean?"

"There isn't going to be a wedding."

She stepped back, her dark eyes lighting with a mix of shock and outrage. Her face reddened until it looked as if her skin were on fire.

Watching her reaction, Tony got the first glimpse of what he was actually dealing with. She wasn't just hurt, she was furious. Hell hath no fury…

The words that came out of her mouth were low and tremulous. "I won't let you go, Antonio."

MELISSA WAITED out on the balcony with the birds. She sat at the table, under the umbrella, absently aware of the

sun beating down on her exposed knee. She was going to
have quite a sunburn. With great effort she shifted her
chair around and moved her entire body into the shade.
Lord, it was hot. She ought to get up and make herself
some iced tea. Her throat felt dry enough to crack.

The poor birds were as listless as she was, perched on
the balcony railing, facing the patio door. Tony had an
entire welcoming party waiting for him. The doorbell had
rung not long after he'd left, and Melissa had nearly died
of heart failure, but it was only the workmen coming to
dismantle the wall-mounted cameras. That's when she'd
come out to the balcony. She hadn't even noticed when
they'd left.

She glanced at her watch, wondering what could be taking so long. Nearly two hours had ticked by. She could
easily imagine Natalie becoming hysterical, and Tony, being Don Quixote, feeling compelled to stay with her until
she was calm. Considering what he'd gone there to tell
her, that could take a good long time. Natalie had not
seemed very stable, and Tony really was too heroic for his
own good. But his poor welcoming party would die of
heatstroke if he didn't hurry.

She shivered reflexively. Thank God for the heat. It
seemed to insulate her. It kept her from moving, from
thinking. All you could do was sit and wait in weather like
this, like a sunstruck bird perched on a railing. Not even
the notion that a dreaded disease was the cause of her
shivering had entered her mind, which was a shame, really.
Nothing could keep you occupied like a good hysterical
illness. The only thing that hurt at the moment was her
knuckle, where the skin was raw and fiery.

"MELISSA, it's Jeanie. Tony just called me from Kennedy."

The phone receiver nearly slipped from Melissa's hand.

It was wet with perspiration. "Kennedy? What's he doing there?"

"He's going back to London."

"He's leaving?" Melissa whispered. "With Natalie?"

Jeanie cleared her throat. "Yes, sweetie, I'm afraid so."

A crushing weight pressed on Melissa's body. For a moment she couldn't think or breathe or do anything. The weight felt heavy enough to snuff the very life out of her, but then it was gone, and she began to shake.

"Of course, he's gone," she said, fighting to get the words out. "What man wouldn't go anywhere with that exotic creature."

"Melissa, *you're* the exotic creature. And he didn't go with her because she's beautiful."

"Why, then?"

"I wish I knew. He doesn't love her, I'm certain of that. He was at the airport, and either she was right there with him, or he couldn't hear me well. He thanked me for trying to help, but he didn't answer any of my questions."

"What questions?"

"Like what the hell he was doing? Like had he lost his mind?"

No such luck, Melissa thought. "Tony knows what he's doing. He knows." She swallowed over a raw, aching lump. "Why didn't he call *me?*"

"I don't know, but he asked me to tell you how deeply he regretted not being able to come back. He said he'd kept his promise, and one day you would understand. He also said that he'd kept his promise to me, although I don't know what he meant."

"What was his promise to you?"

"That he would protect you and not let you be hurt."

Laughter stabbed at Melissa's throat like a thousand

sharp stickpins. "He promised *me* that everything would be all right. I'd say he fouled out on both of those, wouldn't you?"

"This has to be devastating for you. I'm sorry, baby."

"So am I, Jeanie." It was all Melissa could manage. Her eyelids burned, but she couldn't let herself cry. That would be admitting how bad this was, that it *was* devastating. It wasn't pride stopping her, it was pain. How would she ever deal with that much heartbreak? It would snuff the life out of her.

"Can I ask what you're going to do now?"

She unwound her legs and sat forward on the living-room couch where she'd been curled up since she'd come indoors. Her whole body ached. This may have been the first time she'd moved in several hours. "Go back to Kansas, what else?"

"Why don't you stay in New York a while longer? I haven't canceled all the appearances yet, and it would be easy to book more. At least you'd be busy and not sitting in your apartment brooding. You could even stay in the suite, if you wanted."

"I can't stay in this suite, Jeanie."

"Does that mean you'll stay in New York? I'll make arrangements to get you moved immediately. Another hotel, maybe the Peninsula. It's lovely there."

Jeanie was gone before Melissa could protest. How many times had that happened? Melissa sat there, shaking her head, dazed. She couldn't decide whether to call Jeanie back or go and pack her bags. She chose the latter. It seemed certain she was going somewhere, and that was all she cared about right now.

The last rays of sun slanted through the living room as she rose from the couch and stretched the stiffness from her body. A rich amber glow lit the room, magnified by windows that stretched from floor to ceiling. It was an effect worthy of a cathedral. Melissa should have been savoring it, but another flash of light had caught her eye.

She let out a little gasp of relief. Or was it dread?

Something gold glinted in the white carpet.

"WELL, it's all over now. You're free to go back to Kansas, Dorothy." Jeanie reached over to pat Melissa's hand. "If you want to, that is."

A brave smile seemed to be in order, but Melissa wasn't feeling particularly brave. She stared out the window of the limo, wishing Jeanie hadn't just reminded her that they would soon be back at the Peninsula Hotel, and some decisions were in order. She'd just completed her last day of book signings and the tour was officially over.

"Click my heels, and I'm home?" she said. "Maybe that's exactly what I should do."

"You're sure that's what you want to do? Go back to Kansas?"

Melissa shrugged. "What else is there?"

Jeanie peered at her with concern. "In case you haven't noticed, you have a hot book that's only going to get hotter after they air your reality TV show. The world is your oyster, Melissa. Be a celebrity, get a place here in the city and go to A-list parties. You can stay with me until you get settled. I have plenty of room."

"And the fact that my 'husband' walked out on me? That he's having our marriage annulled so he can marry someone else? What's going to happen to the book when that gets out?"

Melissa had received the latest missive from Tony's attorney that morning. He seemed determined to kill her, little by little, just the way he'd seduced her. Or had she seduced him? She didn't remember anymore. All she knew was the growing bitterness she felt toward someone she had once loved dearly.

In the two and a half weeks since he'd left, Melissa had kept the emotional demons at bay—barely—by working from dawn to dusk. Sleepless nights had been spent jotting notes for a new book idea that had nothing to do with sex, men or marriage. She'd titled it *The Joy of Celibacy,* but her heart wasn't in it. What joy?

When the attorney letters had started coming, complete with legal forms for her to fill out and sign, she'd wondered why they didn't just clamp her to a revolving board and start throwing knives.

"Okay, the annulment could be scandal fodder," Jeanie admitted. "At some point the media's going to find out, and we have to prepare ourselves for that. But it's not necessarily a bad thing. The fact that your husband deceived you takes nothing away from the book."

Melissa could hardly believe what she was hearing. How could it not affect the book? "To be honest," she snapped, "I don't give a damn about the book anymore, but that's *all* you seem to care about. And Tony didn't deceive me. You did."

Melissa's outburst surprised both of them. She'd been too stunned by Tony's abrupt departure to deal with it until now. She hadn't even realized how angry she was at Jeanie.

"I apologized for that," Jeanie said, quick to defend herself. "In fact, several times."

"I know you did. I just wish you'd told me about Tony's engagement. None of this had to happen, Jeanie. I wouldn't have let myself get involved with him—and I wouldn't be feeling like roadkill on the highway." Grief washed over Melissa, and her chin began to tremble. "Oh

God. Just forget it. Let's change the subject, okay? Could we talk about something else, please?''

Jeanie brought her fingers to her mouth with a look of absolute horror. "I didn't realize, Melissa. Really, I didn't. I could see that he was falling for you, but I didn't know you were in this deeply. You seemed to be doing fine."

Pain thickened Melissa's voice and made it throaty. "Of course I'm doing fine." Of course she wasn't doing fine, but Melissa had to say it. Jeanie finally understood what she'd done, but it really wasn't her fault that Melissa had fallen in love.

"What can I do?" Jeanie asked. "How can I help? Please, tell me."

Melissa shook her head. What could anyone do? "I don't want to live in New York, that's for sure. I want to be as far away from the city and its memories as I can get, even if it means falling off the edge of the earth."

Melissa pulled at the ring on her finger, and then saw what she'd done. It wasn't there. Phantom-ring syndrome. People who lost a limb felt it for years afterward, sometimes their whole life. In her case, the sensation of wearing the tight band had burned itself into her nervous system. Was she doomed for the rest of her life to feel a ring that wasn't there?

"What are you doing?" Jeanie asked when Melissa bent to reach into her purse.

"Looking for something." Melissa's purse was on the floor by her feet. She kept valuables in a hidden zipper compartment, and it only took her a moment to find the delicately scrolled band.

"Here. Send this back to him." She put the ring in Jeanie's hand. "You must know where he is."

"Melissa, I can't. Ask me to do anything else."

"But you're the one who created the terms of the agreement—book tour, quick annulment, remember? You should send it back.''

''He didn't give it to me.''

Melissa was doomed. The ring seemed to symbolize her greatest downfalls and mistakes in life, and apparently it would always haunt her. She returned the band to her purse and then made another painful request of Jeanie.

''Tell me what he said before he left.''

''Are you sure you want to hear it again?''

Melissa nodded. ''Tell me. I'm still trying to make sense of it.''

Jeanie went through the brief conversation again, and by the time she was done, Melissa was staring out the window once more, her vision blurred by tears. ''I just don't understand. If you'd heard the things he said to me, Jeanie, his passionate declarations of love, his promises.''

''Melissa, don't go there. You'll only make yourself miserable.''

''Like I'm not miserable already?''

Jeanie sighed. ''Maybe it was some kind of honor thing. He made vows, had obligations over in Europe, and he believed he had to keep them. He's staying true to who he is, his culture, and what he promised to do.''

''He promised to be with me. He said he was going to make it right for us.''

''Maybe he couldn't.''

''Then he should have told me himself.''

''Maybe he couldn't do that, either.''

Melissa brushed away the tears and turned to Jeanie. ''Do you know something? Are you holding back again?''

''I wish I did, sweetie. I'd tell you in a minute. I promise I would. I'm guessing just like you are.''

Melissa's conflict about Tony and the ring was so great she felt as if she had to do something to resolve it. He'd told her the ring wasn't supposed to come off. It meant their love was unending. But the ring had come off, and their love had ended. He was marrying someone else, and she couldn't hang on to a wedding band from a sham ceremony anymore. Even if she didn't realize it, she'd probably been trying to keep hope alive when the situation was hopeless. She was afraid to end it and face the pain. But she hadn't been protecting herself from the pain, not really. She'd been prolonging it.

By the time they'd reached the hotel she'd made a decision. "I don't want to guess anymore, Jeanie. I want to get on with my life. Give me Tony's address, and I'll send back the ring."

14

Don't stare too long out to sea. What you're looking
for may be right behind you.

101 Ways To Make Your Man Beg

"TO MELISSA, whose dirty mind has vastly improved my
love life!" Kath Crawford raised her Lemon Drop martini
high and saluted Melissa, who sat across the table.

Renee Tyler chimed in. "Guess who's retired her vibrator, thanks to chapter thirteen."

Pat Stafford followed suit, and the toasts got more ris-
qué.

Melissa smiled as her faithful friends lifted their glasses
and drank. The four of them were at Maggiano's in Kansas
City, an Italian restaurant where they'd met to celebrate
Melissa's return home. She'd actually been back over three
weeks, but with four busy women, it had been difficult
coordinating schedules.

It had been nearly double that time since she'd seen
Tony or heard from him. Six weeks today. The time she'd
spent with him felt like a fever dream now, something
dredged out of her unconscious by extreme circumstances.
The first time had felt that way, too. Maybe such intensity
was never meant to be permanent, rings and legends not-
withstanding.

"My pleasure," Melissa said, bowing her head. "Literally."

Kath grabbed her menu. "Which pasta is it that looks like a big long tube?" she asked. "Cannelloni? I'm craving it."

Pat snorted. "We'd better warn the waiters to wear codpieces."

"Their loss," Kath rejoined. "I have that Velvet Tongue thing down."

Melissa winced. "Do you think we might order dinner, *ladies?*"

Everyone deliberated over their menus, and Melissa finally decided on eggplant parmigiana, mostly because it bore absolutely no resemblance to the male organ. It turned out to be a good choice, but she had little appetite. Fortunately the dinner chatter was brisk and funny. Prior to the get-together, Melissa had caught up with each one of the girls individually on the phone—and made one request for tonight. No talk of Tony. She desperately needed to be distracted, she told them. She'd received the final annulment papers yesterday. She didn't tell them it had knocked the breath out of her. They were friends. They knew.

"Excuse us, but aren't you the nice lady who wrote this book?"

Melissa looked up to see a beaming older couple, hovering near the table. The white-haired woman was holding Melissa's book and a ballpoint pen. "Sorry to interrupt your dinner," she said, "but would it be possible to have your autograph?"

"Of course." Flattered, Melissa took the book and the pen. As she inscribed the title page, the woman chattered nervously about her husband, an elderly, stooped gentleman, who was leaning heavily on his three-pronged cane.

"Howard here doesn't have a flat tire anymore since we

tried that Over the Moon game," she said. "He really liked that one. His shoulder's out, though. Could be dislocated."

It took Melissa a moment to figure out what a flat tire was. "I'm so sorry about your shoulder," she told Howard, genuinely concerned as she returned the book. Perhaps she would have to write one for seniors. "Maybe the Sexual Scrabble game would work better for you?"

"No worries," Howard croaked. "The doc's going to put me in a sling. We can hardly wait to see how that works, right, babe?"

His wife blushed. "Right, Howie."

Melissa's friends had gone quiet, but she could feel their eyes burning into her.

As the happy couple left, Renee stifled a giggle. "Your book should come with a disclaimer, Sanders. 'Don't try this at home!'"

It got a laugh, but Melissa wondered if Renee was right. Had the whole world gone sex crazy? And was her book responsible?

By the time dessert was served, the discussion had moved to the next getaway.

"How about Alaska this year?" Pat suggested. "Anchorage has a very favorable ratio of men to women."

"Men," Melissa grumbled. "Haven't you girls got anything else on your mind but penis-shaped pasta and men?"

"You may have had something to do with that," Kath reminded her.

There was little Melissa could say, especially with all of them looking at her again. Apparently she'd improved everyone's love life but her own. Certainly her parents had never seemed happier. After they'd heard at church about their daughter's best-seller they'd immediately gotten satellite TV in order to catch her appearances.

"You know we've read *101 Ways* from cover to cover," her mother had said proudly. She and Melissa's father had showed Melissa their dog-eared copy the day they welcomed her home. She already knew about her dad's sacroiliac from the *Nice Girls Do* show. Thank God they hadn't given her any more specifics.

They'd also been supportive when she'd explained about Tony. Her mother had hugged her hard and said something about time being the healer. Her gentle father had talked about finding his gun—and Melissa had loved him for it.

The Maggiano party didn't break up until midnight, and Melissa got teary as she said good-night to her friends. She drove back to her apartment feeling less alone than she had in some time. She had loving parents and supportive friends. She'd written a book that was changing people's lives, hopefully for the better. Surely her father's back and Howie's shoulder were exceptions in her readers' experiences.

She had much to be grateful for, much to look forward to—and in time she might even believe that. Right now the irony of her situation was almost too much to bear. Everyone in her life was blissfully happy, and as much as she wanted to be able to share in their happiness, it made her feel all the more lonely and bereft. Nor did it help that they were happy because of her. What kind of cosmic twister was that? Right now all she wanted to do was go home and sleep, and maybe not wake up until the clouds cleared and the sun came out again, however long that took.

But as she pulled up to her apartment house and parked at the curb, she noticed a limo taking up the space of several cars. It was parked a couple cars in front of her, and just inside the glass doors of the building, waiting in the small lobby, was someone Melissa knew.

Melissa's heart broke into a run that winded her before she was even out of the car. *What was Natalie de la Cruz doing in Kansas?*

"Ms. SANDERS," Natalie said as Melissa entered the lobby. "Thank God, you're here. Can I talk with you? I know it's late, but this is important."

"Of course." Melissa hesitated, wondering if it was safe to invite her up to the apartment. The beautiful Natalie de la Cruz looked drawn and disheveled. Her delicate features were pinched, her jet hair tousled. Red flags had gone up the moment Melissa had seen her anxious expression. Still, she was Melissa's only link to Tony, and what if something had happened to him?

Not five minutes later, Natalie was seated on Melissa's living-room couch, fidgeting with the gathers of her plunging peasant blouse, while Melissa fixed them both a drink. Natalie had asked for cognac, and it just happened that Melissa had been given a bottle for Christmas some years ago. She'd never tried the stuff before, but this might be a good time to start.

Melissa handed Natalie a snifter with two fingers of cognac and sat down next to her. "Are you all right?"

Natalie took a slug of the brandy, rocking the snifter in both hands. Or was *she* rocking? Her nerves were contagious, and Melissa could have used a slug herself, but she could barely get the snifter to her mouth. The fumes were so strong they made her want to sneeze.

"I've made a terrible mistake," Natalie said. "And I've left Tony." She'd begun to shake. Even another healthy drink of the cognac didn't help.

"Leaving him was your mistake?" Melissa asked a bit confused.

"No, I had to leave, or he would have."

Now *Melissa's* hands were unsteady. She gave the cognac another try and failed again. The fumes burned her eyes. "I don't understand."

Natalie looked up from the swirling liquor. "The day I came to your hotel suite I did something terrible. Tony called it emotional blackmail, and maybe it was. I threatened him with the one thing I thought might get to him…and I was right."

She stared at Melissa so intensely that Melissa finally said, "Me?"

"Yes, you. I told him I'd ruin you unless he came back to London with me that very day. I threatened to call a press conference and tell the world that your marriage was a fake, that you'd married Tony on a dare and hadn't seen him in years."

She slugged down some cognac, her mouth twisting bitterly. "That was all it took. He agreed to go with me and to say nothing to you about his reasons. I insisted on that, too, because I wanted to hurt you as much I wanted him back. But, of course, the instant he agreed, all was lost. His willingness should have told me how much he loved you—and that he would do anything to protect you—but I was too angry to see it then." Natalie presented her hand defiantly. "See, no ring. It's official. Tony and I are done."

"I—I'm sorry." This time Melissa got the snifter to her mouth and took a deep drink. The fumes didn't faze her. She probably wasn't breathing.

"Don't be. It would have happened whether you came into his life or not."

Natalie rose and walked away, her back to Melissa. She

stopped by the bookshelf on the far wall and began to leaf through the collection of magazines that had published Melissa's articles.

"Tony and I grew up together," she explained. "Our fathers were business partners, and it was always assumed the two of us would marry. I was several years younger, quite naive and completely enthralled with the idea. I think Tony went along with it because it was expected of him. But when our parents pushed him, he stood up to them."

"Why? He thought you were too young?"

"I wish it had been that. He said I was like a sister to him, and he refused to marry me. His father kicked him out, and none of us saw him again until his mother died last year. He arrived just before she passed, and she begged him to marry and carry on the family name. It was her last wish."

"And he proposed to you?"

She released a sigh. "He did, and of course, I said yes. I was still naive. I believed the arrangement would work, but you can't force someone to love you. Tony agreed to go through with the marriage, even after what I threatened to do to you, but it would never have worked. He became remote and distant. He even opted out of a business deal with my father that would have made him a fortune." She hesitated, her posture rigid. "One day I woke up and realized that he would never love me the way I needed to be loved—the way he loved you."

Something brought her around to face Melissa, maybe just the relief of getting the story all out. "It would have been a marriage of convenience at best. At worse, he might have ended up hating me. I didn't want that."

Melissa wished she had something more than sympathy to offer. Natalie had done more damage than she would ever know, but she'd been deeply hurt, too, and it couldn't have been easy for her to come all the way to Kansas to admit these things.

Melissa tried to thank her, but Natalie waved her off. "I had to," she said. "I couldn't have lived with myself otherwise."

"What will you do now?" Melissa asked.

"Who knows? One day there will be someone else. But perhaps I'll read your book first."

"101 Ways?" Melissa feared for the men in Natalie's future. The drink had warmed her up considerably. She flirted with the idea of another slug, but wasn't sure she'd be able to get up from the sofa. Pretty good stuff, that cognac.

"Do you have a place to stay?" she asked Natalie. "There's only one bedroom here, but the couch is comfortable."

Natalie glanced at her watch, a heavy stainless-steel piece with an incongruous diamond-encrusted face. "Thanks," she said, "but the limo waiting outside is mine. I'm catching a red-eye back to New York, and I'm late."

As Melissa rose to walk her to the door, Natalie thought of something else. She spun around, her dark eyes glinting with purpose.

"I almost forgot to give you this," she said, fishing in her jacket pocket. "It came in the mail after Tony had already moved out. He doesn't know you sent it back."

Melissa recognized the ring box immediately. Her throat burned with resignation as she opened it. The lacy gold ring glowed, picking up every light in the room. She would never escape this ring. Even if Natalie hadn't returned it, somehow it would have followed her the rest of her days.

"Here, take this, too," Natalie said. "It's a letter Tony started to me when he realized he'd fallen in love with you. It will mean more to you than it ever could to me."

She drew a crumpled piece of paper out of her pocket, and Melissa recognized it as stationery from the Hotel Da Vinci.

Melissa took the letter, wondering if she would ever be able to bring herself to read it. She began to smooth the paper's edges.

"You'll find Tony at a lovely old restaurant in Brussels," Natalie said. "If you still love him, you'll know what to do."

"What? I should go there?"

"Of course you should! He's pining for you, Melissa. But he'll never make the first move. He believes he's ruined your life, and you're better off without him."

With that, Natalie dashed out, leaving Melissa to stare at the door and wonder what she should do. Had Tony ruined her life? It was true that he'd disappeared with barely a word, but she'd done the same thing to him. Maybe there was some kind of balance in that? It was all so confusing.

She went to the couch and sat down, cradling the ring box in her lap while she opened the letter.

Natalie, by the time you read this, I will be on my way back to London to meet with you and try to explain what's happened in my life. I know you haven't heard from me recently, and I apologize for that. I've had some realizations that we need to talk about. How do I explain my heart to you? How do I tell you all that has happened to me since I've been gone? Please let me try. And if you can, read this letter with an open mind. First, know that I have always cared deeply about you. I wish I could love you the way you deserve to be loved. But those feelings aren't there. I would have given you my heart gladly, except that I didn't have it to give. I lost it two years ago...

That was as far as he got with the letter, but Melissa didn't have to read another word.

BRAMBLE ROSES lay like a coverlet across the cottage's thatched roof. Spilling over the eves in lacy bowers, fat pink blossoms created an awning for the row of shuttered windows below. A tourist on the cobbled lane would never have taken the quaint old structure for an exclusive restaurant. It looked as if it had sprung life-size from the pages of a Grimm's fairy tale.

Fourteen Rue des Fleurs. Street of flowers? Even the address was quaint.

Melissa might have missed the restaurant if not for the sign painter working out front. He'd just finished painting the establishment's name on the Dutch door's glass upper panel, and now he was hard at work on something below it. Melissa couldn't read what it said, but she thought it might be the proprietor's name.

A hand-written card filled one windowpane, pronouncing the restaurant open for business. People milled around inside, but Melissa couldn't tell if they were waiters or customers. Was Tony one of them? Her heart seemed to float at the possibility. What would she do when she saw him? Probably expire. All the blood in her body would rush to her toes, and she would go into cardiac arrest and have to be taken to the hospital, where they would hook her up to life support. Doctors would huddle over her, fighting to save her life, and Tony would pace the halls, cursing, begging, tears in his eyes.

That's how she would make her husband beg.

Chill, woman! She gave her imagination a mental thwack, silencing it.

The sign painter gallantly opened the door for her as she approached.

"*Merci,*" she said as she slipped inside. It was two in the afternoon, and a number of diners still lingered over lunch and glasses of wine. Delicious smells of sizzling butter and garlic emanated from the kitchen, making Melissa's stomach rumble. She'd flown all night, and she'd slept and eaten very little. It had been a whirlwind decision and a whirlwind trip. But now that she was here she had no idea what she was going to do.

The restaurant was as charming inside as out, with long white linen tablecloths and fresh-cut roses everywhere you looked. Lining the walls were intricately carved wooden booths with curtains for privacy. Everything down to the china appeared to be handcrafted. But no sign of Tony. She hoped he still worked here. He seemed to have an almost nomadic existence—Cancún, London, now Brussels.

She spotted a table near a large potted plant that looked as if it might give her some cover. A place to observe without being observed. Head ducked, she walked over and sat down. The menus were parchment sheets, handwritten in a beautiful script that resembled calligraphy. Fortunately, they were plenty large enough to shield her face.

She could read very little of the totally French menu, but pretended to study it anyway. Within moments, she heard someone coming her way.

"*Que voudriez-vous?*" her waiter asked in a deep, sensual voice.

"I don't speak French."

"What would you like, *mademoiselle?*"

A glance beneath the bottom edge of the menu revealed the man's shoes. They were woven leather sandals. Although she couldn't see his feet well enough to recognize them, she did recognize the voice. If he'd whispered at that moment she would probably have had an orgasm.

"What's your special?" she asked.

"Special, *mademoiselle?*"

"Yes, don't you have a luncheon special?"

"Ah, the seafood stew with mussels. Would you like that then?"

She continued to speak into the menu. "No, thank you. I'm not fond of mussels." *Unless they're attached to a certain man. Those I rather like.*

"Do you see something you are fond of?"

"Yes, I do."

"What would you like, *mademoiselle?*"

In a very soft, very deliberate voice she said, "Actually, I'd like you on a skewer for leaving me the way you did. If I can't have that, perhaps you'd like to propose. Again."

The menu dropped and so did Antonio's jaw. Melissa dangled her high heel from her toe and casually played with the pearls at her neck.

"How many times does a man have to marry you?' He laughed out loud. "How many times, my lost-and-found wife?"

He pulled off his apron, tossed it aside and tugged her to her feet. "Smile for me," he said, holding her at arm's length so he could look at her. "Smile and set fire to my heart."

Melissa smiled through tears of joy. She burned with happiness and another emotion that might have surprised him—pride. He would never know what courage it had taken for her to make the trip, not having any idea what to expect or whether he would even want to see her. Two years ago, she had run from him as fast as she could, but today she was facing her fears. Today she'd run to him. In the past few weeks, with everything they'd been through and all the risks they'd taken, she'd grown enough to open herself to love.

He brushed a tear from her cheek, and his own eyes got misty.

"I want this relationship," she whispered. "I want you. I'm not afraid of my feelings anymore."

"I'm scared to death of mine." He shook his head, laughing. "Isn't that great?"

"It's perfect."

The rays that crept through the windows filled the room with gold, and reminded Melissa of something. "Look." She held up her hand to show him the ring that sparkled almost as brightly as she did. "It does seem to bring us back together."

"Never take it off. I want it to keep us together this time."

She nodded. "Let's don't mess with the legend."

Tony seemed to realize that they were attracting attention. He led her over to a quiet corner where Melissa gave his face a tender touch and draped her arms around his neck. She couldn't resist the impulse. She didn't want to jeopardize his job with a public display of affection, but she had to be close to him. She ached to be close.

Desire growled in his throat as he kissed her, a fiery little touch of his lips that left her yearning for more. Just as she was going to whisper something desperately erotic in his ear, he eased them apart, holding her at arm's length.

"Are you hungry?" he asked. "Would you like something after your long trip?"

"Hungry for you," she whispered. All she really wanted was him and one of the bottomless feather beds the country was noted for, but he obviously wanted to feed her—and cooking really was the sexiest form of foreplay when he did it.

"Yes, I'm starving—and this place is beautiful," she assured him.

"You like it?" He swung around, throwing his arm out, as if to introduce her with pride to his place of employment.

Melissa looked around her, taking it all in again. The lowering sun filled the room with a rich pink haze. Bramble roses curtained the windows, and outside at the door, the sign painter put the finishing touches on the last of his handiwork. He'd just finished painting the proprietor's name on the glass panel.

DNOB OINOTNA?

Melissa had never been able to read backward, but she glanced at Antonio and noticed his secret smile. What was that all about? she wondered. Next he would be telling her that he wasn't really a waiter.

Epilogue

One year later...

"TONY! What have you done to me?"

Melissa awoke to an alarming discovery. She couldn't move her arms. They were above her head and held fast by what felt like silk tethers. Her legs weren't going anywhere, either. Her ankles had been hitched to the bedpost with what appeared to be black silk scarves. When she raised her head and looked around, she could clearly see the predicament she was in. What she couldn't see was Tony.

"Tony? Where *are* you?"

He didn't answer, and her mind began to spin, whipping up its favorite dish. Panic. Maybe he didn't leave by choice. They were in a foreign country. What if he'd been kidnapped? It could have been revolutionary forces, if there was any such thing in Cancún. Whoever took him intended to hold him for ransom, and they'd left her bound to keep her from calling the police. But they wouldn't have used silk scarves, would they? And they probably wouldn't tie her to the bedposts, either, in her satin teddy.

No, this was the work of a cunning criminal, the same safecracker who'd stolen her heart.

She tugged at the ties and felt them tighten. Slipknots! She really *couldn't* move. Screaming probably wouldn't do any good. Tony had taken the hotel's honeymoon suite for old time's sake, and it was in a wing by itself. This was the room where they'd spent their wedding night, the room she'd fled.

So where had he gone? And what was she supposed to do in the meantime? Admire the red satin canopy above the bed? Count the folds in the ruched silk? Fat chance with her bent for paranoia. She'd already thought of several natural disasters that could happen while one was tied to a bed, helpless.

Screaming didn't seem like such a bad idea as the moments wore on. She took a couple of preparatory breaths, readying herself to shout, "Fire!" when the door to the room swung open. Tony walked in with a tray of breakfast rolls, coffee, juice and the morning paper.

"I see you're awake," he said as amiably as if he always brought breakfast to bound, half-naked women.

"You see that, do you? Do you also see that I'm tied up?"

He set the tray on the chest at the foot of the bed and barely gave her a glance as he poured coffee and slathered crusty Italian rolls with butter and jam. Finally, a cup of coffee in hand, he took the time to check out the situation, *her* being the situation. He actually folded his arms like an artisan inspecting his handiwork, and she detected more than a hint of self-satisfaction in his expression as he perused her spread-eagle legs. She must have kicked off the sheets sometime during the night.

He probably felt pretty good about himself that he'd managed to lash her to the mast without even waking her up. The pirate.

"You should wear black silk more often," he said. "It's good with your coloring."

"You mean my bright red face?" It would have given her great satisfaction to stick her tongue out at him, but

that could have been mistaken for an invitation. The very
coolness of his manner told her that he was in a dangerous
mood. Her husband didn't ignore her unless he wanted her
attention.

Okay. Two could play this game. She could be cool.

"May I ask why you did this?" she said. "And may I
assume that you weren't going for a Scout badge?"

"It's this room," he admitted, looking around. "The
last time we were here together, you disappeared on me.
I wasn't taking any chances."

Melissa caught his fleeting smile and realized that he
wasn't kidding, not entirely. It would kill him to lose her
again, and this was his way of telling her. Her throat tightened so swiftly that she couldn't clear away its huskiness.

"The last time we were here, I was young and foolish,"
she said.

"And now?"

"Now I'm young and hungry." She strained against the
ties, forgetting they were slipknots. "Get me out of here,
m'lord, *please.*"

"Not so fast, vixen." He brought a bowl of fruit from
the tray and sat down next to her on the bed. "Maybe I
should feed you?" He plucked two grapes and popped one
in his mouth. The other he kissed and offered to her.

Melissa allowed him to caress her lips with the grape,
but she refrained from opening her mouth. Make him wait
for it. What chapter was that anyway?

"Apparently she's not that hungry?" he said. "Then
perhaps she'll appreciate my other surprise more—and re-
ward her captor with a kiss."

"Your *other* surprise?"

Melissa didn't bother to hide her nervousness as she
watched him take a newspaper from the tray. What was

he going to do? Swat her like a naughty house pet? Now, *that* had possibilities.

He sorted through the sections until he found the one he wanted, and then he thumbed through several pages and snapped open the paper. "Here we are."

The page he showed her was in the arts section. And right before Melissa's eyes was an ad for her latest book, *Begging Is Half the Fun!* It took up the entire page, and Melissa was totally dazzled by it. There were quotes from reviews she hadn't seen yet. Good quotes. A couple of raves even.

She tore her gaze from the ad and looked up at him, thrilling to his proud smile. "Untie me and we'll celebrate," she said.

A wicked gleam lit his eyes. "Let's celebrate and then I'll untie you."

Her face really must be bright red by now, heated by what his idea of celebrating might be. "How would we do that, m'lord?"

"Here's a thought." He bent closer. "Maybe we should make a baby so you can write a self-help book for parents."

That *was* a thought. She had a better one. "Maybe we should make a baby because it'll have your beautiful dark eyes."

"And your luscious lips."

He leaned over and kissed her, and Melissa no longer cared that her hands were tied. In fact, she rather liked it. That was the beauty of being a writer. *Research.*

HARLEQUIN® *Blaze*™

Look for more

...before you say "I do."

#126 TAKE ME TWICE
Isabel Sharpe (March 2004)

&

#134 THE ONE WHO GOT AWAY
Jo Leigh (May 2004)

*Enjoy the latest sexual escapades
in the hottest miniseries.*

Only from Blaze

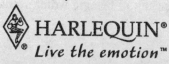

HARLEQUIN®
Live the emotion™

If you enjoyed what you just read,
then we've got an offer you can't resist!

Take 2 bestselling
love stories FREE!

Plus get a FREE surprise gift!

Clip this page and mail it to **Harlequin Reader Service®**

IN U.S.A.	**IN CANADA**
3010 Walden Ave.	P.O. Box 609
P.O. Box 1867	Fort Erie, Ontario
Buffalo, N.Y. 14240-1867	L2A 5X3

YES! Please send me 2 free Blaze™ novels and my free surprise gift. After receiving them, if I don't wish to receive anymore, I can return the shipping statement marked cancel. If I don't cancel, I will receive 4 brand-new novels each month, before they're available in stores! In the U.S.A., bill me at the bargain price of $3.80 plus 25¢ shipping and handling per book and applicable sales tax, if any*. In Canada, bill me at the bargain price of $4.21 plus 25¢ shipping and handling per book and applicable taxes**. That's the complete price and a savings of at least 10% off the cover prices—what a great deal! I understand that accepting the 2 free books and gift places me under no obligation ever to buy any books. I can always return a shipment and cancel at any time. Even if I never buy another book from Harlequin, the 2 free books and gift are mine to keep forever.

150 HDN DNWD
350 HDN DNWE

Name	(PLEASE PRINT)	
Address	Apt.#	
City	State/Prov.	Zip/Postal Code

* Terms and prices subject to change without notice. Sales tax applicable in N.Y.
** Canadian residents will be charged applicable provincial taxes and GST.
  All orders subject to approval. Offer limited to one per household and not valid to current Blaze™ subscribers.
  ® are registered trademarks of Harlequin Enterprises Limited.

BLZ02-R

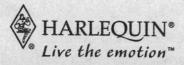

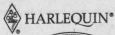 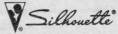

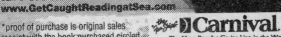

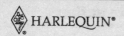

Carnival Elation
7-Day Exotic Western Caribbean Itinerary

DAY	PORT	ARRIVE	DEPART
Sun	Galveston		4:00 P.M.
Mon	"Fun Day" at Sea		
Tue	Progreso/Mérida	8:00 A.M.	4:00 P.M.
Wed	Cozumel	9:00 A.M.	5:00 P.M.
Thu	Belize	8:00 A.M.	6:00 P.M.
Fri	"Fun Day" at Sea		
Sat	"Fun Day" at Sea		
Sun	Galveston	8:00 A.M.	

TERMS AND CONDITIONS

PAYMENT SCHEDULE:
50% due upon booking. Full and final payment due by July 26, 2004.
Acceptable forms of payment are Visa, MasterCard, American Express, Discover and checks. The cardholder must be one of the passengers traveling. A fee of $25 will apply for all returned checks. Check payments must be made payable to **Advantage International, LLC** and sent to: Advantage International, LLC, 195 North Harbor Drive, Suite 4206, Chicago, IL 60601.

CHANGE/CANCELLATION:
Notice of change/cancellation must be made in writing to Advantage International, LLC.

Change:
Changes in cabin category may be requested and can result in increased rate and penalties. A name change is permitted 60 days or more prior to departure and will incur a penalty of $50 per name change. Deviation from the group schedule and package is a cancellation.

Cancellation:

181 days or more prior to departure	$250 per person
121—180 days or more prior to departure	50% of the package price
120—61 days prior to departure	75% of the package price
60 days or less prior to departure	100% of the package price (nonrefundable)

U.S. and Canadian citizens are required to present a valid passport or the original birth certificate and state issued photo ID (driver's license). All other nationalities must contact the consulate of the various ports that are visited for verification of documentation.

<u>We strongly recommend trip cancellation insurance!</u>

For further details call 1-877-ADV-NTGE or visit www.GetCaughtReadingatSea.com

---

For booking form and complete information
go to www.getcaughtreadingatsea.com
or call 1-877-ADV-NTGE

Complete coupon and booking form and mail both to:
Advantage International, LLC
195 North Harbor Drive, Suite 4206, Chicago, IL 60601

Harlequin Enterprises Ltd. is a paid participant in this promotion.

THE FUN SHIPS, CARNIVAL DESIGN, CARNIVAL AND THE MOST POPULAR CRUISE LINE IN THE WORLD ARE TRADEMARKS OF CARNIVAL CORPORATION. ALL OTHER TRADEMARKS ARE TRADEMARKS OF HARLEQUIN ENTERPRISES LTD. OR ITS AFFILIATED COMPANIES, USED UNDER LICENSE.

Visit us at www.eHarlequin.com

GCRSEA2